The Alcuin Letter

An International Intrigue Novel

Jeff Raymond

Also by Jeff Raymond:
The Medici Quest
An International Intrigue Novel - Book 1

jeffraymondfiction.com

Published by Take Me Away Books, an imprint of Winged Publications

Editor: Cynthia Hickey

Book Design by Winged Publications

Fiction and Literature: Inspirational

Action and Adventure

ISBN: 978-1-962168-89-2

Here halt, I pray you; make a little stay,
O wayfarer, to read what I have writ,
And know by my fate what thy fate shall be.
What thou art now, wayfarer, world-renowned,
I was; what I am now, so shall thou be.
The world's delight I followed with a heart
Unsatisfied: ashes am I, and dust.

Alcuin of York
Opening stanza of self-composed epitaph inscribed
over
Alcuin's tomb in St. Martin's Church, Tours, France
804 AD

On the cover:
The Aachen Cathedral in Aachen, Germany

PROLOGUE

Near Paderborn (Germany), October of 799 A.D.

A brilliant moon blessed the diverse group on the final evening of their arduous journey. The bright orb provided a welcome change after traveling under the cloak of dark and gloomy skies for more than a fortnight. First gathering many days ago outside of Rome, the four travelers now approached their destination on the edge of Paderborn.

The central figure of the foursome appeared dirty and disheveled, his clothes serving as a costume, of sorts, in contrast to his normal exalted attire. Though his face may not have been known to most inhabitants of the small towns and villages they passed, the need to keep his identity hidden remained necessary in a land filled with robbers and others wishing to harm.

Two in the group were soldiers, also dressed in plain and well-worn clothes. The brave souls joined the trek to serve as protection, knowing they could be overpowered if waylaid by greater forces.

As the long journey neared its end, the band of weary travelers entered a dense forest where the light from the luminous moon struggled to break through. Any glimmers that found a way through the canopy only created an eerie canvas of moving shadows that danced like imaginary goblins. The horses carrying the quartet were as skittish as their riders in this dark territory; their hooves stamping down unseen foliage as they trotted along the winding trail.

Few words were spoken during the final leg of the journey, the silence hiding a great anticipation of what was to come. A request would be presented and an offer made. A priceless gift would be given, both for incentive and for safekeeping.

Just as the gloomy forest began to succeed in dampening spirits, the four riders entered a large clearing, allowing the moon to become visible again. Ahead, the shapes of additional horses and riders emerged, the snorts and whinnies of the mounts announcing the new arrivals. The two parties approached each other with caution, still anxious for the discussion that was to come.

This was not the usual meeting place for a king and a pope.

A white steed, standing at least two hands taller than any other in the clearing, moved forward carrying a rider who appeared in proportion with the large animal. In contrast to the travel-sodden attire of the group from Rome, the man on the white horse was splendidly dressed, even at this odd hour. The King of the Franks—also known as Charles the Great or Charlemagne—blocked out a portion of the moon as he approached, his size exceeded only by his reputation. He was the ruler of more lands than any other person on earth; protector of Rome; benefactor of the Popes.

"Holy Father, we are honored with your presence," King Charles said. "I am aware of the situation in Rome and am sorry for the threat to your safety. I am pleased you found others to accompany you and managed safe passage."

"I am the one who should be honored," replied Pope Leo III. "Please forgive our appearance. My travails have made me an outcast to some who used to praise me, making it necessary to refrain from drawing undue attention as we traveled." The King nodded his understanding. The Pope continued. "I am most grateful for your willingness to meet at this unusual time and place. I thought it better to have our initial discussions away from curious eyes and ears, even those loyal to you."

"You have nothing to fear in Paderborn, your Excellency. Nor any of my lands," added the King. "The man elected to lead the Holy Church and be God's voice on earth will come to no harm. That is my solemn vow."

"Your kindness and dedication are a great tribute," said Leo, who breathed easier than a few moments earlier. A resolve to complete his intended mission now replaced the fear of rejection by the great King of the Franks.

The Pope turned his horse and returned to his small traveling group. He asked the final member of the party for a special package; an item secured before the Pope was assaulted and driven from Rome by those who hoped to force him from his exalted position. Winigis, the Duke of Spoleto, unwrapped the strips of cloth protecting the package and offered it with great care to the Pope. The two pairs of hands shook during the exchange, giving testimony to the historical act that was about to take place.

Winigis served as a guard for the item—encased in a wooden box—for the past weeks. He and the Pope had engaged in frequent discussions concerning the priceless relic; discussions that began while the Pontiff took shelter at the Duke's estate before embarking on the journey to Paderborn.

"Winigis, you have been a trusted and valuable servant to me and our Lord," said His Holiness. "Your sacrifices to make this journey and to protect this holy item will not be forgotten."

Pope Leo took the wooden box and led his horse beside the large mount carrying the King. The Holy Father leaned in close and spoke so no others could hear his words. The King of the Franks soon nodded and informed those who remained in the clearing that the Pope would join him on a short ride. No one should follow.

CHAPTER 1

Present Day

Each step on the pavement brings me closer to my goal. Since some steps produce more pain than satisfaction, keeping a picture of that goal in my mind is often the real battle.

Ten years past my days as a college track athlete, I am slogging through a five-mile run, battling the afternoon heat and humidity. I'm making this effort because I accepted a challenge to run a half marathon in a few months and plan to follow through as long as my body cooperates. Two students in my class challenged me, saying they would train over the summer and return to campus ready to race. After initially declining their offer, I found myself saying *yes* on the final day of the semester.

It's a funny thing about challenges. They can give you a new focus, a new purpose, and a new sense of accomplishment. For one person it might be climbing a mountain or earning a promotion. For another, it could be giving up sweets or caffeine. For me, the biggest challenge for most of the past year has been the simple act of getting out of bed in the morning. I met that challenge every day, despite the sensation of walking in a haze and feeling inadequate most of the time. Running—even with the aches and pains—is somehow helping me find my way through the fog of life.

My run takes me near the local college where I have been a history professor for the past five years. Bannister College, located in its namesake of Bannister, Indiana, has played a key role in the close-knit community of fifteen thousand for over a century. Bannister can give off a bit of a Mayberry vibe, but I enjoy the lifestyle after growing up surrounded by the traffic, noise, and harried lifestyle of a large city. If I want more excitement, the state capital of Indianapolis is less than an hour away.

Now, in the third week of my training regime, I notice the landscape as I run. At first, I didn't pay attention to my surroundings, too caught up in my own issues. Day by day, I am becoming aware of the beauty of early summer flowers, the smell of freshly cut grass, and the joy on kids' faces as they play in the park. I am becoming almost human again.

No one needs me to make that transition more than Maddie.

An exclamation of "Daddy" greeted me as I jogged up the driveway of my in-laws' home. Arms and legs not quite in complete unison, my three-year-old daughter burst out of the front door, moving with a toddler's speed to greet me. She didn't worry that I was dripping with sweat as she grabbed onto my legs.

"You wet daddy. You wet," she repeated.

"I know sweetie," I said as I picked her up. "Now we'll both need a shower."

I carried her into the house where my mother-in-law Karen waited inside the door. The two women in my life were born more than fifty years apart, but their similar genetics were apparent. Both had prominent cheekbones, an engaging smile, and dark curly hair, although Karen's had more hints of grey as the years passed.

The two shared ocean-blue eyes that captured your attention. But their eyes also remained tinted with sadness. One lost a mother and the other a daughter a little over a year ago when a drunk driver tried to pass on a narrow country road. The third woman in my life—my wife Rachel—was killed instantly, sending me into a downward spiral that I was just beginning to climb out of.

"Dinner will be ready shortly," said Karen as she took Maddie from me. "Matt, you should take a shower. Donnie will be home soon to join us."

My father-in-law was Donald Henderson to everyone else, but Karen had called him Donnie since they started dating as teenagers.

Maddie and I have stayed at the Henderson's on most weekends for the past year. My parents live near Denver, making them too far away to provide anything more than moral support. Karen and Donald proved to be invaluable since Rachel died, unselfishly supporting Maddie and me despite their own sadness and other responsibilities. I breathe easier at the end of each week, knowing that I will have a two-day respite from the memories that assault me each time I enter my own home.

After a shower, I sat on the floor to join Maddie in front of the television. She was enthralled with *Curious George* on PBS Kids and the never-ending antics of a monkey who found trouble in any situation.

"Hey Matt, since you're staying here this weekend I stopped by your house and picked up the mail today," Karen said as she leaned in from the kitchen. "A package arrived from overseas; England, I think."

"Thanks. It's probably from my friend Ashton. I expected a message from him concerning the conference I'm attending. I'm not sure why it didn't email me the information, but I'll look at it after dinner."

Ashton and I met in grad school, both working on master's degrees in history at the University of Illinois. He arrived from London, and we hit it off the first time we studied together. We stayed in touch over the years as our lives moved forward. Ashton completed his Ph.D. and became a professor at the University of Leeds, about 200 miles north of London. He's not married, but always jokes about finding a *Yankee* wife when he makes trips to the States.

A year ago, Ashton came to the U.S. as a guest speaker for the Midwest Medieval History Conference, hosted at our alma mater. I attended the conference to support him and we hung out in our old surroundings for a few days. I shared with him the joys of married life and bragged about my then two-year-old daughter. Ashton promised he would settle down and find a wife soon.

Less than a month later, Rachel died.

I plan to travel to England in a few weeks as Ashton's guest at the International Medieval Congress held yearly at the University of Leeds. I have to admit that I am looking forward to the trip. Medieval history is more an interest than a vocation for me, but the thought of getting out of the bubble I've been in for the past year is exciting. The protective bubble was one of my few comforts for many months but lately has become like a weight that never leaves my shoulders. I'm hoping that travel and new surroundings combine to relieve some of that pressure.

My father-in-law made it home from his job as the publisher of the local newspaper and sat down for dinner. We bowed our heads as Donald said the prayer of thanks—a tradition in the Henderson household—and then started on lasagna, garlic bread, and salad. I was starving after my run and my cravings only deepened after smelling the food for the past thirty minutes.

Karen cut some lasagna into small pieces for Maddie and the three-year-old dug in. Maddie managed to get some into her mouth, but the remnants slipped through her small hands and fell to the floor.

"So how was the run today?" asked Donald. "I saw you go by our office and out toward the campus."

"It's getting better. I made it the entire five miles without stopping, which is encouraging. That's a long way from thirteen miles, though. I still have a ways to go."

Karen cleaned off Maddie's fingers for the first of many times during the meal. "I'm glad you're doing this running thing," she said as she moved the napkin to Maddie's chin. "It gets you out of the house and active again. You used to run a lot, before…uh... Maddie was born."

We all knew Karen meant to say '*before Rachel died*', but speaking about Rachel in everyday conversation remained difficult. Mentioning her in reverent terms was okay, but talking about her in the flow of a common conversation still felt like minimizing her death. It's hard to explain unless you have been through a similar situation.

"So is your trip all planned to England?" asked Donald, breaking an awkward moment.

"I've confirmed my tickets and will fly out of Indy and have a brief layover in New York before taking off for London. Ashton is driving down to London to pick me up. He sent me a package today, which I assume includes some more details about the conference."

An hour later I had given Maddie a bath and her grandmother was reading her a story before bed. Donald and I were enjoying an NBA playoff game on his large-screen television.

"I know you're looking forward to seeing your friend Ashton and traveling to England, but I'm curious how this conference will help your teaching?" inquired Donald.

"All history is somewhat related," I explained. "Many of our ancestors came from Europe, and the medieval times encompassed a thousand years of history, right up to the time of Columbus. A vast amount of key events happened during the era, including the rise of the Catholic Church, the Crusades, the Black Death plague, the Italian Renaissance, the Reformation, and….." I stopped myself. "Oh, you don't care about this. Sorry, I was in my lecture mode."

"That's fine Professor Kincaid," said Donald with a smile. "A person's never too old to learn."

I went to tuck Maddie in and kiss her goodnight. As I returned to watching the game, I remembered the package from Ashton.

Ashton could have emailed me the schedule of the conference in Leeds, so he must have a good reason for sending the information through the mail. Once I opened the package, I found a scribbled note and a copy of an old manuscript or letter. I looked again in the envelope and found a flash drive stuck in one of the folds.

Donald took notice of the strange look on my face. "Not what you were expecting."

"Uh, no. There's a copy of an old manuscript in a foreign language. It looks like Latin. And a small flash drive. Maybe Ashton's note explains."

I read the short note. Then read it again. My mouth hung open.

"What are you looking at?" asked Karen as she came into the room, seeing the surprised look on my face.

"This is strange," I replied. "Ashton said he might have made a significant historical discovery and didn't want to leave a digital trail, so put the information in the mail. He didn't explain himself further, only asking that I keep the flash drive and the documents secret until I hear from him."

"Can't you just call him and find out what this is all about?" asked Karen.

Even though it was 4 a.m. in London, I dialed Ashton's number. After several rings, the call went to voice mail and I left a message, asking him to call me.

"He didn't answer, which isn't surprising due to the time change."

"What do you think is on the flash drive?" asked Donald.

"I have no idea," I said. "My laptop is still in my office on campus, but I'll go there first thing in the morning. Hopefully, I'll get a reply from Ashton by then."

One Week Earlier

The blindfold covering his eyes was drenched in sweat but held firm. Not seeing what was coming next felt worse than any of the actual pain. So far.

An academic by trade, being kidnapped was as far from normal for Ashton Collins as he could imagine. Battling other faculty for budget increases and working through disagreements with the college administration were the normal stresses in his life. Being abducted in front of his flat, tied up, gagged, and transported to an unknown location was an unwelcome new realm of experiences.

Ashton inherited his tendency to be a bookworm. His British father was a renowned pediatric surgeon at the Royal London Hospital, while his Spanish-born mother served as a professor of chemistry at the Imperial College of London. His sister Camilla, three years younger, was never enthralled with school. She developed her creative side and found her success as a freelance photographer who traveled the globe with assignments from various organizations and media outlets.

Raised in an upscale home in the Kensington area of London, the Collins kids rubbed shoulders in their private schools with the children of politicians and celebrities. Somehow the two remained grounded and never lost their appreciation for the privileges they experienced growing up.

Ashton was not blessed with any privileges at the moment. With his eyes covered, his other senses were overloaded, waiting to see which pain receptors would be attacked first. He sensed his captors were in the room with him, but the men who abducted him had not said a word since plopping Ashton in his current location: a hard metal chair in an unknown building. His frantic questions of "Why did you kidnap me?" and "Why am I here?" had so far been ignored.

"Dr. Collins, we apologize for this inconvenience."

The words said in a German accent were welcome to Ashton after the long stretch of silence. At least if someone was speaking, he might find out what was happening. Not knowing anything was worse than his fear of what could be coming.

"Why am I here?" asked Ashton again through trembling lips.

"We have a little problem and hope you can help us." His captor spoke patiently, enunciating each word with a drawn-out cadence. The effect was the opposite of calming for Ashton, giving him the impression that the speaker would be willing to do whatever was needed to solve the *'little problem'*.

"Our employer wishes to obtain some information that we believe you possess." The slow tempo of the speaker made *in-for-ma-tion* come out as an intimidating word.

"What information?" shouted Ashton in his heightened state of fear. "I'm just a college professor. What do I know that would make you kidnap me?"

"Now Dr. Collins, don't sell yourself short. An established professor at the University of Leeds has access to many types of knowledge; perhaps some things that would interest others."

Ashton shook his head and felt sweat dripping down the back of his shirt. His logical mind of facts and dates couldn't grasp the abstract reality of his current situation.

"What do you want?" Ashton had his head down and spoke in a voice that indicated he was resigned to cooperate.

Silence filled the room again as Ashton contemplated what information the men wanted. The passing of time did nothing to increase his confidence or bravery.

A sudden slap across his face elicited a cry from Ashton and drew blood from his lips. Before he recovered another slap on the bridge of the nose drew more blood.

"That was just a little wake-up call to confirm that we are serious," said the same voice that spoke earlier.

With his hands still tied behind him, Ashton had no way to wipe the dripping blood from his face. The one positive development was the slaps moved the blindfold just enough for him to see a small sliver of light. He viewed a cracked linoleum floor and a pair of shoes that looked like they belonged to a banker instead of a kidnapper. His captors didn't notice the blindfold had shifted up Ashton's face.

"You recently made a trip to Germany, Dr. Collins, and returned with a special letter. My sources tell me you made an interesting deduction about the true meaning of the letter."

Ashton now understood what the men were after, but his mind raced to determine how they could know. He had told only one person about his discovery: Dr. Ambrose Monteith, his department chair and immediate supervisor. *Who had Monteith told? Was his office bugged? It didn't make any sense.*

Ashton felt jolted with the realization that what only days earlier was a clue to an important historical find, now might trigger his own personal—and permanent—demise.

"So you have two options," continued his captor. "First, we can avoid any more unpleasantness. If you can retrieve the letter in question and any notes about the contents, then this day could have a happy ending for all of us." He paused as if deciding on another option. "Or, you could choose option number two and decide to be stubborn. In which case my associate and I will submit you to more pain than you thought possible, convincing you to tell us what we need to know. That option will not be a happy ending for you, but we will still finish this evening with the items we came for."

Ashton sat in silence for several moments, trying to be brave, but knowing he didn't have the fortitude to challenge these two men. He noticed the *bankers'* shoes move away from his limited vision and be replaced by a massive pair of work boots. If the overall size of the man connected to the boots was proportional to his feet, he could break Ashton's body in seconds.

"I believe my colleague would love for you to pick option number two," said the deliberate voice from across the room. "He doesn't talk much, but he's very good at helping others experience pain."

"I have what you want. It's all in my office," said Ashton in almost a whisper.

Ten minutes later he was back in the van, tied up and gagged. The starts and stops of late evening traffic were taking the trio towards the University of Leeds. They soon pulled to a stop and his captors began removing the bindings. The leader gave Ashton a not-so-friendly reminder just before the blindfold came off.

"You will escort me into the building and straight to your office. We will gather the letter you acquired in Germany, any notes or documents related to the letter, and your computer. If we meet anyone else on the way, you will tell them I'm a friend visiting from out of town. Do you understand?"

"I do," replied Ashton.

"Tell me you understand that your life and the life of your lovely sister depends on your success tonight," the man added.

His captor brought Camilla into the conversation during the ride, making it clear that they knew her address near London and other details of her life. They would keep Camilla out of the equation if Ashton cooperated. He was determined not to let his family be part of this; whatever *this* turned out to be.

"I'll do whatever you ask."

Once the blindfold came off, Ashton stepped out of the van, relishing the ability to see his surroundings. It was evening, so only the streetlights invaded his eyes as they adjusted. When he turned to look at his captors, he saw that the larger man had a crude mask over his face. The other wore what appeared to be a fake mustache and an odd hat.

The van was parked in a lot just north of the Parkinson Building, which served as the beacon of the University. Built in 1951, the massive building sat just inside the main entrance and was topped by an iconic clock tower; a tower that had been incorporated into the school logo a few years earlier.

Ashton and the man in disguise followed the sidewalk to the left side of the Parkinson Building and approached the Social Sciences Building, which housed the offices of several departments. Ashton used his campus ID card to scan in through a side door. While doing so, he noticed his captor kept his head down as they passed the security camera above the entrance. They climbed the stairs to the third floor and entered the Department of Medieval History office suite. No one appeared to be around on the early-summer Saturday evening. Even the housekeeping crew was off for the weekend.

The document Ashton brought back from Germany was locked away in a cabinet in his office, along with a few copies and his scribbled notes. He retrieved those items and put them into a leather satchel—all under the menacing eye of his companion. Ashton unplugged his laptop and slipped it inside the satchel.

"Is that all?" the man asked.

Ashton shook his head.

"Who have you told about your discovery?"

"Only Dr. Monteith, my supervisor," admitted Ashton "I haven't contacted anyone else."

"Your computer logs will be checked, so I hope you're telling the truth." The man's tone made it clear that the threat was real.

While Ashton had not technically told anyone else about the letter and his theories, an envelope he prepared the previous day should be on its way to America. His forethought to send information to his friend Matt Kincaid now appeared to be one of the smartest things Ashton had ever done.

"Nine minutes," said the man, checking his watch as they retraced their steps back to the van. "Very good, Mr. Collins. Your speed and cooperation were exemplary."

Once inside the vehicle, the door slammed shut and the men replaced Ashton's blindfold. Ashton hoped this nightmare was about over and he would soon be released. As the van pulled away, his hands were jerked behind him and tied, followed by his feet. Finally, a gag went back in his mouth.

"We appreciate your assistance with our assignment, Mr. Collins," said his captor in a satisfied tone. "Be assured that we will take your findings to someone who will reap the fruits of your labor. Unfortunately, you will not be around to see it."

CHAPTER 2

Present Day

I called Ashton as soon as I awoke in the morning, realizing the five-hour time change made it early afternoon in Leeds. His brief note and the unusual documents—plus the fact that he failed to answer my calls to his cell phone or office—had me confused and worried. I left brief messages and prayed he would call me back soon.

I planned to use Saturday morning to cut the grass for the Hendersons and help spread some mulch in their flower beds, but begged off those tasks and drove to my office after breakfast. Karen and Donnie agreed to watch Maddie and then drop her off across town at a birthday party for a girl in her daycare class. I would pick Maddie up by mid-afternoon and bring her back in time for a nap.

My office is the quintessential professor's space: a ten-by-ten cubicle with book-filled shelves and a paper-covered desk. The one neat spot in the office is the ledge along the window where I keep pictures of Rachel and Maddie. Over the past year, I developed a habit of sitting and staring at the pictures for several minutes each morning. Sometimes it was hard to pull my focus away and move on with my day. At other times, though, I was inspired to do my best because that's what Rachel would have wanted.

"Hey Matt, what are you doing in your office on a Saturday?" I was settling in at my desk and turning on my computer when Ethan Montgomery startled me.

"Uh, you know. Just trying to catch up on things," I replied. "I hope to get some grading done for the online summer class I'm teaching." I didn't want to delve into the topic of Ashton's note and the flash drive in my pocket.

Ethan served as a professor of Renaissance history and had an office down the hall. He and his wife, Chloe, often invited me to their house and offered to care for Maddie when I was overwhelmed. The couple moved to Bannister from the Washington D.C. area a year ago to be closer to Ethan's family. A rumor swirled around campus that the two were involved in uncovering a priceless manuscript in Europe a few years back, but neither could be convinced to talk about it. Now, their big adventure was Chloe's pregnancy and the impending birth of their first child.

I met Ethan regularly for lunch, our conversations usually focused on subjects outside the realm of our professional jobs. Sports, politics, and religion were three of our favorite topics. We also ventured into discussions about handling loss, faith, and the depth of our beliefs. As our friendship developed, I knew when Ethan stopped by my office and asked "How are you doing?", he wasn't being rhetorical. He wanted an honest answer.

"How's that beautiful daughter of yours?" asked Ethan. "Chloe and I haven't seen her for a few weeks."

"Maddie's doing well. She's going to a birthday party today, so I expect her to have a great time and eat way too much sugar."

"Hope you two can join us at church in the morning. And you should take Maddie to our Vacation Bible School in a few weeks. We have preschool programs for three-year-olds."

"I'll see how things work out," I replied, not wanting to commit.

"Okay. I'll send you the details about VBS." Ethan invited me to his church almost weekly for Sunday services and other special functions. I took him up on the offers a few times. He was never pushy and never seemed hurt or judgmental when I turned him down.

"Hope to see you in the morning," Ethan said again as he left the office.

Once he was gone, I ignored the grading I needed to do and pulled out the flash drive from Ashton. It took a few seconds to load after I plugged it into the USB port of my laptop. Once the contents loaded, an icon titled *The Alcuin Letter* appeared.

I recognized the name Alcuin as a scholar and teacher from the Middle Ages. It wasn't unusual for my friend Ashton to have information on Alcuin, as the scholar influenced Charlemagne, perhaps the greatest ruler of medieval times. If I remember correctly, his namesake Alcuin College was part of the University of York in England.

I wondered how a file on Alcuin could be a significant discovery. Maybe this is material for a special lecture.

When I clicked the icon, a low-quality video appeared, most likely made on a computer webcam or a cell phone. Ashton's face filled most of the screen as the video began. He appeared either agitated or excited or a combination of both. His blue eyes were so wide open that they almost looked dilated. His dark hair was uncombed and he wore an old Beatles t-shirt.

After watching for only a minute, I knew this wasn't lecture material. Ashton believed he had found something big.

Dr. Monteith, I know you are out of the country, but I hope you will be checking your emails. Sorry for the video, but I wanted you to be able to see my face when you hear what I have to say. I didn't think a simple email would do this message justice and didn't know if I would be able to reach you by phone. Sorry if I ramble, but I am so excited I can hardly think straight.

Ashton rotated his head as if he was checking to see if anyone else was in the room. He took a deep breath and then continued.

I went to Germany last week after receiving a call from a friend who deals in antiquities. He came across an item he thought might be special and wanted me to look at it. I made a quick trip to Frankfort and my friend showed me a letter that was allegedly written by Alcuin to one of his former students named Rhabanus.

Ashton took another deep breath and seemed to gather himself.

Well, I looked closely at the letter and the Latin script appeared to be similar to other writings from Alcuin. Even though reading Latin is not my forte, I made out enough of the contents to know it wasn't a normal letter between teacher and student.

I asked my friend if I could bring the letter back to England on loan to examine it further. He was hesitant, but I convinced him to let me have it for a week. I arrived back on campus earlier this week and studied the letter almost nonstop. There's some amazing stuff here that you won't believe.

A loud sound happened off camera and Ashton's head jerked around and he left the frame of the camera for about twenty seconds. He came back and continued without an explanation.

The letter mentions Pope Leo III and Charles the Great and the passing of a special gift during a meeting at Paderborn. I have studied the letter for hours and looked for any way to confirm it's a fake, but everything points to it being genuine. I still have to do more research, but Dr. Monteith, I think I know what the gift is that Alcuin talked about.

Once again Ashton looked around and then leaned in close to the monitor. He almost whispered his next words.

Sir, this might sound crazy, but I believe Alcuin is

talking about the cup Christ used at the Last Supper; the so-called Holy Grail. He claims the Catholic Church possessed the cup until Pope Leo III presented it to Charles the Great at their Paderborn meeting. I think this is real and believe I can follow the clues to determine if the cup exists.

The video went blank for a few seconds and I was ready to turn it off, but Ashton's face popped again.

Sorry, Dr. Monteith. I accidentally hit the stop button. I hope you're still watching. I haven't told anyone else about the letter because I thought we needed to get more testing done before we say anything about this find. Please contact me as soon as you get this message.

The video ended and I sat in stunned silence. Was this for real? Was my friend Ashton truly on the trail of the cup of Christ? And why did he send me the pictures and the flash drive? The package had to take a few days to arrive from England, so why had Ashton not called to explain? The questions kept flowing at hyperspeed.

The need to get in touch with Ashton was now even more important. I tried the numbers I had for him again, still not getting an answer. No one would be around his office on a Saturday afternoon and he lived alone, so there was no one to call at Ashton's home. Maybe I could try his parents or sister, but I didn't have any phone numbers for them.

I went online and found a site that searched for phone numbers in England. I tried Ashton's father's name, but Dr. William Collins's number was unlisted. Then I plugged in his sister's name. Ashton often talked about Camilla so I was somewhat familiar with her background. Fourteen hits came up for a Camilla Collins in the London area. I wasn't sure where she lived, so the attached addresses meant nothing to me. There was no way to judge how many people would be home on a Saturday afternoon, but I began dialing the international code for the first number.

My initial three calls went to voice mail, forcing me to leave brief messages introducing myself as Ashton's friend and asking for a return call. Someone answered the next two calls, but both sounded like elderly women and neither knew anyone named Ashton Collins. I left two more messages and was quickly running out of names.

"Hello," said the female voice that answered my eighth overseas call.

"Uh, hello. My name is Matt Kincaid and I'm calling from the United States." I spoke rapidly to squeeze in all the pertinent information before she could hang up. "I'm a friend of Ashton Collins and am trying to contact his sister, Camilla. Do you happen to be the right Camilla?"

A silent pause filled the line. I thought maybe she ended the call. "Yes, I have a brother named Ashton." It sounded like her voice was cracking or maybe the connection was bad. "Who did you say you were?"

Shocked and relieved to finally have the right person, I blurted out, "Matt Kincaid. I know Ashton from when he went to grad school in the States and we've kept in touch. I need to talk to him, but can't reach him on the phone and hoped you could help me."

Another long pause. Her voice sounded strained when she spoke again, like she was trying to hold something back. "Mr. Kincaid, Ashton is dead."

Then her sobs broke loose.

Dominic arrived at one of the most picturesque spots on earth with a heavy heart. Outside the car's window, the Rhone River flowed through a luscious valley of summer green. In the distance were the snow-capped Swiss Alps; the majestic Matterhorn set perfectly in the middle of the Dom and the Weisshorn mountains. Each peak stood over fourteen thousand feet high, providing a daunting lineup of climbing adventures for anyone brave enough and talented enough to make the attempts.

The scenery had little effect on Dominic as he arrived in Saillon, a small village of less than 3,000 people in the southwest corner of Switzerland. The primary language in Saillon was French, but Italian and German were also spoken around the village, a quick drive away from the borders of France and Italy.

Dominic rarely struggled with language barriers, as he was fluent in all three local dialects, plus several others, including English and Latin. Abandoned by a teenage mother at birth, Dominic was raised by the man he was on his way to visit. He showed a knack for languages at a young age and was encouraged to develop his skills, often forced to switch from one language to another multiple times throughout his studies. One day he might have to converse in French during his mathematics lesson and in German for his science class. The next day it could be English all morning, Latin in the afternoon, and Italian after dinner.

The car pulled up to a large stone building with massive ten-foot tall cedar doors waiting at the top of steps rising from the circle drive. Dominic said a few words of thanks to the hired driver before stepping into the cool summer air, carrying a small travel bag and a briefcase. He took a deep breath to calm himself and spent a few moments admiring one of his favorite views: the nearby church tower built 400 years earlier, framed by mountain ranges created by God ages ago.

Dominic pushed open the large doors, which gave little resistance despite their size and age. The foyer he entered was large enough to create its own echoes, and soon the sound of his steps reverberated off the walls. He made his way down the primary hallway and stepped through the final door on his left. A prim and proper woman sat at the desk in the small outer office. She was expecting him. With greying hair pulled up in a bun and a conservative white blouse over a navy blue skirt, the woman stood and took Dominic's suitcase, setting it down behind the desk. She knocked on the door of the inner office, prompting a firm “Enter” from the inhabitant.

“Welcome back, my blessed Dominic.” A large man rose from the antique wooden desk wearing a white priest's robe and a large medallion around his neck. He opened his arms to embrace Dominic, keeping an obvious eye on the briefcase. Dominic accepted the embrace and lifted the case onto the desk.

“I have completed the task you gave to me, Father.”

“The Lord has blessed our efforts,” came the reply from Father Niklaus Griego, the Superior General of the Society of Angels.

At seventy years old, Father Niklaus looked twenty years younger. His face showed only a few lines; lines that added more character to his face than age. His white hair was the only clue to his seven decades on Earth. It was full and thick, not thinning or nonexistent like many of his contemporaries. Griego would claim that fresh air and daily climbs in the Swiss hills were the secrets to his youthful appearance. Very few knew about his secret trips to Milan for procedures often requested by models and actors.

“I have been waiting patiently to study the document you have acquired,” said Griego. “It means a great deal to our movement. We are blessed to have this special opportunity.”

Dominic opened the briefcase, pulled out the twelve-hundred-year-old letter, and handed it to Griego. Despite being sealed in air and water-tight coverings, Griego handled the pages with a unique reverence, showing admiration like they were the tablets of the Ten Commandments. The look on the priest’s face reminded Dominic of a child opening a long-wished-for present.

Griego said, “The delay in getting these back here to Saillon was worrisome, my young Dominic. Now, however, we can move forward with our plans.”

“The two Germans were being especially careful in

leaving England, making sure no one followed," Dominic explained. "They made it to Paris two days ago. Once I confirmed the contents of the package they delivered, I followed your directions and presented them with the second half of their payment. I also passed on your directive that they should return to England and continue to monitor the situation. They agreed to contact you if anyone started to ask too many questions."

"I trust you did not use any names or give any indication that you were part of our Society?" asked Father Griego.

"No, Father. To my knowledge, they have no way to trace who hired them. I am glad to be away from them."

"They are not the type we normally associate with, but in this case, they serve a higher purpose," said Griego. "I also understand from your message yesterday that you are troubled by the loss of life of the college professor. I, too, have been troubled. But in my times of reflection and meditation, I have felt an assurance that this step needed to be taken to ensure our ultimate goal. Unfortunate? Yes. But necessary.

"Do you understand, Dominic?" Father Griego asked.

"I'm trying to, Father. I will keep praying for that assurance," Dominic said, knowing the assurance he sought would remain elusive.

Father Griego continued to admire the document and read through the notes from the college professor. He had already seen the video sent to Dr. Monteith, a man who happened to be a long-standing member of the Society of Angels.

"We are very fortunate that Brother Monteith was wise enough to inform me of the discovery of these pages before the news became public," said Griego. "It can only be God's hand that brought forth this opportunity for us."

"Will we ask Dr. Monteith to help us as we follow the clues in the Alcuin letter?" asked Dominic. "His knowledge in medieval history could be of great assistance."

Griego acted like he didn't hear the question and continued to read Ashton Collins' notes. "No," he finally responded. "I don't think Dr. Monteith will be available to assist us in this endeavor."

CHAPTER 3

My life changed the minute Camilla said that her brother—my friend Ashton—was dead. Not just dead. Murdered.

In the three days since that fateful phone call, I had moved at warp speed to find a way to England. I changed my airline ticket and arranged for a colleague in the history department to finish up the grading for my online class. Next, I made sure that Maddie was taken care of. She would stay with her grandparents most of the time, but Ethan and Chloe Montgomery offered to keep her whenever the Hendersons needed a break.

When the day came for me to leave, saying goodbye to Maddie was harder than I expected. The two of us had barely been apart in the last year. It's difficult to explain to a three-year-old—especially one who had lost her mother—why Daddy needs to fly far away and be gone for several days. Turning away from those big blue eyes and letting go of her tiny hug was an agonizing experience.

On the British Airways flight somewhere over the Atlantic Ocean, far too many things swirled around in my mind to be able to sleep. The in-flight movies didn't hold my attention and I soon found myself mindlessly flipping through the complimentary magazines without reading a word. When most passengers around me were asleep, I pulled out my laptop and powered up the video from Ashton. I plugged in earphones and watched the video for what felt like the millionth time in the last few days. Seeing Ashton, knowing that he died within days of making the recording, was still surreal.

The contents of the video continued to be mind-boggling when I considered that the cup of Christ may be out there somewhere. It was difficult to wrap my mind around that possibility.

I had been a marginal believer in God for most of my life. A fence-sitter. Lukewarm as it says in the Bible. Not a bad person, but not ready to stand behind a pulpit.

Through several conversations with Ethan over the past year and listening to him talk about his faith, I can say that I am leaning toward the true believer side of the fence. However—still being honest—I must also admit that turning my life completely over to Christ continues to be a chasm I am having a hard time summoning the faith to step across.

If I cannot completely accept Christ, why would I have any feelings for a cup He might or might not have held two thousand years ago?

Camilla and I spoke on the phone each day since our initial contact the previous week. She had not been in contact with her brother for several weeks, so had no idea why Ashton would send me a copy of the strange letter and the video. She didn't know about his trip to Germany, the Alcuin letter, or his deduction of where all the new information might lead.

She did, however, keep me updated on the investigation into Ashton's death. He was found stabbed to death in an alley behind a seedy pub on the east side of Leeds, about five kilometers from the University. His wallet and watch were gone, making it initially appear to be a mugging gone wrong. The detectives assigned to the case began to suspect some other motive was in play when they checked with the University of Leeds and discovered Ashton had entered his office building with another man on the same night as the murder. The University's security video was little help in identifying the man, as he wore a large hat that successfully hid his face from the cameras.

The detectives searched Ashton's office, finding an unlocked cabinet and papers on the floor, but not finding his laptop computer. The department's office assistant assured the detectives that Ashton would never leave his office in disarray.

Despite evidence that something much more than a mugging led to Ashton's death, the detectives had not yet come up with a realistic motive.

It was obvious in my mind that Ashton's death had something to do with the Alcuin letter and his hypothesis that the letter held clues to the location of what some called the Holy Grail. Camilla hesitated to speak to the detectives about the Alcuin letter, knowing it would sound like a fantasy. I convinced her to contact the detectives once we had time to look into the letter a little more and were able to talk with Dr. Monteith.

The facts swirled through my mind on an almost endless loop until the plane touched down at Heathrow. According to my body clock, it was the middle of the night, but the flurry of activity around the world's third-busiest airport confirmed that it was 8:00 a.m. in London.

England is on British Summer Time—or BST—which is similar to Daylight Savings Time in the States. The country then switches to Greenwich Mean Time from October through March.

Sometimes the facts I remember make me laugh at myself. Rachel used to tell me that ninety percent of what was in my brain was useless in everyday life but might come in handy if I ever showed up on *Jeopardy*. I guess that's the curse of being a college professor.

I retrieved my luggage and cleared customs before following the crowd through the corridors until I emerged in a large concourse. A throng of people waited to greet travelers from various international flights, but my eyes found Camilla in seconds since her features left no doubt that she was Ashton's sister. She was dressed casually in jeans and a colorful top, with her hair pulled back in a ponytail. Her blue eyes were ringed in red, indicating the time of mourning for her brother was far from over.

We greeted each other awkwardly, feeling like pen pals who knew a lot about one another, but had never met.

We walked to the Short Stay Car Park and found her Fiat, a car I soon realized was too small for my taste. The two of us and my luggage stretched the limit of what the vehicle could hold. Entering the left side of the car as a passenger was strange, only to be outdone by getting up to speed on the M4 highway on the left side of the road. My foot must have hit an imaginary brake pedal a few dozen times as Camilla zipped the car around slower traffic during the forty-five-minute drive to her condo in the London suburb of Dalston.

"You can put your things in the guest bedroom down the hall," said Camilla after we took the elevator from the underground garage to her fourth-floor condo. "Feel free to freshen up. There are clean towels in the bathroom. I will fix us something to eat."

The condo was compact but efficient. There were two bedrooms with small balconies, a general living area, and a small but adequate kitchen. A larger balcony extended from the living room, providing an uninspiring view of another condominium complex next door. Camilla said she didn't spend much time at home as she was often traveling to various places for her photography assignments.

The décor was a modern blend of chrome, leather, and glass, topped off with numerous framed photographs on the wall. The photos—which I assumed were highlights of Camilla's work—were all in black and white; most capturing subjects in a range of close-up emotions. The photos made you want to guess what each person was going through at the time of the picture. I suppose that was the mark of a good photographer.

After showering and changing clothes, I joined Camilla for a late breakfast of eggs, sausages, and toast. A large cup of coffee provided some needed caffeine as I hoped to remain functioning after being awake for almost twenty-four straight hours.

"I appreciate your hospitality," I said after we filled the meal time with small talk. "I could stay in a hotel and not burden you with a visitor; especially with everything else your family is going through."

"I don't mind. I know Ashton was fond of you and, truthfully, I am glad to have someone around. My parents needed to get away after the funeral, so they went to my grandparent's home in Spain and intend to stay for a couple of weeks. Plus, if we are going to work together to follow up on the information Ashton sent you, it will be easier if you're staying here."

"I've been thinking a lot about that," I said. "Are you sure we shouldn't just take all this to the detectives and let them see where it leads? They could find experts to look into Ashton's hypothesis and determine if there is any truth."

"No," she said emphatically. "The authorities are only interested in closing this case and moving on to the next one. Anyway, they probably wouldn't take any of Ashton's thoughts about the purpose of the Alcuin letter seriously. They would file whatever we gave them away and never pursue it. I can't let that happen to something Ashton thought was very important. I need to follow this through to determine if he was on to something and maybe find out why he was killed."

Camilla began to get choked up and turned away to wipe her eyes, trying to hide her raw emotions. The thought crossed my mind that an up-close photograph of her right now would fit in nicely with the others on her wall; her face showing the rough emotions of sorrow, hurt, and confusion, along with hints of inner strength and determination.

I reached across the table and put my hand on hers. “Okay, I’m with you. I have at least a week until I need to fly back home, so let’s see what we can find out.”

Her eyes lifted to meet mine, and I sensed her appreciation.

A bit uncomfortable with our moment of intimacy, I pulled my hand back and cleared my throat. “So, where do we start?”

She gathered herself and reigned in her emotions before speaking again. “Well, I have been trying to contact Ashton’s boss who was the recipient of the video you saw. But Dr. Monteith seems to be on vacation, and no one can get in touch with him. The office assistant is getting a little concerned because she said Monteith normally checks in every few days, even if he’s out of town. She tried his personal cell number a few times and left messages but has not received a response. After Ashton’s death, she’s understandably worried.”

“What about Monteith’s family? Do they know anything?” I asked.

“I guess he’s a long-time bachelor and doesn’t have any close friends around, at least according to Mrs. Barclay, the office assistant. She said Monteith is usually either working at the University or off doing research in various parts of Europe. To her knowledge, he didn’t have much of a social life, and she seemed the type that knows everyone’s business.”

“Monteith must do something outside of work or have some live human being who would know where he is.”

Camilla thought for a second and then mentioned, “Mrs. Barclay did say that Monteith was involved in a church in Leeds pretty heavily. It was called something unusual.” Camilla closed her eyes and tapped her forehead trying to recollect what she’d been told.

“Oh yes!” she exclaimed. “It’s called the Society of Angels. At least I think that’s what she said.”

"Society of Angels. What kind of church is that?" I asked. "Sounds more like a club for high society ladies who sit around drinking tea and telling inspiring stories."

Camille laughed at my comment. "No. I have been around plenty of high society ladies and most would not be described as angels. They sit around and drink tea, but the only stories they tell are all the gossip they collect on everyone in their social circles."

"The Society of Angels—whatever kind of church it is—doesn't sound like a great lead. Maybe we should skip Dr. Monteith for now and go in another direction." I stated.

"Any ideas?" asked Camilla.

"I think we have two other paths to follow. First, I believe we can trace Ashton's footsteps, so to speak, and try to deduce any clues in the letter. Second, we should attempt to find the antique dealer who gave your brother the letter in the first place. The fact that Ashton never mentions the guy's name in the video makes that challenging."

We discussed both options and decided to split the responsibilities. Camilla would do some digging and try to find the name of the antique dealer in Germany, while I would work with the Alcuin letter and do historical research.

With our plan of action in place, Camilla began to track down phone numbers for Ashton's colleagues, assuming others at the University might have had contact with the unknown antique dealer. I set up my laptop on Camilla's table and began researching Alcuin online.

After more than an hour I needed some fresh air, so stood to stretch my legs and moved to the condo's balcony. I pulled out my phone and called back to the States, hoping to talk to Maddie. The time change made it early in the morning in Indiana. Karen Henderson answered and was pleased to hear from me. I told her about meeting Camilla at the airport and that we were already busy looking into the mysterious information sent to me by Ashton.

Satisfied I was safe and sound, Karen put Maddie on the

phone and we communicated the best we could. My heart leaped when she recognized my voice and clearly and excitedly pronounced "Daddy!" I told her over and over that I loved her and would be home soon. It was hard to tell if she grasped the depth of my emotion. Karen assured me before we ended the call that Maddie was getting along just fine.

I remained on the patio after the call, lost in thought while sipping on my second *Coke* of the afternoon. My eyelids were getting heavy when Camilla shouted, "Matt!"

Startled, I almost fell out of the chair getting up. I bolted back inside, thinking something had happened to Camilla, nearly running into her as she came around a corner. "What's wrong?"

"I found him. I found him," she said. We were both breathing hard amidst the sudden flow of adrenaline. "I found the antique dealer."

"Okay, calm down," I said, leading her toward the couch in the living room. "Sit down and tell me about it. Did you talk to one of the other professors at the University?"

"No. I only got in touch with one other colleague in the department and he had no idea who Ashton dealt with. Most of the professors are on holiday, so I ended up leaving a lot of messages."

"So, how did you track the guy down?"

"After being frustrated by my lack of success with the phone calls, it finally dawned on me that Ashton might have interacted with this antique dealer via email. I thought not having Ashton's laptop prevented us from checking his messages, but then I realized there was another way."

She looked at me, wanting me to ask the 'how" question, but I just nodded for her to continue.

"It hit me that even though I don't have his laptop, I could get into Ashton's work email account at Leeds."

After a brief pause, I asked, "But wouldn't you need his password?"

Camilla was smiling now, obviously proud of the

knowledge she possessed. "Yes, but I figured it out. Ashton was extremely smart, but he was also a man of habit and simplicity."

Again she paused, waiting for me to ask the next obvious question. "So…," I prompted.

"His campus email address was the login name so I just needed the password. It's p-a-c-m-a-n," she said, spelling out the letters.

I looked at her strangely, trying to figure out if I heard correctly.

"He played the arcade game of Pac-Man endlessly when he was a kid," she explained. "He played so much that Pac-Man became his nickname, and it stuck."

Ashton never mentioned to me his passion for the 1980s arcade phenomenon. "What did you find out?"

"I searched through hundreds of emails going back several weeks and finally came across a message from Germany." Camilla was still excited and talked in spurts. "There was only one message, but it gave some specifics about the location and time for a meeting to examine a letter from the ninth century. The message arrived about three weeks ago, which lines up with the timeframe for Ashton's trip to Germany."

"Who was the email from?" As excited as Camilla was, she seemed content to draw out the revelation of what she found.

"The message came from a Dennis Simons at Simons Antiquities, Inc. I looked up some information and found out he's an American who owns a small antique shop in Frankfort. Nothing about his business looks remarkable, but at least we have the phone number."

We decided there was no time like the present, so Camilla dialed the number for Dennis Simons. When he didn't pick up, Camilla left a quick message, blurting out a synopsis of the entire situation, including Ashton's death. She hinted that his murder may have been because of the

Alcuin letter.

I wouldn't have provided so much information in a phone message, but Camilla had it out before I could stop her.

Now, we just needed to wait.

CHAPTER 4

I offered to take Camilla out for dinner as a small payment for her hospitality. She suggested a pub within easy walking distance and we ended up at a place called The Duke of Wellington. The outside looked like a classic London street corner pub, but the inside had been remodeled to meet the tastes of the younger, hipper clientele that lived in the area. A decent crowd filled the seats on this weekday evening, so we slipped into a booth in the back, hoping to avoid the rowdy patrons watching football—soccer to those of us from the States—on the big screen. Camilla ordered a spicy chicken dish, while I settled on the traditional British meal of fish and chips.

Camilla put her cell phone on the table and stared at it frequently throughout the meal, waiting anxiously for Dennis Simons to call her back.

She was in the same outfit as earlier but had taken a few minutes to spruce up her appearance before we left for dinner. Her hair was styled a bit, hanging down below her shoulders. She found time to put on some makeup—which accentuated her crystal blue eyes—and added a simple silver necklace and matching bracelet.

I couldn't remember the last time a woman's appearance had been on my radar.

"Do you want to know a little about the man named Alcuin?" I asked once we had finished our meals.

"Absolutely," replied Camilla, giving me her full attention.

"I thought I would do some research on Alcuin to make sure the timing of the letter and some of his claims match up with historical facts. I knew a little about him, but spent this afternoon digging."

"Do you still believe that it could be the real thing?"

"I've only completed a rough translation of the Latin text in the main body of the letter. So far I haven't come across anything that looks out of place historically. Also, your brother mentioned in the video that the handwriting looked genuine. From samples I've been able to find online, I would have to agree with him."

The brief mention of Ashton caused a flicker of sadness to show on Camilla's face. I could tell she was thinking about seeing her brother on the video and realizing he died shortly after he made it. She gathered herself and asked, "So who was Alcuin and how could he possibly know the location of the cup of Christ?"

Despite the jet lag beginning to win the battle for my consciousness, I went into my professor mode and spent several minutes giving Camilla the background on Alcuin of York.

"Alcuin was a great scholar and teacher who earned his scholarly reputation by rising to a leadership position at the York School in England, which was a renowned center of learning. On his way back from a trip to Rome in 781, Alcuin met Charles—better known today as Charlemagne—in the Italian city of Parma and was persuaded to join Charlemagne's court.

"Charlemagne reigned over a massive amount of the continent, including all of what makes up the current countries of Germany and France, plus parts of Spain, Italy, Switzerland, and Austria. He welcomed Alcuin to the Palace School in Aachan in 782, a school set up for the education of the royal children. Alcuin not only enhanced the education of the royal family, including Charlemagne himself, but he also helped establish educational standards in cathedral schools and monasteries throughout the kingdom.

"Alcuin was with Charlemagne in 799 during the well-documented visit of Pope Leo III. Leo had been attacked in Rome by those who wanted to overthrow his papal crown and then traveled to Paderborn to request Charlemagne's assistance. No one knows for sure what transpired during the meeting in Paderborn, but it's often been assumed that the two made some type of deal. According to Alcuin's letter, Leo privately presented Charlemagne with a gift at that meeting; a gift that held great importance for the church.

"A little more than a year later, a ceremony took place in the original Basilica of St. Peter in Rome. That's when Pope Leo III bestowed the title of Holy Roman Emperor on Charlemagne and placed an imperial crown on his head.

"By the time Charlemagne was crowned in Rome, Alcuin was over sixty years old and requested to relinquish his duties at the Palace School. Charlemagne put Alcuin in charge of the Abbey of Tours in France. At Tours, Alcuin continued to draw students who wanted to learn from the great scholar until he died in 804. One of the students was Rhabanus, who became the Abbot of Fulda in Germany and took over Alcuin's mantel as one of the most learned men of the age.

"Wasn't Rhabanus the recipient of the letter from Alcuin?" Camilla asked, breaking up my lecture. At least she was listening.

"Yes. From what I've learned from the letter so far, I believe that it must have been written around 804, a few months before Alcuin died. The letter reads like a deathbed confession."

Camilla yawned and I couldn't help but catch it.

"As exciting as your history lesson is, we better head back and get some sleep," she said. "Something tells me that this will be a busy week."

That turned out to be a massive understatement.

The night was as black as Father Niklaus Griego's mood. He stood on the balcony of his large estate located five kilometers outside Saillon and stared up at a starless sky. He often had an enviable view of the moon hanging above an alpine vista, but tonight a summer storm was moving in; the smell of rain forecasting the coming deluge.

Griego spent the last two days doing nothing but studying the Alcuin letter and following the research initiated by the professor in England. He began the process assuming that Ashton Collins had figured out the Alcuin letter and knew the final location of the cup of Christ. That assumption turned out to be incorrect. While Griego was well-informed about men like Alcuin, Charlemagne, and Rhabanus, he was not an expert and increasingly became frustrated as he tried to decipher the scribbles and vague notations made by Collins.

It turned out that asking the German enforcers to help Dr. Ambrose Monteith disappear—a task even Dominic didn't know about—was a mistake. The distinguished professor's expertise on medieval history would come in useful right now, and Griego was hesitant to bring in other outsiders. He wanted to keep news of the possible discovery quiet until he held the artifact in his hands.

Father Griego's research was at a standstill. As a man used to getting results quickly, he was not handling the lack of progress very well.

The man the world now knew as Niklaus Griego was only thirty-two years old; at least the name had only been around for a little more than three decades. Formerly known as Niklaus Schaeffler, he took over his father's local trucking business near Munich, Germany, as an eager twenty-five-year-old in 1979. Through willpower, intimidation, and many back-room deals Niklaus expanded the transport business across Europe and into parts of the former Soviet Union. *Schaeffler Transport Logistics* grew into a multi-million dollar company by 1990.

A year later, following the death of his wife from a rare form of cancer, Niklaus unexpectedly sold the company and disappeared. Most assumed he was going through a mourning period and wanted his privacy. As time passed and world events moved forward, Niklaus Schaeffler was forgotten; only mentioned in a few obscure business journals. Without any children and as an only child himself, very few relatives were concerned with his whereabouts. To most of the world, he simply didn't exist anymore.

Niklaus grew up believing in God and regularly attended mass with his parents at St. Peter's Church, the oldest church in Munich. Once he grabbed control of his father's business and it began to expand, Niklaus became a more infrequent visitor to St. Peter's. Privately, the gods of wealth and success became his inspiration more than any heavenly calling. Still—through habit more than inspiration—he managed to go to confession at least once a month, unloading the many burdens that came with running an international business.

Then Niklaus' wife died. Even though the marriage was forged out of convenience—Natalia Schaeffler was the daughter of a former competitor in the transport business—she was the one constant human relationship in Niklaus' life. With her gone, the drive to expand the company and acquire more wealth was no longer present. Niklaus soon found a buyer for his thriving business and went into seclusion with a net worth approaching $250 million. The day that he signed the final papers for the sale of his business was the last day Niklaus Schaeffler existed.

Niklaus Griego emerged three years later with a new face—thanks to plastic surgery—a new passion, and a young adopted son named Dominic. He spent two of those years studying at the Monastery of Yuste, an obscure outpost in the small village of San Yuste, Spain. Yuste was kept open by Father Enrique Fortuna, a once-proud Catholic Cardinal who left the church because of disagreements about policy and doctrine. Still a believer in God and the value of faith, Fortuna took in many religious wanderers looking for a secluded place to study and to heal. Several of these wanderers just happened to have the resources to donate a substantial monthly tithe to the monastery.

Niklaus received lessons in religious doctrine, church history, and languages. He learned the lessons but also questioned everything. Long and sometimes heated discussions with Father Enrique were commonplace. The two debated the existence of God, the role of religion as the 21st century approached, and the problems with the current Catholic Church and other denominations. They also spent many hours discussing the potential of starting a new religious movement based only on the positive messages from scripture: no fire and brimstone; no cumbersome rules; only love and acceptance with a small dash of actual Biblical learning.

During his final months at Yuste, Niklaus took in a young boy abandoned at the entrance to the monastery. He considered the opportunity a calling and accepted the chance to raise the boy under his watchful influence. In a way, the boy would be his grand experiment. Niklaus planned to prove that his ideas on faith and religion resulted in a positive impact on the people of the world—even one abandoned at a young age.

After leaving Yuste, Niklaus spent a small portion of his wealth paying off the right people to develop a new identity, complete with a birth certificate, passport, and fictional family history. With his altered identity solidly in place, Father Niklaus Griego appeared. His new passion would be an organization he called the Society of Angels, named after something his wife used to say when she heard about good deeds being done: "*There are still angels in our society if you know where to look.*" Natalia said those words often even as she was dying from cancer.

Griego's first steps included the purchase and renovation of an abandoned abbey in Saillon, Switzerland, to become the headquarters and training ground for the Society. He also built his estate outside of the village. Through connections made during his time at the Monastery at Yuste, Griego recruited several influential individuals to serve as his public relations arm. Soon the Society of Angels had a small following. The positive, feel-good message Griego espoused found its niche among the upper class and well-educated crowd. The growth of the internet as the 21st century approached provided another avenue to promote his doctrine, and Griego took full advantage.

Griego insisted that the followers he trained to help spread his message be called *priests* and that they wear robes similar to those in the Catholic Church when on official duty. He believed such touches of tradition gave the message of the Society more legitimacy and provided an aura of familiarity for those who might initially be uncomfortable with the more modern take on religion.

By the time the Society was ten years old, it boasted pockets of followers in Switzerland, Spain, Germany, Italy, and France. The movement continued to expand with growing numbers in England and other parts of Europe. Approaching thirty years of existence, the society's membership numbers were nearing one hundred thousand; small compared to some denominations, but very powerful when considering the collective wealth and influence held by the Society's members. Father Niklaus—as most called him—was now much more powerful and influential than he'd ever been as a millionaire businessman.

That power and influence were doing him very little good right now as he sat at the massive mahogany desk in his study and stared again at the materials retrieved from

Leeds.

A week ago he had been convinced that the time for the Society of Angels to become a major world movement was just over the horizon. The call from Brother Monteith about the Collins's video and the Alcuin letter was unexpected. But just as he had done as a successful businessman, Griego jumped on the opportunity, using his vast network to make anonymous contact with a German duo known for being quick and discreet. The pair completed their assignment with ruthless efficiency, snipping off loose ends and delivering the requested materials. Now, if Griego could hold the actual cup of Christ as proof that God blessed the Society, the Society would gain a layer of legitimacy that it currently lacked among mainstream religious circles. The exposure would also cause an explosion of growth in membership around the world.

For those things to happen, however, Griego had to find a way to connect the clues sitting in front of him. He was confident a breakthrough was agonizingly close, much like how one feels when a name is on the tip of the tongue but refuses to leap from the subconscious to the spoken word.

Weary and growing in frustration, Father Niklaus was ready to retire for the evening when a cell phone chimed, startling him. He opened the top drawer of his desk and removed a phone with a number known to only one person.

"Yes?" he answered after several rings.

"Do you know who this is?" said the caller in German.

"Yes," said Griego. "Why are you contacting me?"

"We promised to inform you if any noteworthy inquiries or unwanted scrutiny arose after our previous assignment," the man said calmly and slowly. "Something came up today that we felt you should know."

"Explain," said Griego, trying to remain cool, but already running unpleasant scenarios through his mind. Was there some way the actions against Monteith or the other Leeds professor could be connected to the Society? He couldn't comprehend how that would happen, but the Germans were calling for some reason.

"We kept tabs on the sister of the professor in Leeds, just in case we needed extra leverage to entice his cooperation," the man explained. "The voice-activated bug we put in her flat near London had a two-week lifespan. The bug sends a wireless signal to a receiver we stashed outside the flat, which then transmits any content to a secure server we can access from anywhere."

'Okay. I am impressed with your technical knowledge," Griego snapped sarcastically. "Now tell me what you have found."

"This evening we checked the server one more time before the bug ran out of power," the man continued, still pronouncing each word patiently and distinctly. "We heard some interesting conversation from earlier today between the sister and another man."

Griego did not respond, but took a deep breath to calm himself, waiting for the man to continue.

"First, the woman talked about trying to track down Monteith, but had hit a dead end," the man snickered to himself, obviously considering his use of the words *dead end* as a pun. "Then she made calls to other professors from Leeds, this time trying to locate an antique dealer in Germany. She came up with the dealer's name and left him a phone message. We believe the man with her is a history professor. He was researching the Alcuin guy who wrote the letter we retrieved for you. The man sounded American, though, not British."

Father Niklaus wondered how the sister and the American man were aware of anything related to Alcuin or the antique dealer. A wealthy member of the Society of Angels paid the greedy antique dealer in Frankfort very well for his silence. And from all he had determined, Ashton Collins told nobody but Dr. Monteith about his discovery.

The German continued. "The pair mentioned something

about a package sent to America. It also sounded like they gained information from a video, but I couldn't determine the origin of the video."

Griego knew exactly what video the man was talking about. Again, he was perplexed by how the woman and her new friend came into possession of a copy. He would need to worry about the *how* later. Right now he needed to take action to ensure the pair in England did not create any additional complications.

"It sounds like I have another assignment for you," Griego said after taking a few moments to think. "The sister and her American friend need to be out of the picture and it needs to look like an accident."

"We can be at the sister's home in London tomorrow," replied the German. "Accidents are a bit trickier, though. Our fee will need to be adjusted."

Through gritted teeth, Griego agreed. "I'll add twenty-five percent to your fee after seeing satisfactory results. And this accident needs to happen soon."

"Agreed," said the man. "We'll be in touch."

Griego tossed the phone back in the drawer and resisted the urge to shout out words not normally heard from a priest. He sat and stared out the window, the night still clothed in darkness, the rain now falling in torrents.

CHAPTER 5

It feels good to run again. What started as a daily chore several weeks ago is now something I almost look forward to. With all that was going on, running lent a sense of normalcy to my life; even during my first run in Dalston, England. It would also give me some time to think.

Despite rushing over to England, I still am not convinced I'm doing the right thing in helping Camilla unravel the mystery of her brother's death. Am I trying to be noble or only acting out of a false sense of responsibility because I'm the one who received the package from Ashton? Is it rational to leave my three-year-old daughter at home to get involved with something that could be dangerous? Or, am I listening too much to the small voice in the back of my mind telling me how cool it would be to make a major historical discovery?

It took me about a mile of running to feel fully awake. The beautiful, cool morning, was unlike the summer heat and humidity I often battled at home. I ran along Heyworth Road, turned left on Napoleon, and then continued on Queensdown Lane until I arrived at the entrance of Hackney Downs Park. The park was not large but had several trails that all came together in a central pavilion and playground area. From above, I imagined it looked like a wagon wheel. I ran down each *spoke,* then along the perimeter to the next *spoke*, which I followed back to the center. After forty-five minutes, I stopped for a drink from an outdoor fountain and found a nice spot on the grass to stretch.

While my body cooled down a bit, my mind drifted back to this quest Camilla and I were on. I still have a hard time comprehending the fact that we might be on the trail to the actual cup Jesus used at the Last Supper; the occasion where he compared bread and wine to his body and blood. Could it be the cup used at the first communion service two thousand years ago?

Along with doing research on Alcuin, Charlemagne, and others in medieval times, I also looked into the theories concerning the cup of Christ. It turned out there were as many theories as there are denominations in the Protestant church. The theories varied widely in their origin, their conclusions, and their believability.

Not surprisingly, none of the theories mentioned anything about Pope Leo III and Charlemagne. Only one claimed the cup was ever in possession of the Popes or the church at all, theorizing that Pope Sixtus II in the year 258 put the cup in the hands of a deacon to save it from being taken by the Roman emperor Valerian. After centuries of being acquired, hidden, and rescued through various means, the *Santo Caliz*—or Saints Chalice—found its way to the Cathedral of Valencia in Spain, where it still resides. The *Santo Caliz* gained notoriety when Pope John Paul II used it during Mass while visiting Valencia in 1982.

Of course, the theory has been shot down by scientific claims that the materials in the Valencia cup are not old enough to have come from the first century A.D.

Then there's the plethora of theories and conspiracies surrounding the Holy Grail, which has been described as anything from the cup used at the Last Supper to the secret offspring of Christ.

I always thought the idea that Jesus didn't die on the cross but covertly slipped away with a woman and started a family was a bit mind-boggling. As a person who could be described as a marginal Christian, the idea that the entire

Christian faith was predicated on a *savior* who skipped town is hard for me to fathom. After all, the Christian movement spread because of a handful of dedicated followers in the first century who were under the very real threat of persecution and death. Who would put their life on the line for a man who made outrageous claims, then found a wife and slipped away? Even if a person had absolutely no Christian faith, the theory that the Holy Grail is a descendant of Christ should come across as ridiculous.

Associating the Holy Grail to the Cup of the Last Supper happened in the 12th century when Robert de Boron penned a long poem titled *Joseph d'Arimathie*. Boron's story told of Joseph of Arimathea receiving the Holy Grail from an apparition of Jesus and passing it to followers of Jesus who took it to Great Britain.

Over the last eight centuries, stories and theories about the Grail became all the more implausible; more like fairy tales than anything a rational person would believe. Unless, of course, money could be made by making those fairy tales into books or movies.

Thoughts of the cup, Ashton's death, and my part in this little adventure battled in my mind as I jogged slowly back to Camilla's condo. By the time I made the final turn on Heyworth Road and the condo was in sight, I had made a decision: I would stay two more days and help Camilla and then fly back to the States and to a normal life. Despite my friendship with Ashton and my genuine sorrow at his death, I couldn't risk something severely disrupting my life, and by extension, Maddie's life. My daughter had already been through enough.

Before crossing the final street I stopped as a slow-moving work van passed by. The side of the van advertised an internet television company, and I happened to see the driver and his passenger as it passed. Both of them were looking toward the condo complex. I thought it odd that one was dressed in a business suit and the other in work clothes.

Maybe the boss was doing a ride-along today. I jogged across the street as the van pulled to the curb about half a block ahead.

I took the elevator to Camilla's fourth-floor condo and heard a man's voice when I entered. "Camilla. Where are you?" I called out, instantly on alert.

"Shhhhh. Matt, get over here," she said in a kind of emphatic whisper.

I followed her voice into the kitchen and found Camilla staring at her phone. The man's voice coming out of the phone was rushed and breathless. The high-pitched tenor sounded more a result of anxiety than a normal speaking tone. By the time my brain registered who the voice most likely belonged to, it was gone.

"Was that who I think it was?" I said, looking at Camilla expectantly.

"Dennis Simons called me back. He called when I was in the shower and left a message. I just noticed the message light blinking before you came in." Her words came in short bursts, making it painfully obvious she was still frazzled by this whole situation.

Who wouldn't be? Losing a brother to murder; finding out he might have been on the trail of a major historical discovery; looking for clues in a twelve hundred-year-old letter; hosting a foreigner you barely know in your condo. The combination of those things would be tough for anyone to handle.

"What did he say?"

"He didn't know the value… heard about Ashton's death… was paid off..." She wasn't making much sense. "Oh, listen for yourself," she finally said and pushed a button on her phone.

This is Dennis Simons. I need to make this quick, but I got your message and wanted to say I know about Ashton, and I'm sorry. I shouldn't be contacting you, but you deserved to hear from me after what happened. I didn't know the true value of the letter I gave him. I acquired it from a contact at the Grey House in Winkel and was just hoping to make a few bucks. A man stopped at my house last week asking about the letter and wanting to know where I found it. I didn't tell him the truth because I didn't trust him. He ended up paying me a lot of money to forget about the letter and warned me not to talk to anyone about it. Honestly, the man scared me. Also, I think I'm being watched, so I have already said more than I should. Please don't try to contact me again. And be careful.

The message ended. Camilla and I stared at each other for a long moment.

"Play it again," I said. So she did.

"What do you think," she asked, once the recording ended.

"I think he sounded scared," I replied. "I'm sure hearing about Ashton's death and getting an intimidating visit from a stranger has to be unsettling. I'm surprised he called you back."

"I agree," Camilla said. "I also keep thinking about the timing and scope of everything that has gone on. We assume Ashton's death was related to the Alcuin letter he received from Simons, a person none of Ashton's colleagues knew about and we had a hard time tracking down. Ashton died about ten days ago in Leeds. A short time later Simons gets a visit in Frankfort, is warned to keep quiet about the letter, and is bribed to assure his silence. Whoever is doing all of this must have some resources."

"Just the fact that they knew about the letter shows some inside knowledge," I added. "Plus, we believe they were able to kidnap Ashton and make his death look like a mugging gone wrong. I would think an operation like that had to take some planning and experience. When you include the contact and payoff to Simons, I agree it adds up to something much bigger than a local thug trying to make a big score by stealing a medieval artifact."

We both considered the seriousness of what we were doing. Did we want to move forward or play it safe? My decision to give it two more days was still feeling like the best move. One day might even be smarter. And safer.

"What do we do next? What can we do with the information we have?" Camilla asked, obviously making up her mind to push forward with our search.

"Well, I'm going to take a quick shower," I said, hoping a few minutes alone would give Camilla the chance to reconsider. Plus, I didn't exactly have a pleasant aroma after my run.

"Hey, what was that Simons said about a grey house?" she asked as I walked toward the spare bedroom.

I turned in the hallway, thinking about the exact words in Simons' message. "I think he said he got the Alcuin letter from a contact at a grey house in Winkel. I know Winkel is a town in Germany, but not sure about the grey house reference. There are probably a lot of grey houses in Winkel.

"Why don't you look up Winkel online while I'm in the shower and see if any possible connection with a grey house comes up?"

Twenty minutes later I was clean. When I returned to the front room of the condo, Camilla's face showed a smile of satisfaction. "What?" I asked.

"I know what the grey reference is about," she replied proudly. "Maybe you should hire me to do historical research for you."

"Okay, impress me with your knowledge."

"The reference is actually to the Graues Haus," Camilla said with her best German accent, "which translates literally to the Grey House that Simons mentioned. It's considered one of the oldest stone houses in Germany.

"Here's the key fact," she continued. "Although there's still debate on when the house was originally built, some theories say it was erected in the 9th century and was the place where Rhabanus Maurus lived his final years until he died in 856. That's the same Rhabanus who studied under Alcuin and was the recipient of the letter Simons gave to Ashton.

"Good job, Camilla. I didn't know Rhabanus died in Winkel," I admitted. "I guess I stopped my research of him once I learned he had a connection to Alcuin. The fact that he died in Winkel lines up with what Simons said about the Alcuin letter and gives me more confidence in the authenticity of the document."

"I wonder who Simons' contact was at the Grey House?" said Camilla as if she was thinking out loud. "I wonder where, exactly, the letter was found and why someone would give it to Simons?"

"All good questions. But, at this point, I don't know if they're relevant; at least as far as following the clues in the letter are concerned. As I said, this information helps give us confidence the letter is real. That's worth something. At least we don't have to worry that we're on a wild goose chase."

"On a what?" she asked with a perplexed look.

It took me a second to realize what she was asking. "Oh," I said with a snicker. "A wild-goose chase. You don't know what that means?"

She shook her head.

"I'm surprised since the saying started with your countryman William Shakespeare." I am back to showing off some of my worthless storehouse of knowledge. "I think he used it in *Romeo and Juliet*. We use it now to describe a worthless and often lengthy pursuit."

Camilla's red cheeks indicated a slight bit of embarrassment, but her jaw was set with determination as she thought of a reply.

"Okay, Professor", she said, laying on the sarcasm. "What if I said '*the cake is a lie*' in relationship to the letter? Would you know what I meant?"

The cake is a lie. What is this woman talking about? "No," I finally acknowledged. "I have no idea, but I bet you're going to tell me."

"Well, I once knew a gaming nerd whose favorite game was called *Portal.* I don't remember exactly what was going on in the game but '*the cake is a lie*' was a warning. Some gamers picked up on it and used the saying to mean something was unattainable or the promised reward was false. The saying became one of those aphorisms that made its way around the internet and even out into some everyday usage."

"I guess I also learned something new today, so thanks for teaching me," I said, matching her sarcastic tone. Then turning serious again, "I hope this cake we're chasing is no lie."

CHAPTER 6

Winkel, Germany, March of 856

The old man wrapped a worn blanket around his shoulders, trying to fight off the chills that seemed to be his constant companion. The final remnants of winter were stubbornly holding on as a brushing of snow formed a thin layer on the pine trees surrounding the small stone house.

The young monk who attended to the aged man built a roaring fire in the fireplace and brought a steaming bowl of soup to the table.

"This should help warm you Father Rhabanus," said the monk as he helped the former Archbishop of Mainz to his seat at the table.

"Thank you, my young Marinus. Your continued kindness and assistance have been a blessing to me in my final days."

"Do not talk like that Father. You have many more days ahead."

Rhabanus tried to laugh, but it came out as a wheezing growl. "Oh, you know lying is a sin," he said with a weak grin. "The Lord has blessed me with a long life. What is it now? I believe I have been on this earth for seventy-five years, which is more than most men. I am confident my final breath is not far away and am content with that knowledge."

The old man ate his soup in silence, his coughing spells

causing the process to take several minutes. When finished, Rhabanus motioned the young monk to his side.

"Marinus, you have proven yourself faithful in the little I have asked you to do," Rhabanus said in a weak voice. He needed to catch his breath between each sentence. "Now, I must present you with a task that is of great importance." Another breath. "I have held onto a secret that needs to be told. It is time."

Marinus sat silently and waited for Rhabanus to catch his breath and continue.

"I have been in possession of an important letter since I was about your age, more than fifty years. The letter came to me from my teacher, the great Alcuin of York. The letter tells the story of a priceless relic Pope Leo III secretly presented to Charles the Great; an act that took place when Alcuin accompanied the great King in Paderborn."

Marinus' eyes grew large and his mouth hung open as he recognized the names of three people revered by many: the great teacher Alcuin, the mighty conqueror and leader Charles the Great, and the former holy leader of the Catholic Church Leo III. Marinus knew of Rhabanus' past as a Bishop but never imagined he had any connections to such iconic men from recent history.

"Alcuin hides the location of the relic in the words of a poem, which he included in the letter. I want you to take this letter to Rome," continued Rhabanus, "and deliver it personally to Pope Benedict. I will write you a letter of introduction so he will welcome you for a private meeting."

"What is this relic the letter talks about?" asked Marinus.

Rhabanus seemed to ignore the question. "Help me to my bed, my young friend," he said, barely above a whisper.

Marinus essentially carried the frail man to his bed. He covered him in several blankets and added more wood to the fire.

"I will answer your questions in the morning," said

Rhabanus. "Come at first light and I will send you on your journey."

"Yes, Father," replied the monk as he began to put out the candles that provided light to the small cottage.

"Leave the candle burning by my bed as I might want to read from the scriptures for a few moments."

Marinus finished his chores and left the cottage to return to the nearby abbey for the evening.

In the dim light of the single candle by his bed, Rhabanus managed to sit upright and then stand. He made the short walk to the fireplace, his age making each step like walking against a gale-force wind. He found the right stone on the outside edge of the fireplace and used his bony fingers to twist and pull until the stone came loose. The effort drained what little energy Rhabanus had. He stayed motionless with his head bowed for several minutes, his breath coming in raspy and uneven intervals. He finally steeled himself and reached into the gap left by the removed stone. A small metal box emerged from the gap. Clutching it close to his body, Rhabanus shuffled back to his bed.

He opened the box and gently removed the letter he had read often over the years. On many occasions, Rhabanus had been tempted to pass the letter on to someone else, mostly so he would not have to live with the weight of what the letter contained. He was confident that he was the only man alive who knew what had taken place so many years ago in the forest near Paderborn.

Knowing his final breath on Earth would not be far into the future, Rhabanus would now entrust Marinus to take the letter to Rome. And he would pray the current Pope would have the ability to not only find the relic but also use it wisely.

He read the letter through, even though the words were ingrained in his mind almost as well as passages from scripture. Rhabanus then used his remaining strength to put the letter in the box and return it to its hiding place. Once back to his bed, he extinguished the lone candle and laid his head down, hoping for a restful night's sleep. The familiar words Alcuin wrote in the letter hung in his mind as he balanced between consciousness and slumber.

My dearest Rhabanus,

Greetings to you from your friend and teacher. Word arrived of your great success at the school in Fulda and I know you and your students will fervently pursue learning and scholarship. I pray the Lord continues to bless your efforts and encourage you always to seek knowledge with diligence and purity of heart.

My days on this Earth are coming to an end. Before my time comes to cross that bridge between earthly life and the promise of eternal life, I must release a burden. In releasing that burden through this letter, I regret the knowledge I possess will now become a yoke around your neck. My solemn prayer is that you have the wisdom and insight to protect the knowledge and pass it on when appropriate.

During my final days of leadership at the Palace School in Aachen I was asked to join King Charles in Paderborn where a new cathedral was being built. Within months after my arrival, Charles asked me to accompany him on a late evening ride. The ride took us into the forest, where we met a small group of men. I was surprised when I realized one of the men was Pope Leo III. The Holy Father revealed a small wooden box and asked to meet with Charles in private.

Charles remained silent about the contents of the box for several days as he continued to hold meetings with Pope Leo in Paderborn. When the king finally sent for me to join him in his chambers I sensed he was troubled. He revealed to me the gift that Pope Leo had given him and I was astonished. According to Charles, very few people knew the Church had possession of this holy relic. Each Pope was made aware of its existence on the day of his coronation and tasked with protecting the secret. Each Pope also went through the internal battle of deciding whether making the existence of the relic widely known would be a blessing to the Church or provide more motivation for the Church's many enemies.

Pope Leo had already been attacked in Rome and had a tenuous hold on the Papal throne when he visited King Charles at Paderborn. Charles accepted the special gift from Leo for safekeeping. The King was wise enough to understand the unspoken request that he also protect Leo when the Pope returned to Rome.

During our time together over the next several months, Charles often asked my advice. Despite his great position and many accomplishments, King Charles experienced a crushing burden when he took possession of a relic that had such significance for those of the Christian faith. Much like the Popes throughout history, he was torn between openly honoring the relic's significance and securing it to protect it for centuries to come.

After long discussions, we agreed the relic should be preserved at all costs. To my surprise and dismay, Charles asked that I secretly arrange to secure the relic and personally carry out the plan. He did not want the burden of knowing where this priceless gift would reside. Although he was unaware, the King played a part in helping me complete that task.

King Charles' final request was that I ensure the item's location be passed on to someone I trusted before my death. I am using this letter to fulfill that request. I pray you will do the same when the time is right.

In all my years of teaching, Rhabanus, you were my most impressive and diligent student. Therefore, I am confident your knowledge and wisdom will allow you to interpret the following words. I use the verses below to help protect the identity and location of the relic from all those of lesser insight and intellect who might read these words.

From God comes a son;

From the son comes blood;
From the blood comes life;
Drink from the cup of life and be saved.
From the house of wisdom come gifts;
From the gifts comes a golden vessel;
From the vessel comes a hiding place;
Open the vessel of life and be saved.
From a king comes a journey;
From a journey comes a place to rest;
From a place to rest comes a gift;
Discover the gift of life and be saved.
From a martyr comes a church;
From a church comes constant praise;
From praise comes redemption;
Find redemption in life and be saved.

My deepest apologies for putting this burden upon you, though I am confident you are capable of fulfilling this calling. May God bless your life and your efforts in this endeavor. I look forward to meeting again in the heavenly realm.

Your friend, Alcuin

Rhabanus deciphered the sixteen lines of verse many years ago, but it took much effort. He understood that with the number of years passing since the creation of the letter, the answer would be more difficult for others to uncover. He prayed, though, that the secret would be discovered and the hidden relic revealed to the world. He never believed himself worthy to be the one to make such an announcement.

Rhabanus finally drifted off to sleep, content that the letter would be on its way to Rome in the morning.

Marinus knocked on the door of the stone house just as the sun inched its way above the horizon. The chorus of birds singing nearby attested to the dawn of a glorious day. Not hearing a reply, which was not unusual, Marinus opened the large wooden door and saw Father Rhabanus still in his bed. That was unusual. The elderly man was known to be up well before dawn each day to study the scriptures and pray.

A gentle touch to the hand of Rhabanus was all Marinus needed to confirm his fears. The coldness proved only the body of the former Archbishop of Mainz remained; his soul had departed sometime during the night.

Marinus remembered that Rhabanus wanted him to deliver something important to Rome. Pushing back his grief and hoping to fulfill that final request, he looked carefully throughout the small house. He found nothing except the sparse belongings of a man who dedicated his life to God, learning, and teaching.

CHAPTER 7

Camilla and I debated our next move for the second time in less than twenty-four hours. She wanted to follow up with Dennis Simons, go meet him in person, and talk about the origin of the Alcuin letter.

I didn't think that was the best idea.

First, we would have to travel to Germany, which would take time and money. Both of those things were in short supply for me, especially if I was going to meet my two-day timeline to return home. Second, I wasn't excited about walking into a situation that seemed uncertain, at best, and dangerous, at worst.

She countered that we could fly to Frankfort in the morning and visit Simons' antique shop. After looking up the distance, Camilla said we could even make the forty-five-minute drive to Winkel, if necessary. She volunteered to cover the cost of the flight, as her freelance photography career allowed her to build a huge cache of frequent flyer miles.

Camilla failed to soothe my fears about the possible danger, but her actions hinted the motivation to find out more about her brother's death was serving as a kind of emotional Novocain, numbing her sense of fear. I would have been the same way if Rachel's death would have been anything other than a tragic accident.

I reluctantly gave in to Camilla's argument, figuring I could at least spend the rest of today trying to decipher the verses in the Alcuin letter. I hoped to be able to provide another direction for our search; a direction that would take us closer to the relic Alcuin and Rhabanus protected. I also hoped we remained one step ahead of whoever else was involved with the same search.

My fear came from knowing we were already behind and the other party in this search was not playing nice.

Camilla wasted no time planning our trip to Germany, checking on flights from Heathrow to Frankfort for first thing in the morning. As someone who grew up in the middle of the United States, the ease and reality of traveling between European countries was difficult to fathom.

As she was in the process of booking our flights, Camilla's phone rang. She let it ring several times before picking up and resting the phone between her shoulder and ear. "Hello," she said while continuing to make our reservations. Her fingers stopped typing and she turned to look at me abruptly, confirming something the caller said caught her attention.

I tried to mouth "Who is it?" but she shook her head and listened intently.

"I'm so sorry," Camilla said. "Did they tell you what happened?"

She listened again for several minutes. I tried to wait patiently, wishing I could hear the other side of the conversation.

"Yes. Yes, I would be interested in seeing them," Camilla suddenly replied to the caller. "Will you send them to me?"

Camilla gave the caller her e-mail address and then repeated it, slowly. "Thank you for calling me. I am sorry you have to deal with all of this. I will let you know if the email doesn't come through." Another nod of agreement with the caller before ending the call.

Camilla looked at me for a few seconds, attempting to process whatever she heard during the call. I tried not to rush her, but being the third person in an important two-person conversation can be frustrating.

"Monteith's dead," she finally said, wiping the single tear rolling halfway down her cheek. "That was Mrs. Barclay from Leeds. She said Monteith was found at the bottom of a cliff in a national park near Rugen, Germany."

"Was it an accident?"

"According to Mrs. Barclay, the authorities have told the administration at Leeds that there are no signs of foul play. Monteith was staying at a resort on Rugen Island and they believe he went for a hike in Jasmund National Park and slipped while walking too close to the chalk cliffs."

What are the odds that two professors in the same department meet untimely deaths within weeks? At least two people we believed knew about the Alcuin letter are now dead. In one case, the detectives considered a street mugging as a possible explanation, while the other is considered an accident.

"I guess he fell into an area not easily accessible," continued Camilla. "They believe Monteith had been dead for several days when a hiker and his dog discovered the body."

"What is the secretary planning to send you?"

Camilla's demeanor perked up as she answered. "She said the university started cleaning out Ashton's office. When the cleaning crew moved the desk, Mrs. Barclay found a handwritten sheet of notes that had slipped behind a drawer. Not recognizing them as anything related to the classes Ashton taught, she asked if I knew anything about a guy named Alcuin. I'm not sure what the notes say, but she's going to scan them and e-mail them to me sometime this morning."

"I hope the notes give us more information," I said. "But listen, Camilla, we should think about what we are doing. Two people connected to the Alcuin letter are now dead. Common sense says their knowledge of the letter had something to do with their deaths, regardless of what the authorities say."

She stared straight into my eyes, and I half expected her to call me a coward and say she would go on by herself if needed. She started to say something, but then the strength in her gaze faded as a bit of fear and reality crept into those bright blue eyes. Too many things were happening for her to push forward foolishly.

"I know you're right," she said, fighting away tears. "I just cannot stand for whoever these people are to get away with murder. But I can't blame you for wanting to go back to your daughter and your life. I also can't take causing more sorrow for my parents. If something happened to me, I don't think they would get through it."

She found a tissue and wiped her eyes and nose. "Let's wait and see what we find in the notes Mrs. Barclay is sending," she suggested. "If there's no significance to Ashton's notes, we will call it quits and move on with our lives."

"I can agree with that. What about the trip to Germany?"

Camilla went back to her computer. "I didn't confirm the reservations, so I'll hold off until we decide."

She moved the mouse to wake up the screen, logged off the airline site, and then pulled up her email account. "Hey. The e-mail's already here. Mrs. Barclay must have scanned it as soon as we hung up."

I stood behind her as she opened the attachment and displayed the page of Ashton's notes on the screen. At first glance, the page looked like an unorganized bunch of scribbles. Camilla printed off a copy of the notes for each of us.

Ashton spelled out ALCUIN LETTER in block letters at the top of the page. The sixteen lines of the verse Alcuin created as a guide to finding the relic were written out in Latin. Several keywords from the verse were translated into English on the edges of the sheet. Ashton separated the verse into four distinct parts by drawing a box around the first four lines, then the second four lines, and so on.

Next to the first box, Ashton had written *Cup of Christ.* Even with my limited translation skills, I came to the same conclusion about the first part of the verse. That was the easiest part because none of the other three sections made any sense to me so far.

The second section started with the phrase *Ex domus si spientia adveho munia* in Latin. My one attempt at the translation ended with the nonsensical line *From the household of wisely carried gifts,* confirming my lack of expertise in Latin. Ashton had scribbled several words in English above the phrase and then scratched most of them out. The only words remaining from his scribbles were *House of Wisdom, with* a line drawn to the right side of the paper pointing to the words *Baghdad,* and what looked like *Al Rashid.*

I didn't know what those words were referring to but would research them soon.

The next line in Latin was *Ex munia adveho a aureus vas*, with the words *Golden cup* written at the end. The third line in the verse was the last on the page with any additional words written around it. *Ex vas adveho quietus locus* was followed by Ashton's scribbled words *quiet resting place* out to the side.

"Does any of this mean anything to you," Camilla asked after we both took several minutes to look at our respective copies.

"The lines in Latin come straight from near the end of the Alcuin letter. I believe it's a poem or verse that gives clues to the location of the relic Alcuin talked about in the rest of the letter.

"Ashton circled the four main sections of the verse and indicated his belief that the first section talks about the cup of Christ. I was pretty sure of that fact, but his notes about the next section are new information to me."

"What do *House of Wisdom*, *Al Rashid,* and *Bagdad* have to do with the cup of Christ?"

"I don't know yet, but it's something new for us to research," I answered. "I hope it will take us another step forward."

A *large man* was the simplest and most accurate description of the person sitting in the driver's seat of the van parked down the street from Camilla's condo. Close-cropped hair covered his oversized head, while his workman's overalls barely contained his massive frame. His meaty hands grabbed the steering wheel, looking like they were able to snap it off the steering column with minimal effort. A scar ran down his face from below his left ear to his collarbone. His nose showed signs of being broken multiple times.

There was no chance this guy would be front and center in any family pictures. In truth, his most recent photo op was more than five years in the past when authorities snapped his mug shot before sending him to serve three years in a German prison. His crime? He beat a bartender to within an inch of death. Why? He claimed the bartender was watering down the drinks.

"We might have a little problem," said the well-dressed man sitting in the passenger seat. He had a computer open and was listening to the conversation from the fourth-floor condo less than a hundred meters away.

The massive driver grunted and shook his head. He was a man of few words.

"The bug we planted proved beneficial," said the passenger. "We need to discuss what we've heard with the man paying the bills."

The man in the passenger seat was the polar opposite of the driver: well-dressed, well-groomed, and boasting a face that could be called moderately handsome. He wore a steel blue pinstripe suit, silk tie, and shoes shined to a high gloss. The only thing that broke up the illusion of a well-to-do gentleman were the tattoos showing on his wrists and the back of his hands.

The number he dialed had a French country code, but he had no way of knowing it was connecting to a cell phone in a secluded town in Switzerland. The call was answered after several rings and he described the conversation that had just taken place in the Collins woman's condo. He listened for another minute and then ended the call without another word.

"No more planning for an accident," he reported to his oversized friend. "The boss man—whoever he is—wants us to move as soon as possible and take care of Ms. Collins and her friend. We are also supposed to get a copy of the notes they have been discussing."

The two men spent the next several minutes making plans before stepping out of the van and walking toward the condominium complex.

"Why don't we get out of here and do our research somewhere else?" I suggested to Camilla. "Is there a café around that has Wi-Fi? We could get lunch while we work."

"There's a great place a couple of kilometers away. We might be able to sit outside. We don't have enough sunny days in London, so you should experience some of our nice weather before you go home."

"Sounds like a good plan. Let me pack up my computer and grab some notes."

I headed to the bedroom and Camilla began shutting down her computer and putting it in a backpack. I organized my notes and slid them into the bag with my laptop. I slung the strap over my shoulder just as the doorbell rang. I heard

Camilla respond 'Who is it?' and the safety chain rattle on the door. There was a muffled reply from whoever was at the door, followed quickly by the sound of the front door crashing open. Camilla let loose a brief cry of surprise before it was stifled.

My first reaction was to run toward the front room, but something made me stop.

With the door ajar in the bedroom, I saw down the short hallway. An enormous man in work overalls had a huge hand clamped over Camilla's mouth; hence the brief nature of her scream. Another man crossed my field of vision. The suit he was wearing sparked a memory of the pair in the work van I saw as I finished my run this morning.

"Where is your boyfriend?" the well-dressed man asked Camilla in accented English.

I pulled away from the door, hoping she didn't inadvertently glance my way.

"I don't know what you are talking about," Camilla managed to say once the big man removed his hand. Her answer earned her a slap across the face.

"Do not waste my time," said the man. "I know your friend from America is here. Maybe if my friend here begins to break a few of your bones, your gentlemen friend will show himself. What do you think?"

"He left to pick up our lunch. He'll be back in a few minutes." Camilla surprised me with her reply, saying it with a level of sincerity that had to be difficult to muster considering the circumstances. She was stalling for me, but what was I supposed to do? I had nothing to fight these guys with, and I couldn't exactly jump out of the fourth-floor window. Or could I?

One of the special features of the condo complex was each bedroom had a small balcony. I moved quietly to the sliding door in my bedroom, pulled it open, and slipped onto the small outside space.

I heard movement in the hallway as one of the intruders

looked for me. He entered Camilla's bedroom first, providing me with more time. After pushing the sliding door closed, I knew the balcony wouldn't hide me for long, but there was now only one way off.

I swung a leg over the railing and tried not to look down at the thirty-foot drop. I pulled my other leg over and stood outside the railing looking back into the room, the computer bag still over my shoulder. Just as the door to the bedroom began to open I shimmied down with my hands and let my feet drop into nothingness. I couldn't hold myself in this position for long and would be easily noticed as soon as anyone opened the balcony door.

Looking down, my feet hung only about a foot above the railing from an identical balcony on the third floor. I let my hands slide down a few more inches, but my toes would still not reach the railing below.

What I would give to be a few inches taller right now.

My grip started to give out, providing only seconds to decide. If I tried to pull myself up, I would be found by the men in Camilla's condo. If I tried to drop the last few inches to the balcony below and then lost my balance.... well, let's just say I don't want to test the laws of gravity and sudden deceleration due to hitting a solid object. In this case, the solid object would be a concrete sidewalk.

With no time left to debate with myself, I swung my legs away from the building and as they began to swing back, I let go from the railing above. My move wouldn't earn high marks from a gymnastics judge for form or style, but I managed to stick the landing on the third-floor balcony. I checked that all my body parts were working and my computer bag had made the leap unscathed. I only had a few scratches on my fingers from gripping the railing so tightly to show for my high-wire performance.

Fortunately, the balcony door was unlocked. I'm sure most people don't expect someone to sneak in from outside the third floor. I stepped into an empty room and could hear no sounds coming from the condo, which had the same layout as Camilla's. I walked straight down the hallway and out the front door. The residents would wonder why their door wasn't locked when they came home, but would most likely chalk it up to forgetfulness when they realized nothing in their condo had been disturbed.

I moved swiftly to the end of the hall and bounded down the stairs two at a time until I crashed through the exit door on the ground level. I was out of the building safely, but what next?

CHAPTER 8

My temporary safety wasn't doing anything for Camilla. I could try to find some help, but what would happen to Camilla before help arrived?

I wasn't sure my phone would call 999, the actual emergency number in England. Another bizarre fact I somehow remembered. It's strange what goes through your mind when fear and adrenaline are flowing in equal parts.

I dialed 999 as I made my way back to the front of the building. The call went through, and I breathlessly told the dispatcher that a woman was being attacked in her condo and gave them the location.

As I rounded the corner and had the condo's entrance in sight, the man in the blue suit came out the front doors. I jerked myself out of sight but peered around the edge of the building. I watched the man walk calmly toward the work van parked on the street, climb in the driver's side, and start the engine. The van made a U-turn, before pulling in the entrance to the condominium's underground parking garage.

They must be bringing Camilla out in the garage where the chances of being seen are much less. I needed to do something to delay them until help arrived.

Without conscious thought, I began to run toward the van waving my arms. The driver glanced at me and looked away again. I came right up to the side of the van as it neared the garage entrance and indicated the man should roll down the window. He tried to ignore me, but I slammed my hand on the side of the van. The man turned, obviously not recognizing me as Camilla's friend, but also not pleased I was disrupting his plans. He rolled down his window and told me to move away.

"Hey mister," I said. "My internet is on the blink. Can you fix it?"

The look on his face told me he didn't remember the internet TV logo on the side of the van. When that fact registered with him, he said, "Not now," and began to roll up the window.

I needed to stall him a while longer, so I jumped in front of the van and banged on the hood. "I said I need my television to work," I yelled like a crazy man, which wasn't too far from the truth at present; crazy with fear as much as anything.

I could see the man's face turning red with rage. I'm sure he was torn between doing something drastic and trying to resolve the situation without any unwanted attention. His eyes shifted to look over my shoulder. I glanced behind me and saw the behemoth from Camilla's condo standing at the edge of the entrance to the parking garage. His right arm extended to the side, holding something just out of sight. Probably Camilla.

I was running out of options fast. I began beating on the hood of the van again, screaming about my internet. The driver decided he'd had enough and opened the door. I froze when the barrel of a handgun appeared through the door's partially rolled-down window.

I'm not a gun person, have never fired anything stronger than an Airsoft gun, and certainly have never had a gun aimed in my direction. My pounding and yelling stopped and I sucked in air fast enough to nearly choke.

With my heart threatening to beat right out of my chest, I stood up straight and tried to appear unfazed. I'm sure the act of make-believe bravery didn't fool anyone, especially the man holding the gun.

"I am not going to ask you again," he said forcefully. "Move… away… from… my… van!" Speaking through clenched teeth, his German accent seemed even more menacing.

The sound of sirens reached us with their distinctive wail before I responded. Considering the current situation, those unique European sirens were among the most beautiful sounds I had ever heard.

The guy in the suit and his muscled sidekick were not so enamored with the sirens. They stared at each other for a few moments, giving the appearance that messages were passing between them telepathically. The driver gave a small nod of his head and his large friend immediately headed toward the van, leaving Camilla crumpled inside the parking garage. The pair sped off about thirty seconds before a police car arrived.

By the time the police were done interviewing us, Camilla and I had come down off of our adrenaline high and felt exhausted. We gave the police all the descriptions we could remember about the two men and their vehicle but stayed away from the *why* question as much as possible. We denied knowing why they broke into Camilla's condo, which was partially true. Even though we were sure the two were after information about the Alcuin letter, Camilla told me they never mentioned the letter specifically. They only demanded she gather her computer and the notes on her table into a bag and bring it with her. We were fortunate that she managed to keep possession of the bag when the two men retreated.

Before the police left, word came back that the van had been found abandoned along a little-used side road just minutes away. The vehicle was wiped clean and when the police ran the plates they found it had been stolen the night before on the other side of London. The police planned to check some of the thousands of traffic cameras spread around the city, hoping to catch a lucky break and capture a good look at the culprits. They promised to keep a car on patrol in the area for the next twenty-four hours but suggested we consider staying elsewhere for a few days.

Camilla, boasting a nice bruise on her cheek where she was slapped, opened up her computer as soon as the police cleared out of her condo.

“What are you doing?” I asked.

“I'm confirming our tickets to fly to Germany. We need to get away from here for a while," she stated. "We can continue to research the letter as we try to make contact with Dennis Simons.”

Two things ran through my head as Camilla responded. First, I admired her bravery and her ability to put aside the fact that she was almost abducted earlier today. Second, I thought that this woman was nuts.

“No way, Camilla!” I practically shouted. “This ends right now, at least for me. You were attacked in your condo today, and I had a gun pointed at me for the first time in my life. As much as I want to see this venture through, I need to go home and be with my daughter. Whatever we do won’t bring Ashton back, but it looks more and more like it could get us killed.”

Her head turned away from me and I thought she would explode in anger. Instead, her shoulders begin to shake; gently at first, but then more pronounced as she began to sob. Once she turned back to face me, the confident, focused woman from a few moments earlier now looked insecure and frightened. The dam around her persona broke.

Camilla stood and came towards me, tears streaming down her cheeks. “I can’t do this alone,” she said between the sobs. She tried to say something else, but couldn’t get it out. The next thing I knew her arms wrapped around me and she wept on my shoulder. If I didn’t believe Camilla was sincere, I would say this was manipulation at its best.

By eight o’clock in the evening, we were boarding a plane to Frankfurt, Germany.

It was after midnight when we checked into a hotel not far from the airport and went to our separate rooms with barely a *good night* spoken. The day's events had been draining, and we desperately needed sleep.

Despite being tired, my mind still raced, making it hard to fall asleep. I called and talked to my in-laws, explaining the situation, but leaving out many alarming details. They put Maddie on the phone, and I reminded her how much I loved her. I also called and talked to my parents in Colorado for a few minutes.

After the calls, I lay back on the bed and reviewed the past few days. Was it really less than forty-eight hours since I'd flown to London? So much had happened: identifying the antiquities dealer Dennis Simons, receiving a message from Simons warning us not to get involved, finding out Ashton's boss had mysteriously died in Germany, and receiving a copy of a lost page of notes from Ashton's research. Then, of course, there was the attempted abduction which we were fortunate to avoid.

The two men involved were still out there somewhere. Since at least one of the men had a German accent, the fact that we were now in Frankfurt wasn't the most comforting thought, despite the long odds that they could follow us.

When Camilla and I met for breakfast, we both admitted that sleep had been fitful, at best. Neither of us felt rested, but knew we needed to keep moving forward. She had already tried to call Simons, but—not surprisingly—he had not answered his phone. We planned to go to his small antique store when it opened later in the morning. Until then, we would try to research some of the clues we pulled from Ashton's notes on the Alcuin letter.

We sat eating a traditional German breakfast of coffee, fresh rolls, jam, a soft-boiled egg, and various sliced meats and cheeses. Between bites, Camilla asked, "Matt, what do you think about the cup of Christ?"

When I didn't respond immediately, she continued. "Can we truly be looking for the cup Christ used when meeting with his disciples, and if so, does it hold any meaning?"

These were the questions I had asked myself for several days. For me, though, the real question was not if such a cup held any historical significance—which it would—but if such a cup would hold any significance for my faith. Would finding such an artifact nudge me off the fence and fully commit to faith in God? It makes no sense in my logical mind that a man-made object could affect belief in an eternal God. But part of me is convinced that seeing and holding an object touched by Christ and mentioned in the Bible would solidify my belief. Would others tell me I didn't have real faith if I needed to see and touch something to believe?

"I think finding the cup of Christ would hold significant meaning to those from the Christian faith," I replied to Camilla. "I guess the cup's significance would depend on each person's beliefs."

"What do you believe?" she asked. "Not just about the cup, but faith in general."

I've never been one to open up about personal things. Even when Rachel was alive it was sometimes tough for me to speak openly about subjects that went much deeper than normal daily events. She worked hard to pull me out of my communication shell and urge me to talk about deeper topics. Since her death, I've returned to being a master of talking about things on the surface of life, rarely diving into more profound discussions. The few exceptions were my periodic talks with Ethan Montgomery. He usually found a way to prompt me to open up, at least on some subjects.

Taking another bite of my breakfast and a drink of coffee, I tried to delay my response. I sensed, though, that Camilla wasn't letting me out of this discussion.

"What do I believe about faith?" I said, re-wording her question, still stalling. "That question might be difficult for me to answer. Mostly because I'm not completely sure what I believe."

I hoped she would accept that non-answer, but she leaned forward on the table with her elbows and cupped her chin in both hands. Though she didn't say anything, the look in her eyes communicated that she was waiting for a more complete and honest answer.

"Deciding where faith fits into my life has been a struggle for me," I said while looking away from her. I didn't want the additional intimacy that comes with looking someone in the eyes when speaking. "Even before Rachel died, I was never completely comfortable with religion and the formality of most church services. I never knew the right things to say. It was like someone forgot to tell me all the correct religious code words. At the same time, though, I continued to be pulled toward the faith others talked about."

This was the first time I remembered putting these thoughts into words. It was strange. But good at the same time.

"Since Rachel's death, any level of faith has been a struggle. I went through times when it was hard to make it to the end of each day without breaking down. The biggest influences on me during the past year—at least where faith was concerned—were the discussions I had with one of my colleagues. He's been a Christian for most of his life and the best thing he did was let me vent my anger toward God. It took a while for me to open up to him, but he didn't try to preach to me. He answered my questions and gave me advice only if I asked for it."

"So, I'll ask you again. What do you believe?" She was intent on dragging a full answer from me.

The waitress came by, giving me a brief reprieve. Once our coffee cups were filled and the empty plates cleared away, Camilla asked again.

"What do you believe?"

"You are persistent," I said with a smile. She smiled back, but didn't say anything; just looked at me with those expectant eyes again.

I cleared my throat, looked at my watch, and then acted fascinated by something over Camilla's shoulder. All classic stall tactics that would make any teenager proud. "As you can tell, I'm not good at stuff like this. I'm better at talking about other people's beliefs and actions, usually from a few centuries ago."

She reached across and put her hand on mine until I looked her in the eyes. "Just tell me what you believe, Matt. I might disagree with you, but I won't judge you."

I took a deep breath and exhaled slowly. "I believe there's a God," I started. "And I believe a higher power created this crazy world we live in. I think it takes much more faith to believe that we are all a cosmic accident than it does to believe in a creator. I also believe in Jesus and that he is the son of God. I don't pretend to understand how that's possible, but I guess that's where faith comes in.

"I'm still working through the whole formal religion thing. There are so many different denominations and traditions that it's hard to know what is right and what is opinion. My friend Ethan and I have talked about this a lot. He keeps saying faith isn't about religion, a certain denomination, or a list of dos and don'ts. He keeps emphasizing that faith in God is about a relationship."

I felt self-conscious as I opened up, not accustomed to talking about deep subjects for an extended amount of time. Camilla remained quiet, waiting for me to continue.

"I guess the relationship part is where I continue to struggle. You're now witnessing how tough it is for me to talk openly with another human being about anything substantial. Imagine how I feel thinking about communicating with the God who created everything; a God who is supposed to love me unconditionally. I suppose I sometimes don’t believe I'm worthy of that kind of relationship.”

We were both quiet for a while, letting my words settle. I didn’t have much more to say and I think Camilla was satisfied and maybe surprised by my words.

“Are you going to tell me what you believe?” I asked, putting the proverbial ball in her court.

“I believe in my brother and want to prove Ashton was right in his deductions about the letter,” She responded with more anger than conviction. “I want to prove he was killed because of his knowledge.

“I don’t care about the cup of Christ,” she added, looking away and giving off the same body language as I did when I didn’t want to talk.

She stood and began walking toward the door before I had a chance to object. Looking back she said, “Right now I believe we have some more research to do before we go to Simons’ place.”

CHAPTER 9

We settled back into our rooms to continue our research. The connecting door remained open to allow easier access back and forth. Camilla had her computer set up on the desk in her room and was focusing on the notes Ashton had written about the verse in the Alcuin letter. I had a similar setup in my room as I attempted to decipher some more of the Latin text.

We asked a few questions through the open door, but pretty much remained silent in our own little worlds of research for an hour.

"I think I have some of this figured out," Camilla said as she walked into my room. "I'm not sure what it all means, but at least I have a few answers."

"What did you find?"

"Well, Ashton wrote *House of Wisdom* on his notes and mentioned Baghdad and someone named Al Rashid. When I put all of them into my search parameters, I came upon what amounted to the world's first university. The Arabic name of Bayt al-Hikma translates into House of Wisdom. Harun al-Rashid founded it in the late eighth century and the university lasted for over four hundred years. The school supposedly had the largest collection of books in the world at the time."

"What does an ancient university in Baghdad have to do with Alcuin and his letter to Rhabanus? Alcuin was a very learned man, but I never read anything about him traveling to that part of the world."

"I guess al-Rashid and Charlemagne had some type of relationship," she stated. "I read how they each needed the other as allies to help defend against various rivals. They were known to send extravagant gifts to one another. One site I looked up mentioned that al-Rashid sent Charlemagne an elephant."

"An elephant? I bet that caught people's attention in Germany in the Middle Ages," I said with a smirk.

I turned and made a few quick notes. "Okay. Here's what I have so far." I held up a copy of the verses from the Alcuin letter and pointed to the first few lines much like I would do in a history classroom.

"For the first four lines of these verses in the letter, I believe the translation would be: *From God, there comes a son; From a son, there comes blood; From blood there is life; Partake from the vessel of life and be saved.*

"That's the section we can all agree is talking about the cup or vessel of Christ. The cup was used to hold wine, which Jesus related to the blood of life. It makes sense to me, anyway. Do you agree?"

"It sounds right," Camilla replied. "What about the next section?"

"Your new information helps here. Now it looks like it starts with, *From the house of wisdom comes gifts*. That would fit with what you found out about al-Rashid sending gifts to Charlemagne. I believe the second line of the section should now read, *From gifts comes a golden vessel*.

"Did you read anything about one of the gifts from al-Rashid being a gold cup?" I asked.

"I don't think so, but we can dig into it some more later."

"Okay, so we have a gold vessel of some type being sent as a gift from al-Rashid who founded the House of Wisdom. We can assume it's a gift to Charlemagne." Pointing to the next line of text, I moved on. "This section of the verse concludes with lines that say, *From the golden vessel comes a hidden place,* and *Enter the vessel of life and be saved.*"

Camilla was looking at my notes on the verse and appeared to be thinking intently.

"Here's a thought," she said. "Maybe this section says that a golden vessel from al-Rashid was used as the hiding place for the cup. If we can get inside the vessel, whatever it is, then we can find the cup."

Now it was my turn to think for a minute. "You might have nailed it. Your explanation makes a lot of sense. The first section talks about the cup and the second section tells us where the cup was hidden. Now, we need to figure out what this *golden vessel* is and if it still exists."

She looked at her watch. "Well, we will have to work on that later. It's time to leave for Simons' antique shop."

We arrived at the antique shop thirty minutes later. Camilla drove our compact rental car, directed by a mapping app on her phone. Her freelance photography job took her all over the world, so she was comfortable driving in most countries.

Called *Simons' Antiquities*, the shop was located in the Sachsenhausen district on the north side of Frankfurt. Old Sachsenhausen, featuring cobblestone lanes and historic homes, was nearby so an antique store fit in well. The exterior of the building featured bricks that looked to be well over a hundred years old; maybe closer to two hundred. It was a little run down on the outside, but maybe that look appealed to an antique dealer. A dark-stained wooden door greeted each visitor and a small bell jingled when we opened it and stepped inside.

No one acknowledged us at first. "Anybody here?" I said loudly.

A door toward the back of the shop opened and a small

man appeared. He looked to be about forty years old, with very thin, wispy hair. As he approached, I noticed a two-day growth of beard and dark circles under his eyes. His eyes shifted back and forth between Camilla and me, having no idea who we were.

"Can I help you?" he said in a voice matching the message left on Camilla's phone.

"Mr. Simons?" inquired Camilla.

"Yes, that's me," he said. "What can I do for you?"

"You can start by telling us everything you know about the Alcuin letter you loaned to Ashton Collins." Camilla was nothing if not direct. She wasn't wasting any time.

The statement startled Simons. His body language became defensive—and perhaps a little scared—within seconds. "Who are…. Wait. Are you Ashton's sister?" he asked, noticing the family resemblance.

Camilla began to answer, but Simons jumped in. "I told you not to contact me. Turn around and get out of here. I cannot talk to you!" He was visibly shaken, looking over our shoulders and out the front window.

"We just want some answers," I stated. "Only a few minutes of your time."

"You don't understand," he said, looking at me, clearly agitated. "I already said too much when I left a message on her phone." He pointed toward Camilla. "The guy who paid me money to keep quiet stopped in here yesterday and asked if I was keeping my end of the bargain. I got the sense he already knew I made that call."

"Did he threaten you," asked Camilla.

"Not in so many words, but he made sure I understood there would be consequences if I talked." Simons began rubbing his temples and shaking his head. "I wish I had never laid my eyes on that blasted letter," he said almost to himself.

"We appreciate your situation, Mr. Simons," I said, trying to calm him down. "We had a situation of our own yesterday, but we are here now and need a couple of questions answered."

Simons continued to shake his head. He was about to say something when the front door opened, causing the bell to jingle. Camilla and I were looking toward Simons, while he looked over our shoulders at the entrance.

"I will be with you in a minute," he said. I guess he expected all of his customers to speak English.

"No, I believe you will be of service to us right now." The voice coming from behind us sent a shiver down my spine. I looked at Camilla and her expression told me she recognized the voice as well. I think both of us were hesitant to turn around, wishing we could melt into the woodwork.

"Miss Collins and your American friend, it is so nice you came to my country for a visit," the man said sarcastically as we turned around to face him.

His German accent and methodical diction gave away his identity before we saw his face. The man who tried to abduct us less than a day ago in London was standing in front of us now in an obscure antique shop in Frankfurt. I didn't know what was more disturbing: the fact he and his oversized sidekick found us so quickly, or the fact that the man was now pointing a gun in our direction.

"Who are you? What is this all about?" Simons blurted out without a hint of authority in his voice.

"Who we are, Mr. Simons, is none of your concern," said the man, who was again dressed in a high-end suit and silk tie. "However, what this is all about has very much to do with you."

The big man had yet to say a word, which was not unusual in my brief experience with him. If he got paid by the syllables spoken each day, he would live in poverty. He was, however, able to lock the front door and turn a sign around; a sign in German I assumed translated to *Open* on one side and *Closed* on the other.

The two men—one dressed impeccably and the other in jeans and a muscle-hugging t-shirt—approached us, the gun still prominently on display. "I need the three of you to walk to the back of the store, so we can have a little discussion."

The gun prompted us to do as he said. At the rear of the store was a round table with four chairs. The man pointed for us to sit in the chairs where other antique pieces would block us from being seen by anyone looking in the store's front windows.

At this point, I am more scared than I've ever been in my life. Yesterday's attempted abduction happened so fast, the fear didn't have a chance to build up. Now I was sitting in the back of a store in an unfamiliar foreign city, a gun pointed in my general direction, and no ideas coming to mind of a plan to get out of the situation.

The look on Camilla's face told me that fear was also winning the battle with her tough exterior. Her eyes, which often displayed confidence, were now unfocused, darting randomly around the room.

Simons looked ready to pass out. His face had splotchy red patches and his breathing was coming in uneven gulps.

The man with the gun looked at Camilla and me when he said, "I was extremely upset yesterday in London when our time together came to a premature end."

At this comment, Simons' eyes showed surprise that this man knew us. It looked like he wanted to say something, but either wise restraint or overwhelming fear convinced him to hold his tongue. My bet was on the fear option.

"However, the fact that you made it to Mr. Simons' shop turned out to be a convenient detour," the man continued. "With the three of you together, our work is much easier."

His final comment didn't do anything to ease the fear in the room. I'm sure each of us imagined many bad scenarios associated with the *work* he referred to.

"What do you want from us?" It was the question every captive asked his captors, but I needed to throw it out there and see what response I got.

"I am glad you asked my American friend. We did not get around to that part yesterday." He sat on the fourth chair at the table and laid the gun down softly, keeping his tattooed hand wrapped around the grip. "We need all the information you have on the letter Ashton Collins received from Mr. Simons. That includes notes, files, documents, and computer hard drives. And you, Mr. Simons," he said turning to face the antique dealer. "We need you to tell us exactly where the letter was acquired and who else knows about its existence."

"What happens to us if we give you the information?" This time, Camilla spoke up.

"That is yet to be decided," the man responded. "But I can assure you that you will not like the consequences of not cooperating."

This statement caused what sounded like a sob to escape from Simons' throat.

"Now let's get this question-and-answer session going. Mr. Klein, will you go and stand next to our illustrious store owner." The big man had a name. He moved to stand behind Simons, causing Simons to look even more frightened. I would judge his fear level to be an eleven on a scale of one to ten.

"My colleague is there to remind you of the importance of truthful answers," he said to Simons. "We need to know…."

"I got the letter from a friend in Winkel," Simons blurted out before the man finished his question. "He was working to help restore a fireplace in the Graues Haus. During his work, a stone came loose and behind the stone he found an old box containing the letter. My friend hoped to make a little cash, so asked me to find out what the letter might be worth." Simons spoke in rapid bursts and an uneven rhythm. "I contacted Ashton because I worked with him in the past on some other medieval pieces I acquired. That's it. That's all I know."

Simons slumped over like he was exhausted from his

brief confession. "That's all I know," he said again, his head now resting in his shaking hands.

"I believe you," said the man with the gun. "And I thank you for your cooperation. Now I want you to go with Mr. Klein to your office and let him take a look at your computer. We need to make sure it's clean of any reference to the letter." He nodded to the big man and Klein took hold of Simons' arm like it was a piece of straw. Simons resisted for a brief second, but then compliantly stood and walked toward his office.

Once the two disappeared, the man turned to us. "Mr. Klein is very good with computers. Most assume because of his size and selective use of the spoken word that he is not intelligent. Many have regretted that assumption."

He paused for a moment, moving the gun around, but not pointing it at anything, or anyone, in particular. "I think you two know what I want. I hope you will be as forthcoming as Mr. Simons."

"Why are you doing this? Why so interested in old letters?" Camilla asked, apparently calmer than a few minutes earlier. She appeared to have recovered a bit from the initial shock of being held at gunpoint for the second day in a row. Her eyes were more focused and she showed a hint of renewed resolve.

"I am interested because my employer pays me to be interested," the man replied. "And I am a loyal employee."

That was the only insight we would gain over the next several minutes as the man asked us questions about the letter, our research, and any materials we had in our possession. He also asked how I came to be involved. We told the truth for the most part. Having a gun pointed at you tends to encourage truthful answers.

Our captor appeared satisfied with our answers. He said we would soon be traveling together back to our hotel to retrieve the materials in our possession. I wanted to ask again what would happen to us if we cooperated but decided I didn't want to know the answer.

"Aren't you at least a little curious about how we found you after our premature break-up yesterday?" he asked, obviously proud of his bloodhound capabilities.

We just stared at him, so he went on. "Your condo has been bugged for the past couple of weeks," he said boastfully, looking at Camilla. "We overheard your discussions and the plans you made. We only needed to wait until you showed up here to see Simons."

Camilla was not shocked by the fact her condo had been bugged, but I sensed her fear was in the process of turning to anger.

"We placed the bug while you were out of town on a photo assignment, mainly to keep track of any interaction you had with your brother." It was obvious the man enjoyed revealing these facts. "Once our business was done with your brother, we didn't realize how valuable those little bugs would be. You and your friend here just had to keep digging, but we were able to monitor you.

"By the way," he continued in a mocking tone, looking at Camilla again, "I enjoyed spending quality time with your brother."

Before I could stop her, Camilla lunged at the man with a guttural scream. It surprised him, as well, and he was unable to raise the gun before her fingernails gouged the skin of his face.

The collision jarred the gun loose, and it tumbled to the floor on the other side of the table. I froze in place for a moment, not processing what was going on in front of me. My survival instinct managed to kick in, and I dove under the table to retrieve the gun.

While making my move, the man gained control over Camilla and tossed her across the table. He noticed what I was doing and lunged for the gun at the same time my hand took hold of its grip. We wrestled for control, each trying to find the best leverage while rolling on the floor. I managed to throw a hard elbow into his ribs, which gave me a brief advantage, but he would not let go of the gun. He kneed me in the stomach, causing a wave of pain and nausea that made me lose my grip. As the gun was about to be ripped from my hands, I made one more desperate attempt for the weapon, my finger finding the trigger.

The gun exploded.

CHAPTER 10

It took me a moment to take stock of all my body parts. My ears rang and my stomach felt like it had been hit by a bowling ball, but I didn't see any blood.

Our well-dressed captor was not so lucky. The bullet from the gun scorched the side of his face, leaving a trail from his cheek to above his ear. A half-inch difference in the bullet's trajectory would have taken off much of his face. He wasn't moving but appeared to be breathing. Blood ran down his face and onto the floor.

The big man rushed out of the back office before I regained all my senses. Camilla alertly picked up the gun and waived it around enough to convince Klein not to advance on us. "Don't move!" Camilla yelled in her best television-cop-show voice. "Send Simons out here."

Klein simply smiled and shook his head. Camilla responded by firing a shot which missed but splintered the wooden floor near Klein's size fifteen boots. He didn't even flinch, giving off the distinct impression he had been shot at on numerous occasions in the past. He continued to shake his head and then said, "He dead," in a surprisingly high voice for such a massive man.

Camilla and I looked at each other, wondering if we should believe him. We needed to get out of here while we still had an advantage. At the same time, we couldn't leave Simons behind if he was still alive. "I don't believe you," I said to Klein as he stood stoically about twenty feet away. "I want to see him."

The big man shook his head again, before speaking in halted English. "Is Mr. Schmidt alive?" he asked, pointing to the man on the floor.

"He's breathing."

"I show the shopkeeper. You leave Mr. Schmidt." Mr. Schmidt? I guess the man on the floor did have a name, although who knew if it was his actual name? The name Schmidt was as common in Germany as Smith in the U.S. I think Klein was trying to make a deal to ensure we wouldn't take the unconscious man with us. Schmidt would be pleased to know his companion showed so much concern for his welfare.

I shook my head to indicate agreement. Klein moved slowly toward the entrance to the back office. He reached his giant hand through the doorway and pulled a rolling chair into sight. Simons was sitting in the chair, but his head hung to the side at an unnatural angle; eyes still open staring into nothingness.

Camilla gasped at the sight of the dead antique dealer. "Why did you do that, you monster?" she screamed. "He told you what you wanted to know."

Klein shrugged his shoulders as if to say, '*What's the big deal? I do this all the time.*'

Camilla's whole body trembled as I took the gun from her hand with little resistance.

"Let's go," I said. "There's no more we can do here."

We backed our way to the front doors, keeping the gun pointed in Klein's general direction. He showed no inclination to keep us from leaving, realizing that, despite his size, bullets would still stop him. Camilla unlocked the door and we backed through. I stuffed the gun down the back of my pants and pulled my shirt down once we were on the sidewalk. We took a few hesitant walking steps until breaking into a run, soon reaching our car and pulling away. We saw no one come out of the antique store to try and follow us.

"Oh, my god! Oh, my god!" Camilla said over and over as she drove. It looked like she was still shaking.

"Do you want me to drive?"

"No. No, I'm okay," she said, trying to convince herself as much as me.

She drove for fifteen minutes and then pulled to the side of the road. "What are we going to do?" she asked, her head resting on the steering wheel.

A very good question.

"Right now I think we need to take one step at a time," I said, trying to sound confident. "I don't believe Schmidt and Klein know where we are staying, so we can go back, pick up our stuff, and leave as quickly as we can. We need to go somewhere we'll be safe and have time to think."

"Where can we go?"

"You're the one who knows this part of the world. We need someplace where they wouldn't expect us to go and can't track us."

I couldn't tell if Camilla was thinking or simply ignoring me. She eventually turned her head to look at me. "I might have one option. But I need to make a call."

She told me her idea and I agreed it was worth a try. After a lengthy phone call, the plan fell into place and we were on the move again.

Slightly more than an hour later, we had two coach seats on the Intercity Express train from Frankfurt to Bern, Switzerland, with connecting tickets to Geneva. The train station was located at the airport in Frankfurt, so after rushing to clear out our hotel room we dropped off the rental car and took the first train available. We would be in Bern in four hours and arrive in Geneva less than two hours later.

Camilla's earlier call had been made to Karl Verclammen, the Editor-in-Chief of the magazine *UN Special*. The publication, based in Geneva, focused on topics surrounding the work of international organizations and governance. It's published through joint efforts of the United Nations, the World Health Organization, and other agencies based in Geneva. Camilla was hired a few months ago for a special photo shoot on human rights issues in various parts of the world. She accompanied the UN High Commissioner for Human Rights on a trip to the Central African Republic; a trip that ended with a quick evacuation when the country's civil war almost added the United Nations contingent to its list of casualties.

After Camilla completed the photo assignment, Verclammen asked her to come for a visit, offering her use of his vacation home near Lake Geneva in appreciation for her work. Knowing Verclammen had more than a simple thank you in mind, Camilla declined.

Now, in our current situation, she used Verclammen's previous advances for our benefit. Camilla asked if the home was available for a few days, telling him she needed somewhere to spend time with a friend who was going through some difficult personal issues.

I guess I qualified as a friend, and I definitely had some difficult issues to deal with, so she was being truthful. The magazine editor tried to negotiate some time alone with Camilla out of the deal, but she proved adept at being noncommittal without actually dashing his hopes. After dragging out the conversation, Verclammen agreed to allow Camilla to use the home for three days.

Seven hours after leaving Frankfort we were walking into a very nice two-story home within sight of Lake Geneva. The wood and brick on the exterior gave it a rustic mountain chalet feel, but the inside was modern and clean. Camilla said Verclammen primarily used the home to rent to vacationers or UN personnel coming into Geneva. He lived most of the year in a luxury condo in the center of the city.

As I put what few belongings I had with me into one of the bedrooms, I realized I would be sleeping in my fourth country in the past four nights. Starting at my home in the

States a few days ago, I had since slept in Camilla's condo near London, a hotel in Frankfurt, and now would be sleeping in a pricey lake home in Geneva. As much as international travel appeared to be glamorous from the outside, I would much rather be tucking in my daughter and preparing for bed in my little piece of the world in Bannister, Indiana.

Father Niklaus Griego was once again standing on the balcony of his estate staring out at the picture-perfect view, but not seeing the beauty. His eyes and mind were clouded by frustration. The Collins woman and her companion—whom he now understood to be Matt Kincaid, a college professor from the States—escaped from Schmidt and Klein again. More importantly, they got away with all their notes and research on the Alcuin letter.

The antiquities dealer no longer posed a threat, but the number of bodies being left in the wake of his search for the cup of Christ was beginning to worry Griego. He felt no sadness for their deaths. At some point, however, someone would start to connect the dots between the deaths of a professor in Leeds, the professor's supervisor on an island off the coast of Germany, and a shopkeeper in Frankfurt. There was virtually no way for the dots to lead back to Griego, but any investigation into the deaths could put someone else onto the trail of the cup.

Time was growing short for Griego to both find the cup and cut off any loose ends. If things dragged out much longer, there would be too many people involved. He needed the public relations splash of finding the cup. He also needed to be confident that no one would come forward and challenge the discovery or his methods.

The German pair failed to complete their assignment in Frankfurt, and now two of the key targets had disappeared.

Without the ability to monitor passports or credit cards, tracking them down would be difficult on the European continent. Moving from country to country happened with ease, and at least the Collins woman had experience traveling. She and Matt Kincaid could be anywhere from France to Italy to Holland. They might have even stayed in Frankfurt.

If Griego couldn't find the pair, he must think of some way to make them come to him.

After several more minutes of staring out at the night sky, an idea came to Griego. He made two phone calls, not concerning himself with what time it was and whether he might be waking someone. A pair of short conversations set a plan in motion.

Now it was a matter of being patient, an attribute with which Griego struggled.

A shower and shave felt good after a rough night of sleep. The surroundings made me feel like I was in a five-star hotel with a granite countertop and a large shower surrounded by glass tiles. There were two levels of sprayers, plus a rain-shower option. The stone tile floors could be heated in the colder winter months, while the available towels were fluffy and soft enough to sleep on. I assumed anyone who stayed in this house expected a certain level of luxury.

Camilla had breakfast prepared when I arrived in the kitchen. The house was stocked with food so she took advantage, putting a couple of over-easy eggs and several slices of bacon on a plate and handing it to me. Pastries were already on the table and a Nespresso coffee machine sat on the counter with numerous flavors of coffee pods to choose from. I put in a capsule called Roma, which the package said was an *eight* on the coffee intensity scale. I hope that's on a scale of one to eight because I need a serious caffeine jolt. Once the machine expelled the brew into a tall mug, I added a bit of cream and sugar before sitting down to eat.

"It seems like we've been having a lot of '*What do we do now?*' discussions over meals in the past few days," Camilla stated as she joined me at the table.

"And the answers continue to get tougher," I responded.

We took a few bites of our food and I sipped my steaming hot level eight coffee, which lived up to its intensity rating.

We hesitated to begin the discussion, even though we understood that we couldn't hide out and hope the problem disappeared. We were tired, scared, and way outside of our normal comfort zones. The worst part—at least for me—was the realization that we weren't going to find a way through this on our own and had no idea who to turn to. Would anyone believe our story? We had a lot of little pieces of information and had twice avoided being kidnapped. But, did we have any real proof that we were being chased because of the Alcuin letter? We were confident of that fact but didn't have anything solid to convince someone else.

"Matt, I'm sorry for getting you into all of this."

"What are you talking about? You didn't get me into anything."

"I encouraged you to fly over to London and I have pressured you to stay with me the last couple of days," Camilla admitted. "You have a little girl to worry about. I shouldn't have put you in this position."

"Camilla, listen to me." I waited until she met my eyes. "Ashton was my friend, and I wanted to do what I could to help. There's no way for you to know how this would play out. Yes, I would love to be back home and have this all resolved, but you're not responsible for the decisions I've made. You're certainly not responsible for whoever is behind all of this."

My words mollified her a bit, but the confidence I

witnessed in her over the past few days was waning. The tough, *I'll do it myself* image Camilla normally projected was being slowly swallowed up by our stressful circumstances.

I sensed her tendency to project an outer show of competence developed early in life in her high-achieving family. She likely kept any feelings of inadequacy and self-doubt buried under a mountain of busyness and a list of accomplishments. I could relate, as I spent most of the last year trying to show the world I was doing fine, when inside my doubts and fears constantly threatened to overwhelm me.

"I was awake most of the night trying to figure out what we do next," Camilla admitted. "I've been going at full speed since Ashton's death and there has always been a logical next step. Now, I don't know where we can go from here."

Her final sentence came out like it physically caused her pain to admit; like the weight of the situation was beginning to crush her.

"How about we do this," I said, making her look at me before I continued. "Let's make a list of all we know, starting from Ashton's contact with Dennis Simons several weeks ago. Then we can go through it step by step. Maybe something new will jump out at us, or at least a new direction for us to follow might become clearer. Does that sound like a plan?"

"I guess that sounds good. Let me grab my computer and our other notes."

She left the table, and I cleaned up the dishes. She returned a few minutes later and we spread out the notes we had collected. We worked through the timeline of the last several weeks, noting any breakthroughs we were able to make on the Alcuin letter and what we knew about any others involved. Camilla typed out our timeline and notes as we progressed.

Because of the e-mail Camilla found, we had confirmation this whole thing started when Dennis Simons contacted Ashton. After Ashton traveled to Germany and received the Alcuin letter, it was only a couple of days until he made the video and sent it to Dr. Monteith. Less than a week after that, Ashton was dead and the package he somehow managed to send was on its way to Bannister.

If it wasn't for that package, no one would know anything except that Ashton died tragically.

We figured Dr. Monteith died—probably murdered—sometime during the week after Ashton's death.

I made the trip to London to meet up with Camilla and then things happened in rapid succession. We made contact with Simons and received the missing notes from Ashton's office. Schmidt and Klein made their visit to Camilla's condo, followed by our escape and the trip to Frankfort. We met Simons and ran into the two Germans again, which prompted another escape and led to us finding our current hiding place in Geneva.

Along the way, we learned a great deal about the eighth and ninth centuries and such names from history as Charlemagne, Alcuin, Rhabanus, and others. We also managed to decipher some of the Alcuin letter and at least had a start on tracing the supposed whereabouts of what we believed to be the cup of Christ.

As I looked over the notes I let out a brief laugh. "If I hadn't lived through the last few days, I would never believe this. A few days ago, my biggest worry was getting some grading finished and preparing for my fall classes."

Camilla stood, came around the table, and then leaned over to give me a brief kiss on the cheek. She wrapped her arms around me for a long, tender hug.

"What was that for," I asked as she released me.

"I guess I want to say thanks for staying with me after a crazy few days. Even though you don't know me well, you have stuck by me, and that means more than you can imagine."

Not knowing exactly how to react, I stood and faced

Camilla. I put my hands on her shoulders and looked her straight in the eyes. "I am with you until we figure a way out of this mess. You don't know me that well, either, but one thing I've learned in the past year is sometimes things happen that interrupt our perfect little lives. When those things do happen, we have to keep moving forward and believe we have the strength to find a way through."

Her eyes began to drop, but I lifted her chin.

"My friend Ethan would probably quote a Bible verse right now, but all I will say is I believe the Lord has a plan for all of us. That plan may not be how we envisioned our lives would go, but we still have to trust that in some crazy way, the Lord's plans will ultimately be for our good. That concept is incredibly hard to accept, but deep down it's what I've come to believe."

Camilla continued to look at me as tears formed in the corner of her eyes. A couple of watery blinks and a river of tears flowed down her cheeks. I gently wiped them away and then embraced her, repaying her hug from a few minutes earlier.

We remained in that pose for an extended time. I think we both enjoyed the closeness of another person and the sense of unconditional support.

After we stepped apart, we spent a few moments in awkward silence.

"Is there something we might have missed when making these notes?" I asked, pointing to her computer screen and putting the moment of closeness behind us.

We sat back down and adjusted the computer so we could both read the screen.

"One thing continues to baffle me," Camilla stated moments later. "No matter how many times I run through what's happened, I cannot fathom who's behind all this. Ashton received the Alcuin letter, made his video, and sent it to his boss immediately. Then within a few days, both Ashton and Dr. Monteith are dead. In that scenario, how did anyone find out about the Alcuin letter?"

"Plus, Simons said he had a visit about that time from a stranger telling him to keep quiet about the document," I added.

"What are we missing?" I continued. "From the information we have, it's hard to see where or when the news about the letter leaked out. And, even if it leaked, why would someone go as far as murdering people to acquire the letter?"

"The cup of Christ would be a major find. I'm sure someone could make a lot of money off the discovery."

"I suppose that's true, but why wouldn't they just try to buy the letter and follow the clues? Why eliminate Ashton and the others?"

Camilla didn't respond right away, but stared at the computer screen and tried to process all we had gone through.

"Maybe they don't want anyone left alive who can confirm where the Alcuin letter came from and that the letter was a clue to finding the cup," she said. "Maybe they want to take credit for the discovery and don't want anyone who can deny their claims."

"What about Simons, though? They just paid him off and warned him to keep quiet at first."

"Yes, but he didn't know anything about the cup at that point. He just knew he had a document from medieval times," Camilla pointed out. "If someone announced the discovery of the cup of Christ at a later date, Simons would have no idea there was a link between the discovery and the document he loaned to Ashton."

"You might be right," I conceded. "But, if your theory is correct, a couple of other things are true."

I think Camilla realized where I was going with this train of thought.

"First, Simons might still be alive if we hadn't contacted him." I let that statement sink in. "And, second, whoever is behind this will not want us to stay alive."

CHAPTER 11

Father Griego stood at the pulpit, preparing to address a large gathering of priests and guests of the Society of Angels. His was the keynote address of the weekend and would bring to a close the Society's annual conference.

Priests from across Europe traveled to the Society's headquarters in Saillon for the conference. Joining them were twelve members of the Board of Elders, a group appointed by Griego and consisting of many of the largest contributors to the Society's coffers.

The conference was primarily focused on preparing the priests for another year of service, sharing best practices, and presenting new ideas. There were always small disagreements in doctrine and Society procedures to work out, but most were settled quickly once Griego became involved with the discussion. After thirty years at the helm, the majority of the Society deferred to their leader when a decision needed to be made. Griego's powerful personality often swayed the very successful, wealthy, and influential Elders.

Griego looked out at the audience which filled the former church. While several buildings of the abbey had been redesigned to serve as the Society's headquarters, the church, and its central nave had been left much the same as when it was built in the 1600s. Hand-made wooden pews filled the room, a space lined by stone arches and paved with aged stone tiles. A massive stained glass window looked down upon the altar and all in attendance, its colorful glass panes forming a picture of Jesus and the disciples at the Last Supper. Griego felt the depiction was a sign his search for the cup used at the Last Supper would be a success.

"Brothers and sisters, I am humbled to be standing before you for the annual conference of the Society of Angels. There can be no doubt we are blessed by the Lord."

Griego watched as the heads of practically everyone in attendance nodded in agreement. All eyes focused on him and all were attentive to his words.

"I thank you for your dedication and service to the Society; some for a short time, but several of you for many years. I especially want to recognize two individuals who have been with me since the beginning."

He looked at two people in the first row of pews.

"Father Marcus was the first person to complete the training to become a priest for the Society," Griego said, pointing to a diminutive man in a plain priest's robe. Marcus had only a wisp of white hair on his head and was stooped from age, but accepted his acknowledgment from Griego with eyes that looked very much alive. "He has been at the helm of our church in Leeds, England, for the past five years and previously started our first church in Geneva.

"I also want to announce that Father Marcus is the inaugural recipient of our Society of Angels Excellence Award. The award will be given each year to a deserving priest or church member who displays exemplary service to the Society and others."

Those in attendance showered the surprised Father Marcus with a sustained applause. It pleased Greigo to give the award to Marcus, a presentation that had been planned for several weeks. It also gave Griego a convenient opportunity to reward the older priest for shepherding Professor Monteith in Leeds. That act opened the door for Monteith to make Griego aware of the Alcuin letter and the possible path to Christ's cup. The award would have been a nice plaque and a firm handshake, but now included a substantial monetary gift.

Father Marcus stood and shuffled to the platform to receive his handshake and plaque from Griego. The monetary bonus would be waiting for Marcus when he arrived back in Leeds.

Once the applause died down, Griego continued. "I also must recognize Mr. Helmuth Moltke, a long-time member of our Board of Elders."

A tall, stately gentleman rose to be acknowledged with a polite round of applause. He wore a custom-tailored suit, set off by a bright ocean blue tie and matching pocket handkerchief. His full head of grey hair was professionally styled and topped a long, angular face, recently bronzed by a vacation to the exclusive Cousine Island in the Seychelles. The businessman looked comfortable being at the center of attention and gave off an air of confidence and superiority.

"As many of you know, Mr. Moltke has been instrumental behind the scenes in helping the Society continue to grow and offer our message throughout Europe and beyond. I am sorry to announce he will be stepping down from our Board of Elders to have more time to enjoy his retirement."

Though retired from serving as President and CEO of the largest pharmaceutical company in Europe, Moltke left the Munich-based company with $500 million in stock options and a severance package that added another $200 million to his considerable wealth.

Many in Germany recognized the Helmuth Moltke name. A great-great-great grandfather of the same name was an esteemed military leader in the 1800s and was honored with a statue in Berlin. Unfortunately for the modern-day Moltke, he also shared his name with a distant cousin who was held responsible for military decisions leading to Germany's loss in World War I.

The current Moltke had supported the Society since the beginning but forged an early understanding with Griego that any support came with the expectations of unfettered access. That access included information and possible inroads to markets controlled by other Society members. The relationship proved profitable for the pharmaceutical company, as well as for Moltke personally. Even though he no longer held an official title, Moltke was still very much in the business of making money and being in control.

"I want to publicly thank Mr. Moltke for his many years of service to the Society, for his generosity and also his friendship. His leadership on our Board of Elders will be missed and difficult to replace."

Griego stepped down from the platform as a feigned show of deference. He vigorously shook the businessman's hand, leaning in just enough to whisper, "I will update you later in my office." A brief nod of understanding came from Moltke before he turned to the crowd and raised a hand to acknowledge their applause.

Back in his position behind the altar, Griego continued his address to the gathered assembly.

"For much of the past three decades, the Society of Angels has been taking our message of faith, love, and acceptance to the people of many nations. What started as a small group here in Switzerland has now spread to a dozen countries across Europe. Every person in this sanctuary has played a part in that growth and I am thankful for each one of you."

Griego paused to slowly look at the crowd, making eye contact with as many as possible; seeming to pass on his appreciation with his gaze.

"We are now in a position to expand our ministry to many areas, with new churches in Asia and North America possible before the end of this year. I know many of you have expressed thoughts on expansion and helped develop strategies for growth. I look forward to working with the

Board of Elders to implement those plans soon. It is invigorating to make plans to share with people in these new locations; people who will be excited to hear our message, are hungry for acceptance, and long for a place to belong.

"One thing, though, is more important than any plans for the Society's growth. That one thing is the absolute necessity we continue to emphasize the central message of the Society: God loves us all and God wants each of us to be fulfilled and happy in our earthly lives. Without that focused message, we are just another religious group that occasionally does good deeds.

"Too many organized religions today spend more time telling people what is wrong with them than they do telling people they are loved. Other organized religions expend far too much effort alienating people because of disagreements about lifestyles than they do making them feel welcome. Others want to make a narrow path of rules that everyone must follow, instead of creating a wide path of acceptance.

"I can use the United States—which still calls itself a Christian nation—as a specific example. Numerous denominations argue minute points of scripture while their congregations dwindle. Some churches seem to be more interested in politics and who is right and wrong than they do about who is in need. While they are arguing scripture and trying to elect just the right politicians, their religious freedoms are disappearing rapidly. Much of society is tired of those who preach a message of grace and forgiveness, but fail to show any of those qualities in their daily lives.

"That is not an example we at the Society want to follow."

Griego paused to let his previous words sink in. He also needed to gather himself and make sure the words that were to follow were sufficient to get those gathered in the sanctuary excited about what could soon happen. At the same time, he needed to be vague enough that his words were not able to be used against him if the coming weeks did not bring about the discovery he hoped.

"Brothers and sisters, I now want to speak briefly about something I have shared with only a select few individuals. Not even the entire Board of Elders is aware of the blessing that is on the horizon for the Society of Angels. While I am unable to provide many details at this time, I ask for your prayers and support. I am following a holy trail that can provide an immeasurable blessing to the Society and open many eyes to our message and our ministry. I'm confident the name of our humble Society will be on the lips of millions around the world in the coming days."

Everyone in the audience was now locked onto Griego's words, focused on him, and waiting to hear what more their leader would say.

"I understand many of you will have questions, but for now I need to pursue what the Lord has put before us unencumbered by unrealistic expectations and undue pressure. Be excited about what may lie ahead for the Society of Angels. More importantly, please be in prayer for me as I pursue this quest. Pray for guidance, pray for wisdom, and pray for perseverance. The Lord has put the possibility of an immense blessing in our path. However, that path is not an easy one and there is no guarantee of success."

The animated glances between the priests confirmed they were excited about his words. Griego's main concerns were the members of the Board of Elders who had, up until now, been left out of the conversation about his search for the cup of Christ. Only Moltke was aware of the Alcuin letter and all that had transpired in recent weeks. Griego wanted and needed the support of the entire Board, but didn't feel he could provide details to everyone. There would be too many opinions about how to proceed and too many tongues to be kept silent.

Griego continued. "Even as I speak, plans are being carried out that I hope will take us further down that path. If it is in the Lord's plan, I will have good news to report within the week.

"Again, I encourage you to be excited, but also to be in prayer."

With the most important part of his talk now completed, Griego visibly relaxed and his facial expression softened.

"I will bring my talk and this conference to close by speaking to you not as the leader of the Society of Angels, but as a father. Most of you know my son Dominic and that the Lord brought him into my life shortly before the Society was born. While Dominic is not my flesh and blood, he could not be more loved no matter how he came into my life.

"Dominic, would you please come and stand beside me?" Griego pointed to his son who sat toward the back of the room. Dominic, looking a bit embarrassed, hesitantly stood and began walking slowly toward his father. Griego wrapped his arms around the young man in a strong embrace when he arrived at the altar, an act that felt foreign to Dominic but looked sincere to those watching.

"Dominic has been studying to become a priest in the Society of Angels for the past several years. His academic work has been exemplary and his service assignments have been fulfilled with a loving heart. Therefore, I am extremely proud today to announce that the Board of Elders has approved Dominic as the newest priest in the Society. He will be assigned a church as soon as an opening becomes available."

Many of the priests began to clap and a few "Amens" were heard from the more Pentecostal-leaning side of the aisle. Most had known Dominic for years and interacted with him when they were in the midst of their training in Saillon and other visits to the Society headquarters. They knew him as an incredibly bright boy who grew into an intelligent and compassionate young man. A person would be hard-pressed to find anyone to say a negative word about the Society's newest priest.

"This is my son in whom I am well pleased," said Griego, mimicking the passage from the third chapter of Matthew. "I am confident he will continue to make me proud and be a marvelous ambassador for the Society."

Dominic returned to his seat, struggling to enjoy the recognition. As one of the few in the room who was aware of exactly what his father was referring to when mentioning a potential *blessing* for the Society, Dominic had been fighting his conscience for several days. He understood the positive effect finding the cup of Christ would have on the Society but was having a hard time justifying the means his father and others were using in the attempt to acquire the cup.

Because of the secretive nature of his father's quest for the cup, there wasn't anyone Dominic could talk to about his feelings. His father wouldn't accept or understand his crisis of conscience and would probably say it was a lack of faith. He also couldn't go to Mr. Moltke, a man Dominic had known all of his life but had never liked or respected. There was just something about Moltke that seemed disingenuous and an aura that frightened Dominic most of the time. If Dominic were to speak with one of the other priests and reveal what he knew, his father would never forgive him. This quandary was keeping him awake at night and severely dampened his excitement over officially becoming a priest.

Once Dominic took a seat, Griego called Father Marcus back to the front and asked the elderly priest to close the proceedings with a prayer. Father Marcus prayed in a powerful voice that gave no hint of his age. He spent considerable time praying for Father Griego and the quest that was in front of the Society's leader.

Less than thirty minutes after the gathering dispersed, Griego was back in his office. He looked across his desk at Moltke and the only woman on the Board of Elders, Gretchen Sondheim. Sondheim was the daughter of Geoffrey Sondheim, once a member of the British parliament, and was grilling Griego for more information on his cryptic announcement. She emphasized her belief that all the members of the Board of Elders should be made aware of any activities that could have a substantial effect on the Society. Being left out of whatever was going on was unacceptable to her and was, in her opinion, not the proper way to treat the Elders.

Griego assured her he valued her opinions and would consider her suggestions. His words seemed to appease Sondheim slightly and she left after making the point to the two men that she expected to hear something very soon.

"That woman is beginning to get on my nerves," said Moltke. "Her father was in politics for years, and it seems like she is trying to follow in his footsteps."

"She is inconsequential at this point," replied Griego. "Most of the other elders are not fond of her, so if she continues to press us for more information, we will dismiss her from the board. I think the votes needed to make that happen would be easy to secure."

Griego opened a cabinet behind his desk and withdrew two glasses and a decanter of his favorite single malt Scotch. After pouring two fingers of the dark amber liquid, he offered one glass to Moltke and then raised his glass. "Here's to another successful year for the Society of Angels and to further success in the opportunity that lies before us."

The two touched glasses and then drank to complete the toast.

"Now, I am anxious for the update you promised," stated Moltke. "Have you deciphered the Alcuin letter?"

Griego took a deep breath before answering. "I have

made progress with the letter, but unfortunately, have not deduced the final answer."

Moltke's eyes narrowed, but he resisted the urge to speak.

"Also, some unexpected loose ends have evaded our attempts to tie them up." Griego went on to describe the events of the past few days, including the death of the antique dealer in Frankfort and the escape, once again, of the British woman and the American professor. "Those loose ends possess some information that may assist us in our search."

"I assume you are working to acquire that information?"

"I expect to hear from the two individuals very soon," answered Griego. "Let's just say I have found a way to motivate them to share their information. Once that is done, I have people in place to snip off those loose ends permanently."

"Here's to some successful pruning," said Moltke, raising his glass again. "I hope we will soon be drinking out of a different cup."

CHAPTER 12

A picture window in the front of the home framed a beautiful view of Lake Geneva—or Lac Leman to the locals—and of the Jura Mountains in the distance. The summer sun glistened off the lake and highlighted the sails of a plethora of boats gliding along the tranquil surface. Camilla and I enjoyed the view as we continued to try and untangle our situation.

Completing a quick online search of Frankfort news outlets, we found an article about the death of American-born antique dealer Dennis Simons. The story said Simons, who regularly rode his bike to work, was found at the bottom of a small ravine that bordered the Main River. Although no witnesses came forward who saw the accident, authorities surmised Simons lost control of the bike and fell over the short retaining wall to his death. Simons' bike, with a flat tire, was found resting against the wall at the top of the ravine.

"I cannot believe those two goons killed again and covered it up in a way that no one will even be looking for them," Camilla said with a bit of venom in her voice. "Part of me wishes we would have shot them when we had the chance."

"I'm as frustrated as you, but killing them wouldn't have brought Ashton or Simons back. It wouldn't have helped us learn any more about who's behind all of this. Besides, as much as it might have felt good at the moment,

I'm fairly sure killing them would have brought more trouble our way."

Camilla's features remained hard and foreboding for several moments but eventually softened. "I suppose you are right.

"Hey, whatever happened to the gun we took from Schmidt at the antiques store?" she asked. "With all that was happening when we left the store, I forgot you had the gun."

I walked back to the bedroom I was using and returned holding the gun. "I stuffed it in the bottom of my bag and forgot about it."

"You're lucky it wasn't found when we boarded the train," Camilla said as she took the gun from my hand. "European countries have fairly tough gun laws. If someone found this in your possession, you would probably be in a German jail right now."

She looked over the gun, popped out the clip of ammunition, and laid it on the table.

"This is a Beretta 93R 9mm pistol and looks like it has a thirteen-round magazine," she said. "With the two shots fired in the antiques store, there are eleven rounds left. The 9mm Parabellum is the most popular cartridge for handguns, so we could probably come up with more if needed."

I just stared at her in amazement. "Who are you and how do you know so much about this gun?"

Camilla chuckled. "I guess a mild-mannered photographer is not supposed to know anything about guns."

I continued to stare inquisitively.

"Old boyfriend," she finally replied. "He considered himself a gun aficionado and used to take me to a shooting range. I enjoyed the experience of learning about the guns and shooting them more than I enjoyed his company. The day after I beat him in a shooting contest, he conveniently came up with a reason to end our relationship."

"He must have been intimidated. Beauty, brains, and an itchy trigger finger. That could make a man a bit nervous."

Camilla smiled at the not-so-hidden compliment.

I picked up the gun and the clip of ammunition and slid them into a drawer in the kitchen. When I returned, we continued to work through several scenarios of who might want the Alcuin letter, and by extension, the cup of Christ badly enough to kill for it.

Finding the cup would certainly be a financial coup for an individual or organization, but why eliminate anyone who had information that helped lead to the discovery? What benefit would be gained if no one knew any details except those who announced such a discovery? Was Camilla's assumption true that someone needed to take all the credit for the find to be relevant?

Our discussion came to a standstill, so we decided to get out of the house and take a walk. The exercise felt great after being cooped up on a train most of the previous day. I would love to take a run while in Geneva, but there were more pressing matters to consider. Our walk took us from the house on a street called Chemin de la Marie and over to a nice wide path along the Quai Gustave-Ador, which ran parallel to the lake.

In the distance, we saw the Jet d'Eau—or water jet—near where the Rhone River flowed into Lake Geneva. It was one of the area's most recognizable landmarks and originally served as a water supply safety valve when it was built in 1891. Now, a water stream shot over 450 feet in the air and released 132 gallons of water per second while it was active between March and October. The moisture in the air, combined with the correct angle of the sun, helped create a rainbow around the jet on many summer days. Camilla and I viewed the colorful rainbow as we walked.

In less than half a mile we came up to the entrance of a large green space, called the Parc de la Grange. The park was crowded with families enjoying the luscious rose gardens and unique fountains. There were several areas designed for kids to play and a variety of trails meandering through the foliage and gardens of red, white, and yellow roses. With Lake Geneva at the north end and a refurbished estate from the 1500s at the south end, the park contained scenery and views that graced the cover of many travel magazines. It also provided ample photo opportunities for tourists and locals, alike.

"Here is a thought," Camilla said after we walked in silence for several minutes, simply enjoying the scenery. "What if a church or religious organization wanted to claim they were uniquely blessed by God to possess the cup? If someone else provided the clues and helped them find it, they would lose the chance to claim that *divine* blessing. Such a church would certainly boost interest in its message and probably gain followers almost immediately. We have seen stranger things over the years, like people flocking to see statues which reportedly weep real tears."

"I guess that's one legitimate theory, but I find it hard to believe any mainstream denomination would resort to murder to reach its goals."

"I had those same thoughts," she countered. "Except what if it wasn't a mainstream group, but some type of organization on the fringe? Maybe a denomination that was loosely associated with mainstream religion. One that would get a huge boost if it claimed to find the cup of Christ."

"Maybe," I replied, still unconvinced. "But they would still have to show some proof. People would be very skeptical about a claim like that."

"Whoever is behind all this already has possession of the original Alcuin letter taken from my brother. As far as we can tell right now, that document would hold up to scrutiny. If you and I are out of the picture, then whoever found the cup would just have to demonstrate how they worked through the clues in the letter."

"I suppose you're right. Producing the cup would skyrocket anyone who found it to incredible levels of notoriety within a few days, with the benefits of the find paying off for many years to come.

"The murder thing still confuses me, though," I added. "I can't put the willingness to take an innocent person's life in the same theological arena as the opportunity to benefit from a major religious find."

"Maybe you just haven't seen enough evil and greed in people in your sheltered American life." Camilla's tone was more envious than insulting.

"Perhaps you're right," I said as we started walking back to the house.

"What about the Society of Angels?" she asked as we walked

I gave her a look that must have indicated I had no idea what she was talking about.

"You remember the church Ashton's secretary told me about? The one Dr. Monteith was involved in? You described it as a bunch of old ladies drinking tea."

"Oh, yeah. Now I remember. You think they could be behind this?" I said with a lot of doubt.

"I don't know anything about them," Camilla admitted. "But there's at least a small connection to this situation we find ourselves in. Also, I would assume it qualifies as a fringe denomination that would get a big boost from a discovery like the cup of Christ."

I believed her idea was a reach, but appeased her by saying, "I suppose we can look up some information on the Society of Angels and see what we find out."

The rest of the walk took about fifteen minutes, with barely a word spoken between us, both lost in our thoughts.

"Are you interested in a late lunch?" Camilla inquired as we entered the house.

Before I responded, her phone began to ring. She answered as she moved toward the kitchen.

"Hello Mother," I heard Camilla say. "What? What are you talking about?" There was now an increased pitch in her voice.

I rounded the corner and saw the color drain from Camilla's face as she listened to her mother. While I couldn't make out the exact words, I heard her mother's frantic tone through the phone.

"Yes, Mother I do know what he was talking about. It was something Ashton was working on. We are trying to follow up on some things and complete the project Ashton started."

She listened again. "Matt Kincaid. Ashton's friend from the States."

I assumed she was explaining who the *we* represented from her previous statement.

"No, we are not in London. We have been doing some research in Frankfort."

Why did she not tell her mother we were in Geneva? Seeing Camilla so agitated and not being able to hear both sides of the conversation was frustrating.

"I will take care of it and make sure these people don't bother you again," Camilla said as she found a pen and wrote something on a piece of paper. "What about you guys? What are you going to do?"

Another delay while Camilla's mother spoke.

"All right. I will check in as much as I can. I'm sure Matt and I can handle things, and there won't be any trouble. I love you and tell Dad I love him, too."

Camilla listened to a final comment from her mother and then ended the call. She took a deep breath, and I could sense a lump in her throat as she tried to talk. I restrained myself from throwing questions at her, which wasn't easy.

"They threatened my family," she finally choked out, holding back a sob.

"What? Who threatened your family?"

"Two men knocked on my grandparent's door in Barcelona this morning and asked to see my parents. When my grandfather questioned them, they pushed their way into the house, knocking my grandfather to the floor. The two men waved a gun around until my parents appeared."

Camilla had to stop and compose herself. It was obvious she was both frightened and angry. I waited for her to continue.

"They sat my parents down, pointing a gun at them the whole time, and gave them a piece of paper with a phone number on it. They told them I had some information that others wanted and if I failed to call the number within twenty-four hours they would be back to make their point in a less friendly way. My grandfather was only bruised from his fall and nobody else was hurt, but they are all really frightened."

I approached Camilla and tentatively reached out to embrace her. She hesitated at first, but then let my arms swallow her up as she wrapped her arms tightly around my back.

"I'm so sorry." I knew the words were virtually meaningless, but I hoped she at least felt comforted to know she wasn't going through this situation alone.

"What are we going to do?" she managed to say once calming down a bit but still clinging to me. "These people are everywhere. They were in London, followed us to Germany, and now someone's threatening my parents in Spain. Why did they have to involve my family?"

"I guess they don't know where we are, so they need us to make contact. They're using your family to flush us out."

"How did they know where my parents were?"

"From what the two goons in Germany said, they had your apartment bugged for a couple of weeks. I'm sure they heard you mention your parent's whereabouts."

Camilla picked up the piece of paper with the phone number written on it. "Do I call this number and find out what they want?"

"I think we are well aware of what they want. With all that's happened, though, I just don't see them letting us walk away, even if we give them everything. They realize we probably can't hide forever. The information we have—or at least they think we have—is our only bargaining chip, so we need to be smart and careful."

"I cannot let them harm my parents," said Camilla emphatically. "With all our family has been through, I can't be the reason someone else gets hurt. I couldn't live with that."

"Okay. Let's stop and think for a while. They gave you a twenty-four-hour window to respond, so we have some time to make a decision."

Camilla was now looking out the window that covered much of the living room wall at the front of the house. The yard outside was neatly landscaped with a variety of flowers and had a stone pathway that split in two directions; one leading around the side of the house and the other to the street. I'm sure Camilla wasn't noticing any of it.

"Why don't you sit down and try to relax for a few minutes?" I suggested. "I'm going to call and check on my daughter. With the time change, they should be up by now. Then I will find something for us to eat and we can decide how to move forward."

A nod of the head was the only reaction from Camilla.

Several minutes later Camilla burst into my room. "Matt, I just thought of someone who might be able to help…." She saw my face and froze. "What's wrong?"

"My in-laws got a visit this morning from two men who left the same message your parents received," I said through clenched teeth. "They threatened to hurt my little girl."

CHAPTER 13

There are no words to adequately explain the feeling that engulfs you when your family is threatened with physical harm. When you're several thousand miles away, the feeling of helplessness is only multiplied.

A few short minutes earlier I thought I empathized with Camilla. It took just one frantic phone call for me to realize I was wrong. There is little comparison between empathy for someone else's plight and the sheer terror and frustration when it's your flesh and blood in the line of fire. My late wife's parents and my little girl were now involved in a situation I couldn't have imagined only days ago.

My father-in-law Donald told me about the two men who knocked on the door when he and my mother-in-law were eating breakfast. Similar to what happened to Camilla's family, men waved guns around to gain control and then gave Donald a phone number. The man in charge emphasized that I needed to call the number within twenty-four hours or the two would return and next time wouldn't be so nice. Fortunately, Maddie was still in bed so she didn't have to be traumatized by the intruders.

The jolt of reality served one important purpose. It confirmed what my common sense had been trying to tell me for the past few days.

"We are way out of our league," I said to Camilla once I reigned in my emotions a bit. "We have to get some help."

"Matt, I'm so sorry your family is now involved. Was

your daughter hurt?"

"No. She was still in bed when the men forced their way in and delivered their message. I was able to speak to her for a couple of minutes, and she had no idea anything was wrong. Donald and Karen are taking Maddie and getting out of town for a couple of days."

"Were you able to explain to them what was going on?"

"I told them the basics of the situation, but didn't go into any details."

I think we were both emotionally exhausted. I sat on the bed staring at my hands, while Camilla remained standing in the doorway, gazing out the window. Part of me longed for another embrace like the two of us shared this morning but now was not the time. If there was ever going to be more than friendship between us, it would have to wait until our lives were somewhat back to normal; a state of living that seemed very far away right now.

"I thought of someone who might be able to help us," Camilla said, finishing the sentence she started when she first entered the room.

I turned to look at her.

"I am not sure why I didn't think of this earlier. There is a guy named Brooks Hartley who was in Ashton's class growing up. He and his family lived close to us. I didn't know him well, but Ashton hung out with him, at least until they both went off to college. Ashton mentioned him every once in a while over the past few years. I think they used to get together when both were in London. Anyway, Brooks became a police officer and then an investigator for the Criminal Investigation Department in Manchester. Ashton said he took a job with Interpol a couple of years ago in their main office in Lyon, France. Could someone with Interpol help us?"

"I'm not that familiar with Interpol," I said. "To me, it's just something you read in spy novels. I suppose it would be worth a try, though. Right now I'm totally out of answers, so

I would welcome any help or advice."

"I'll go look up some information and see if I can come up with a phone number for Brooks Hartley."

I continued sitting on the bed as Camilla left the room. Visions of men breaking into Donald and Karen's home and hurting Maddie continued to swirl in my head. I had to get a grip on my emotions or the weight of the situation would render me useless. I needed to focus on the simple goals of staying alive and protecting my family.

I managed to pull myself together before joining Camilla in the front room. She sat on the couch with her computer on her lap, already searching the Interpol website.

"What have you found out?"

"Interpol acts primarily as a liaison between law-enforcement agencies from two hundred countries around the world," she explained as she read the information on the screen. "Their agents do not have any authority to make arrests but can assist with tracking criminals who operate across national borders. They also track crime trends around the world.

"Interpol has a database that maintains one of the largest collections of fingerprints, DNA samples, and lists of stolen travel documents. The member countries can access information at any time through a special secure network."

Camilla's eyes continued to scan information as she scrolled through various screens.

"Do you think our situation would be considered a religious crime?" she asked.

"Why would you ask that?"

"Because it says Interpol doesn't participate in any action involving politics, race or religion, but focuses on key areas like terrorism, organized crime, international fugitives, and computer crime."

"I'm not sure what kind of category our circumstances would fit into. There have been murders in England and Germany, and now we know of personal threats in Spain and the U.S. You and I have personally escaped abduction attempts in two different countries in the past couple of days. We believe all this happened because of a search for a priceless artifact; an artifact that could be hidden anywhere in Europe, or maybe even the Middle East or Asia. All that should qualify as an international crime."

"You're probably right. At this point, I don't think we have much choice anyway. Our twenty-four-hour window is ticking away. I will make the call."

Camilla used her cell phone to dial the main number of Interpol. She asked for Brooks Hartley. No, she didn't know his extension. No, she didn't have a drug-related crime to report. No, she didn't want to talk with someone else.

After being transferred a couple of times, Camilla finally left a message on Hartley's office phone. She identified herself as Ashton's sister and told Hartley of Ashton's death. After a brief description of our situation and especially the deadline we were given, she implored Hartley to call her back as soon as possible. She hung up and we began the agonizing process of waiting.

To pass the time and keep ourselves from going crazy, we pulled out the copy of the Alcuin letter and our notes. We hoped solving the clues in the letter would give us some type of leverage in our situation; maybe some knowledge that would give us a bargaining chip.

We refreshed our memories of the two parts of the verse we already solved, or at least believed we'd solved. It was only yesterday morning in our hotel in Frankfort that we had last discussed the letter. With all that happened since then, it was difficult to get our minds back into research mode.

"I think we agreed yesterday that the first two stanzas of the verse indicate the cup of Christ was hidden in a golden vessel given to Charlemagne by al-Rashid from Baghdad. Is that your understanding?"

Camilla was looking at her watch. She was worried about her parents and the deadline we were under, and hoping her contact at Interpol would return her call. “Yes, I think that’s correct,” she said without much enthusiasm.

“Looking at the third part of the verse, I believe the Latin translates to something like *From a king comes a prize; From a prize comes a place to be still; From a place to be still comes a gift; Find out a gift of life and be saved.*

“Ashton didn’t leave any notes for these last two sections, so I’m stretching my limited knowledge of Latin and trusting my phone’s translation skills.”

I scribbled my rough translation on a piece of paper. Camilla and I both read it several times, hoping to make some sense of the words.

Camilla spoke up. “The only things I can take from those lines are that the *king* is Charlemagne and he gave some type of *gift* that should be found. A *place to be still* might be a church. I’m not sure where a *prize* fits in.”

“Give me a few minutes to look up some additional info and maybe I'll be able to get a better feel for the translation. I know some words have multiple meanings, so there could be mistakes in this basic translation,” I admitted.

Camilla slid the computer across the table to me, stood, and walked to the windows looking out to the small backyard. She checked her phone and glanced at her watch again.

Thirty minutes later Camilla was still standing at the window.

“I think I’ve come up with a better translation of these lines.”

Camilla turned and joined me once again at the table.

“The Latin word *viaticus* was throwing me off.” I pointed to the first line of the third section on our copy of the Alcuin letter, which read *Ex a rex regis adveho viaticus*. “I translated it as *prize*, but an online source said it can have dual meanings with another option being something related to a journey.

“So, with that change, the translation would be *From a*

king comes a journey; From a journey comes a place to be still or maybe *to rest; From a place to rest comes a gift; Find out* or *discover a gift of life and be saved.*

"Can you make anything out of those lines," I asked, trying to get Camilla engaged in the process.

She checked out the new lines scribbled on paper, not commenting at first. The wheels of her brain were turning.

"The king must still be Charlemagne," she said. "He takes a journey and finds a place to rest. While he's there, he leaves a gift."

She stared at the words a few moments longer.

"Possibly the gift was the golden vessel with the cup of Christ hidden inside," she added. "If we find the gift, we will find the cup."

Once again Camilla was able to take a few generic lines and my rough translations and make them spell out a scenario that made some sense.

"If your thoughts are correct, so far we have the cup of Christ in the possession of Charlemagne. He receives a gift of a golden vessel and then hides the cup inside the vessel. Charlemagne then goes on a trip and leaves this vessel as a gift at a location—as yet unknown—where he found some rest. How does that sound?"

"That pretty much sums it up," she said. "I wonder, though, if Charlemagne knew the cup was hidden inside the vessel. Didn't you say the body of the Alcuin letter indicated he was given the cup by Charlemagne and asked to make it secure?"

"Correct. But if we're deciphering the clues correctly, I don't think it matters if Charlemagne knew or not. Alcuin created the clues, so we just need to follow where they lead. Maybe the fourth section will tell us where Charlemagne found his *place of rest."*

"A place of rest sounds good right now," Camilla said while taking another glance at her watch.

There were dark circles under her blue eyes and her

curly dark hair was a bit more untamed than normal. Her face also looked more pale than when I met her a few days ago at the airport. I doubted I looked any better.

The ringing of Camilla's phone startled us both.

Camilla fumbled for her phone, dropping it on the floor once and nearly a second time before she successfully answered. Her eyes met mine and she gave a brief nod to let me know it was Brooks Hartley from Interpol.

I closed my eyes and found myself praying. It wasn't something I did often enough, but right now it was needed. We were running out of options. Brooks Hartley might just be the last opportunity for us to get some help before we or our families face some severe danger. I told Camilla earlier in the day that I believed the Lord's plans were ultimately for our good, so I prayed for some of those *good plans* to be revealed to us very soon.

Camilla told Hartley a condensed version of our last few days, including Ashton's murder, the murder of Dennis Simons, our escape from Frankfort, the phone calls from our families, and the deadline we were given. She described the men who attempted to abduct us and gave Hartley the names the two men used. I could tell Hartley asked a few questions, but mostly he let Camilla talk.

Camilla completed the story and then listened to Hartley before handing the phone to me. "He wants to talk to you."

"Hello," I said.

"Mr. Kincaid, are you doing alright?" Hartley asked in his distinctly British accent.

"As well as can be expected, I suppose. And, you can call me Matt."

"Okay, Matt. Did you hear what Camilla told me?"

"Yes."

"Do you corroborate everything she said and do you have anything to add?"

I thought for a few moments before answering. "I think she covered most of it. Honestly, everything has been happening so quickly, it's hard for me to process it all."

"I can understand that," Hartley said. "It sounds like you two have been through a lot in the past few days, but I will see what I can do to help you."

"That's good to hear. We were running out of options."

"I need to look into a couple of things, but will call back in less than an hour. Then we can discuss some options for the phone call you are supposed to make. Also, I let Camilla know that I will make some calls and get protection for your families. The advantage of being in my position is that I have contacts all over the world."

"Your help is greatly appreciated." I was fighting to keep back my tears. Despite trying to keep it under control since I talked to my father-in-law earlier in the day, fear for my family was eating away at me. Hartley's offer to get them protection almost broke the dam of my emotions.

I gave Hartley my in-law's address in Indiana and confirmed that I would call and let them know protection would soon be in place. Hartley promised that whoever showed up to provide protection would remain inconspicuous, so as not to arouse the suspicions of anyone watching our families. He assured me, however, that while the protection might be out of sight, it would move forcefully if needed.

Hartley gave me a direct line to reach him and assured me once again he would call back within the hour.

After I hung up, Camilla embraced me. I think we were both crying within seconds, releasing tensions and fears built up over the past few days. Hartley believed us and was willing to help us. After feeling like we were alone out in the wilderness, someone was coming alongside us who we hoped would guide us home.

At least one prayer had been answered.

CHAPTER 14

Brooks Hartley went into his super-focus mode. It was something he'd always been able to do and played a big part in his success as a policeman, an investigator, and now in his position with Interpol as Director for Specialized Crime and Analysis. When he needed to narrow down his focus on a particular problem, Hartley often found himself repeating the phrase '*Prepare the mechanism*' several times. He first heard the phrase several years earlier while watching a movie 35,000 feet above the Atlantic, flying back from a conference in New York. The film centered on the American sport of baseball—which Hartley didn't know much about—but he appreciated how the main character in the film used the phrase as a mental cue to block out crowd noise and focus on the task at hand.

The call from Camilla Collins served as the impetus for Hartley's desire to focus. While his main responsibilities for Interpol included such areas as drugs and criminal organizations, the issues of Ashton Collins's death and Camilla's subsequent involvement were personal for Hartley. Unknown to most people in his life, Hartley would not be in his current position without the Collins family; specifically Ashton and Camilla's father.

Hartley's teen years had been rough. His parents owned a string of furniture stores in London that had done very well for several years. The successful business allowed the

Hartleys to live in a large home in Kensington and provided the opportunity for Brooks and his older sister to attend the best private schools. A series of bad business decisions by his father, however, caused serious financial and emotional strain on the family.

By the time Brooks was sixteen, his parents were constantly fighting about money issues and the Hartley household was barely surviving. Brooks worked several part-time jobs to help his family, but when it was time to look into colleges he believed a college education was not financially feasible. Dr. Collins, who was familiar with the elder Hartley's financial woes and had witnessed the young Hartley's character and work ethic, stepped in and offered to provide the funding for college. The offer came with two conditions: Brooks couldn't talk about where the funding came from and he would promise to pay back the money whenever possible.

He lived up to his end of the agreement. Other than his parents, Brooks told no one for several years how he was able to afford college at the University of London. He didn't even tell his friend Ashton until college was completed and he was already in the process of paying back Dr. Collins. Hartley finished paying off the debt more than five years ago but understood money alone would never make up for the opportunities his education provided. He was living comfortably in Lyon, France, with a wife and six-year-old son. He was highly respected in his field and held a significant position at one of the most important police agencies in the world.

Hartley wasn't sure if Camilla was aware of his connection with her father. Regardless, he intended to use all the powers at his disposal to protect Camilla and her friend, as well as find out who was behind Ashton's murder.

He spent the first thirty minutes after his conversation with Camilla and Matt making phone calls to various contacts. By the time forty-five minutes passed, law enforcement crews were on their way to serve as protection for Camilla's family in Spain and Matt's family in the States.

Brooks also received files on Ashton's murder, the death of an antique shop owner in Frankfort, and possible matches for the two German thugs who were most likely responsible for both casualties. He would soon have more information on the phone number Camilla was supposed to call, although he doubted it would lead to a specific person.

Criminals in today's world are rarely dumb enough to use a personal phone for illegal activity. Most of those who did were desperate. Brooks didn't sense that whoever was behind these crimes could be categorized as dumb, although he hoped to find a way to make them desperate. Desperate criminals make mistakes. Mistakes usually lead to getting caught, especially when being chased by someone as focused and competent as Brooks Hartley.

The wait for Hartley to call us back felt like an eternity. Camilla and I were thrilled that he promised to help us but were still worried and uncertain about what might lie ahead.

We each made quick calls to our families to tell them to expect some protection. My father-in-law had been planning to take Karen and Maddie and leave town, but we came to the joint conclusion it would be safer and less traumatic for Maddie if they just stayed in Bannister. They needed to trust in the protection Hartley promised would soon be in place.

Not able to focus on deciphering any more of the Alcuin letter and too antsy to sit around and wait, I decided to call my friend Ethan Montgomery. He was someone I was able to talk to while trying to fight my way through the dark days after Rachel's death. Ethan's a good listener and is never judgmental; great qualities for a counselor, but unusual for a college professor. I found myself longing for one of our deep conversations, filled with personal thoughts and struggles.

Ethan had been there for the most grueling months of my life, and I trusted his advice and wisdom.

Ethan answered on the third ring and was understandably surprised to hear from me. He asked how my trip to England was going and I informed him there had been some complications. I told him a few details, including that Ashton had left behind some information Camilla and I believed was important. Information that could lead to a historical discovery. Other people were also after the same information and were creating some difficult circumstances. I admitted Camilla had made contact with an Interpol agent who was a family friend.

“Ethan, I can’t tell you everything that’s going on, but wanted you to know we are actually in some danger," I admitted. "The people we’re dealing with have even found a way to make threats to our families.”

He was startled by that information and admitted he and Chloe went through a similar experience a few years earlier and also used Interpol for assistance. Ethan gave me the name of their contact at Interpol and asked if there was anything else he could do.

“I would love it if you would stop by and check on Donald, Karen, and Maddie. Just let them know I’ve spoken with you and that you’re available if they need any help. Can you do that?”

Ethan readily agreed and then asked to pray for me and Camilla. It was awkward having him pray over the phone, but at the same time, brought a bit of calmness. It was likely Ethan would have most of his church praying for us by the end of the day. Even the anticipation of those prayers lifted a bit of the weight off my shoulders.

I thanked him when he was done praying and promised to try to keep him updated on our situation, even though I wasn’t sure what would transpire in the next few days.

Once I completed the call, I found Camilla staring out the window, gripping her phone like it was a lifeline. I was about to speak when her phone buzzed.

"Hello," she answered "Yes, we're both here. I can put the phone on speaker. Give me a second."

Camilla motioned me over to the kitchen table and we sat as she tapped the screen of her phone to activate the speaker.

"Can you both hear me?" Hartley asked, his voice strong and clear.

Once we replied in the affirmative, Hartley began to tell us what he accomplished in the past hour. "First of all, both of your families will be protected. Agents from local authorities have been dispatched and should be in place within the hour. You can be confident about your families' safety."

Camilla and I let out big sighs of relief. "Thank you so much," I said, probably speaking louder than I needed to for the phone to pick up my voice.

"No problem," Hartley replied. "Now some other news. I made contact with the authorities in Leeds and convinced them to keep investigating Ashton's case. I explained many of the details you told me and made a case that Ashton wasn't killed by a random mugger."

"Can't Interpol take over the investigation?" Camilla asked.

"That's not how we work. We work through other law enforcement agencies around the world, coordinating and providing information. Interpol, itself, doesn't arrest anyone, but we can be the central component in an investigation. We make sure other agencies receive all the assistance they need.

"I also talked to an investigator in Frankfort," Hartley continued. "I revealed that I heard from eyewitnesses that the antique dealer Dennis Simons was murdered in the office of the antique store. The detective was hesitant to re-open the case, but after I told him the names you gave me of the two Germans, he reconsidered. I guess the two men are well known in certain parts of Germany and are wanted for numerous crimes.

"By the way, the names you gave me of Klein and Schmidt are their real names. Brutus Klein was a promising heavyweight boxer but turned to crime after an injury kept him from making the German Olympic team. He's already served a short stint in jail for nearly beating a bartender to death. He met Gregor Schmidt while locked up in a Berlin jail and the two have reportedly been linked to several crimes since then. Schmidt is the son of a mob boss from Munich and has been trying to break out of Daddy's shadow for years.

"I have put both of them on the Interpol watch list, so wherever they surface we should hear about it."

"You've accomplished a lot in an hour," I interjected. "But what about the phone call we're supposed to make within a few hours?"

"I was getting to that," Hartley stated. "I ran the phone number you gave me. As I expected, it belongs to a prepaid phone purchased in a store on the outskirts of Paris. I have some local contacts checking to see if the store has a record of the sale, possibly a credit card number, or if the store has a security camera. Even if the buyer paid cash, maybe we can get lucky and get a look at them."

"So what should we do?" This time it was Camilla asking the question. "Should we make the call?"

"Yes, I believe the call needs to be made," admitted Hartley. "We can protect your families if you don't do as you were asked, but I think making the connection with whoever is on the other end will give us a better chance to catch them. But before you call, I have a couple of things I want you to do. Are you listening?"

"Yes," we responded in unison.

"First, I want you to purchase a prepaid phone and use it to make the call. We don't know what kind of organization is behind all of this or what kind of capabilities they have. But, if they don't have your phone numbers already, there's no reason to give them easy access by calling from one of your current phones. Understand?"

"Yes," we replied again as if answering a drill sergeant.

"Once you get the phone, you need to download an app that allows me to monitor everything that goes on. We call it *capturing* a phone," Hartley explained. "The app will give me access to all of your phone's features. I can listen in on your phone calls, see your messages as they arrive, and hear your conversation when the phone is not in use. You won't have any privacy if the phone is in your possession, but I will get real-time data. Plus, the program you download has a GPS feature which allows me to see exactly where you are."

Maybe I was naive, but it surprised me that an app like that existed. "It sounds like something from a James Bond movie."

Hartley chuckled. "Much of the same technology is available in apps sold to the general public. Our technology directorate is one of the best in the world and even they have a hard time keeping ahead of the curve. We're lucky if we're able to take advantage of new technology for a couple of months before it hits the open market."

Hartley had us write down a website address that was complicated enough to ensure no one would find it by accident. He said we should log on with the new phone and download the only app available on the site. Once downloaded, the phone would work like normal, but all activity on the phone would instantly be broadcast on Hartley's computer.

We talked for a few minutes longer, getting more information and advice from Hartley. He encouraged us to purchase the new phone as soon as possible and get the program downloaded. He would send a text to Camilla's phone to confirm the program was working.

Once Hartley gave us the go-ahead, we would make the call. A call to the unknown person who was behind the threats, the intimidation, and the murders—all to acquire a holy relic that perhaps was held by Jesus Christ, the holy son of God who gave His life as a ransom for many.

CHAPTER 15

With his conscience in overdrive, Dominic walked quietly down the long hall leading to his father's room. He sensed God tapping him on the shoulder and speaking in his ear, saying *'How can you be a priest when you know the horrible things your father is doing and you're letting them happen?'* It had been a miserable afternoon and evening for Dominic as he struggled with what to do. He wrestled with his conscience and spent time in prayer until he finally built up the courage to talk to his father and attempt to explain his feelings.

The walk from his bedroom seemed to go on forever; like he was walking the wrong way on a moving sidewalk. Dominic almost turned around a dozen times but eventually reached his destination. He was about to knock when he heard his father's voice through the door.

"No, I have not heard from either of them yet." After a short pause, Griego's response rose in intensity. "Yes, Moltke, the threats were made earlier today. I already told you that. And yes, there are still men in place to watch both families and follow through on the threats if they need proof of our seriousness."

There was a longer pause and Dominic almost returned to his room but heard his father speak again. "How dumb do you think I am? The number I gave them is for a phone that has never been used. I had Dominic buy it for me during a trip to France a few months ago. It can't be traced to me."

Silence again.

"I know we have a lot invested in this," Griego said when he spoke, now coming out as an angry shout. "Please don't lecture me, Helmuth. I appreciate the contacts you provided for the operations in Spain and the U.S., but I have much more riding on this than you do. So, let me take care of things.

"As soon as the girl and her American friend surface, they will be eliminated. They know way too much at this point. Even if we don't take possession of the information they have uncovered, putting them out of the picture is the main objective. They have been lucky twice, but I have some people waiting in the wings who will make sure their luck will run out."

Dominic began to walk away as he made out his father saying, "I will contact you when I hear something."

Returning to his room, the newly named priest felt anything but holy. He felt dirty; the kind of dirt that doesn't wash off easily and generally seeps in and turns your life dark and murky.

We found a nearby store selling prepaid phones, loaded the *spy* program, and received a text from Brooks Hartley telling us everything was working properly. Camilla and I then spent significant time discussing who would make the call. Hartley—since he could hear everything we said through the microphone function of the captured phone—called in the middle of our discussion. He suggested Camilla be the one to dial the number given to us, assuming she would come across as more vulnerable and less threatening. Even if that was a sexist assumption, whoever was on the other end of the call needed to believe they had the upper hand and were totally in control of the situation. Hartley also told me to keep my phone close. He would text me any suggestion as he listened to Camilla's conversation, not wanting us to agree to any demands without his input.

With the details worked out, Camilla prepared to make the call. It was nearing ten o'clock in the evening and we were physically and mentally exhausted from an accumulation of stress and worry.

Ten grueling hours into the twenty-four-hour deadline, Camilla deliberately entered the phone number and pushed the green button to connect the call.

She activated the speaker feature on the phone, but after several rings, there was still no answer. Camilla looked at me and mouthed, "What should I do?"

Before I replied, someone picked up. "Hello. With whom do I have the pleasure of speaking?" The man spoke in English but with a strong accent.

"You are speaking with someone who believes you're a coward for threatening our families, including a young girl." Camilla was about to let loose all of her pent-up fear and frustration. I held my hands in front of me, palms out, trying to say, *Whoa, slow down.* She understood the message, paused, and took a deep breath

"Ah. Miss Collins. So good of you to call," said the voice with all the calmness of a telemarketer. "I'm sorry you had to be prompted to make this call. Since you and your friend have been quite unreceptive to the associates I sent, it became necessary for us to converse directly.

"Who are you and why did you kill my brother? He never did anything to you!"

"I assure you, Miss Collins, I had nothing to do with your brother's tragic death. I did hear that he was a victim of a violent mugging. I am so sorry." The voice remained calm but contained an aura of superiority; much like the man was talking to small children.

"The associates you sent—Schmidt and Klein—admitted to killing my brother," said Camilla with the proper sarcastic emphasis on the word *associates.* "Plus Klein killed

Dennis Simons practically in front of us, so please don't play the innocent."

There was silence on the other end of the line. For a moment I thought we had lost the connection. Then the voice returned.

"We don't need to debate the past," the man said. "Right now, we need to discuss the future; in particular, a future where I get information from you and you get to move forward with your life without any more interference. We can both come out winners in this situation."

"I've already lost my brother!" Camilla was having a difficult time keeping her emotions under control. She had every right to her hatred of the man on the other end of the line, but venting her feelings in this setting was not productive. I took her hand in mine and gently squeezed. The act seemed to serve its purpose as she made a visible effort to control her anger.

"What do you want from us?" Camilla said in a much more contrite voice.

"I think you know what I want; everything you have that is associated with the letter from Alcuin and any notes your brother made about the letter."

"We don't have anything you don't already have. I'm sure your *associates* took all the information you need from my brother, including the original letter."

"You might be telling the truth, Miss Collins, but somehow, I don't quite believe you. I have been informed that you have some notes from your brother; notes found after his death by his secretary. I want those and any other documents you might have."

"Even if we agree, how will you know if we give you everything?" Camilla inquired. "What if we give you copies or make changes to throw you off?"

I wasn't sure why she was purposely creating more animosity. When the man spoke again, his tenor had changed from an annoying, but mild-mannered supervisor, to a harsh dictator.

"I know you will do the right thing, Miss Collins, because if you do not, your family will reap the consequences."

My cell phone vibrated, and I read a text from Brooks Hartley. I held it up to show Camilla. It said: *'Don't antagonize him. Set a time and place to meet.'*

She gave me a slight nod and then responded. "Alright. Where can we meet to give you the information?"

"I will send someone to meet you. Just tell me where you are. Assuming you're still in Europe, I can have someone there first thing in the morning."

"You're not brave enough to meet us? You make all the threats, then send others to do your dirty work. You must be so proud of yourself."

I didn't hear all of the man's response because my phone buzzed again. Hartley said: *Tell her to back off! Set up the meeting.* I flashed the message to Camilla again, and her eyes bore into me. She was quickly reaching her boiling point.

"We can be in Geneva tomorrow by noon," I said, breaking into the conversation. "Will that work?"

"Ah, the American professor joins the discussion," stated the man. "I assumed you were there. Yes, I think Geneva will work perfectly. Do you have a spot in mind, or should I make a suggestion? I've been there many times."

"The front steps of the Saint Peter's Cathedral at noon."

"Very well, Mr. Kincaid. My man will make contact with you.

"It goes without saying" he added, "that if he sees any hint of someone helping you, the deal will be off, and your families will be fair game. Understood?"

"Yes, it's understood," I said. "We'll be alone."

"I appreciate your willingness to work with me," the man said in a smug tone. "No offense, but I hope we never talk again."

The line went dead.

I looked over at Camilla as she sat with her head down, rubbing her temples. "Thanks for jumping in for me," she said without lifting her head. "I was having a hard time controlling myself. I kept thinking that the man I was talking to arranged to have my brother killed. I wanted to crawl right through the phone and choke the life out of him."

I moved to sit next to her and placed my hand gently on her back. She sat up and leaned her head to rest on my shoulder. I was about to say something when my phone rang.

"Are you guys doing okay?" It was Brooke Hartley.

I put the phone on speaker, and we both told him we were doing fine. "I think you handled yourselves well, considering the circumstances. Matt, how did you come up with the meeting place?"

"It just came to me. I read about the cathedral this morning in a visitor's guide left on the bed stand in my room. It should be crowded with tourists in the summer, so we can make the exchange without being noticed. I also figured that having all the people around would make it less likely someone would try to harm us in some way."

"Good thinking," complimented Hartley. "Not only tourists, but locals breaking for lunch will be in that area, so there should be substantial foot traffic. You picked a location that will give the people I send some good cover."

"What people?" Camilla interjected. "He said not to have anybody help us."

"Don't worry. You will never know they are watching, and neither will anyone else. The people I'll send are professionals. They will remain invisible when they want to but with the ability to show significant force if the situation calls for it."

"Any more advice as we get ready for tomorrow?" We needed all the help Hartley could give us.

"Right now, I think the most important thing is for you two to get some sleep. I need to get a few people moving, so they can be in Geneva first thing in the morning. I will call you around nine a.m., and we can discuss any further details."

Camilla and I both expressed our thanks to Hartley and then ended the call.

After a few days of frustration, something was finally going right. His plan to force the Collins woman or her friend to contact him had worked. Now Niklaus Griego felt like he had the upper hand in the situation. All he had to do was arrange for the freelance photographer from London and the college professor from America to meet an unfortunate demise in the prominent Swiss city of Geneva. Any information about the Alcuin letter he was able to acquire in the process would be a bonus.

Griego's effort to decipher the letter was moving forward at last. He worked through several of the important lines of the text and had a good idea of where the letter was pointing. Amazingly, that spot happened to be close by; a fact Griego took as further confirmation of his destiny. He would check a few additional details, but he was confident the cup of Christ would soon be in his grasp.

Before that happened, though, he needed to take care of the two people who had become the proverbial thorns in his side.

Griego removed the SIM card from the cell phone he had just used, smashed it on his desk with a large paperweight, and tossed the phone in the trash. He pulled out another prepaid phone from the bottom drawer of the desk and dialed the man who could solve his *thorn* problem. A contact from Griego's previous life as a take-no-prisoners business magnate, this man was known for his competence, his quickness, and, above all, his ruthlessness. Even Griego was hesitant to renew the association, knowing he would be dealing with the worst of the worst; almost like making a deal with the devil.

Ten minutes later, the deal was done.

CHAPTER 16

The sun shimmered through the blinds when I awoke after what was a surprisingly good night of sleep. I suppose exhaustion finds a way to outweigh the highest levels of anxiety. Lifting the blinds enough to look outside, I caught a glimpse of Lake Geneva through the trees that bordered the property. It was still difficult to reconcile the beauty around me with the ugly circumstances currently dominating my life.

I felt an urge to go on a run and enjoy the surroundings while I had the chance. It's funny how only a few weeks ago I struggled with the motivation to complete a daily workout. Now I would give almost anything to be able to go on a leisurely run.

Today, though, I had to settle for a croissant and another cup of level-eight-intensity Roma coffee. Camilla joined me on the wooden deck at the rear of the house and we discussed the day ahead as we finished our breakfast. Then we spent some time gathering all the information we had on the Alcuin letter, including the scrap of notes sent by Ashton's secretary and the flash drive I received from Ashton. We put all of the materials in a nondescript bag and sat down to wait for Brooks Hartley to call.

My phone rang precisely at nine in the morning, Hartley moving right into a list of dos and don'ts for our scheduled encounter at noon. Do notice all the people around you; don't assume anyone is a friendly by outward appearance.

Do take note of all the routes to exit the area; don't agree to go anywhere with the contact. Do hand off the package without hesitation; don't try to engage the contact in a debate or argument. Simply make the handoff and leave.

Hartley texted me pictures of the two agents who would be in the area keeping an eye on the exchange. One was a male who looked to be in his mid-thirties, with a dark, bushy mustache and eyebrows to match. The other was a plain-looking female with shoulder-length blond hair. Hartley said we probably wouldn't see the agents, but if we did, don't acknowledge them in any way. The two were there to make sure Camilla and I stayed safe and would tail the contact once the exchange happened. With any luck, the contact would lead them straight to whoever was in charge.

We called an Uber and the car arrived at 11 a.m. It took only fifteen minutes to get to the section of Geneva known as Old Town and our drop-off point on Rue du Cloitre, a short walk from Saint Peter's Cathedral. With plenty of time before the exchange, we acquainted ourselves with the area, mapped out all possible exit points, and used the basic instructions Hartley gave us to check for anyone following or paying us too much attention.

St. Paul's Cathedral was built between 1160 and 1252 but survived many changes over 860 years. The most drastic came in the 1500s when John Calvin sparked the change from a Catholic cathedral into a Protestant church. Calvin preached in the church from 1536 to 1564 and made Saint Peter's the center of Protestantism in the 16th century.

The architecture of the cathedral was a curious mix of Romanesque and Gothic. Six Roman columns lined the front entrance, and a green spire added in the 1800s soared above everything else. The east side had two non-matching square towers offering visitors spectacular 360-degree city views if they completed the 157-step climb to the top.

The inside was a plain, but pleasing tribute to the austerity of the Calvinist, who had little use for religious images and any kind of excess. A stained-glass window in the chancel remained, as well as a few small statues. The *Saint Peter Altarpiece* painted by German painter Konrad Witz in 1444 survived the Protestant cleansing but now resides in the Geneva Museum of Art and History.

Camilla and I walked hand in hand; partly to look like a couple enjoying a stroll and partly to help calm our nerves. We strolled through the area for half an hour and neither one of us noticed anything or anyone unusual. A few minutes before our scheduled meeting, we ascended the eleven steps that led to the cathedral's main and leaned against one of the six large columns to wait. With the sun overhead on this mid-summer day, there were few shadows to hide the faces passing by.

My mouth was dry and my hands moist as I gripped the bag holding all of our materials on the Alcuin letter. Part of me hated to give up the chase to solve all the clues in the letter, while the wiser side of me would be glad to get rid of the materials that had caused so much grief. With most of the information saved on my computer, someday I might choose to keep working on the clues in the letter. That's assuming we survived the next few hours.

Camilla leaned in close, and I could tell she was struggling like me to remain calm and appear to be a casual tourist.

I glanced at my watch and held my wrist up to show Camilla it was exactly noon. How would the man make contact? Would it even be a man? Maybe a woman would come to make the pickup. Would the person simply walk up and ask for the materials? Would he or she already know our names? We had to assume that the person would have our basic descriptions. Would they take the bag and walk away or check out the contents first?

These and other questions were running through my head when a man walked our way with his gaze locked on us. Short and muscular would be an accurate description. He had dark skin and darker hair with a neatly trimmed beard. My first thought was that he came from Middle Eastern descent, but his looks were generic enough to present many options as to his heritage. He wore a loose-fitting shirt, a pair of light-colored pants, and expensive-looking loafers without socks. On his wrist was a gold watch probably worth a year of my salary. There was also a large, gold signet ring on his right hand. As he moved closer, I noticed his eyes were almost black. They were not friendly eyes.

We braced ourselves when the man stopped in front of us. There were dozens of people in our general vicinity, so we were confident the man wouldn't try anything that would draw unwanted attention.

"Do you have a package for me?" he said with a thick accent, that again made me think he was from somewhere in the Middle East. He knew who we were and didn't waste time asking us our names. He held out one of his large, meaty hands.

I put the bag in his hand without saying a word. Camilla, though, couldn't keep quiet. "Tell whoever you're working for to stay away from our families," she said, louder than necessary.

The man was unfazed and stared at her with his menacing black eyes. The only change in his expression was a slight curling of his lips. Not really a smile; more like non-verbal communication that told us he was in charge and didn't care what we said or thought. With a nod, he moved away, the bag in hand, heading around the side of the cathedral in the opposite direction from which he came.

Was it really that easy? After all the anticipation and worry, the entire encounter was over in less than thirty seconds.

I grabbed Camilla's hand and we walked at a brisk pace. Hartley suggested we alter our route when we left, so we crossed Rue du Cloitre and headed north along Rue des Barrieres toward the International Museum of the

Reformation. The museum was only twenty years old and still drew a decent crowd. It would be a good place to get picked up by another Uber driver.

While waiting for the Uber to arrive, our heads were on a swivel, looking for any danger. As our ride approached, I began to wave my hand to signal the driver when another hand suddenly put an iron grip on my upper arm. I instinctively tried to pull away but was unsuccessful. My head whipped around and saw what looked like a brother—or at least a close cousin—of the man who had taken the package from us in front of the cathedral. This man had the same dark complexion, the same trimmed beard, and the same dark eyes. He was a bit thinner but had the strength to put a vice grip on my arm. Camilla took a quick intake of breath when she saw the man.

"Hey, let go of me," I tried to say with authority. Camilla attempted to push him away, but it looked like she was pushing against a large boulder.

The man just smiled at us. "Come with me, please." The thick accent was the same as his *brother's*.

"I'm not going anywhere with you." I raised my voice, hoping to draw the attention of those nearby. I began thinking there was no way this guy would drag us away in front of all these people, but his free hand reached under his long shirt and pulled out a gun from the waistband of his pants, just enough for me to see it.

"Come with me please," he repeated himself, this time with a sarcastic emphasis on *please*. "I would not want anyone to get hurt."

This was not a good situation. There's no way this man wanted to go somewhere and talk. If we left this crowded area with him, it was likely that we would never be seen again. I had no way of knowing whether Hartley's agents were still watching us, and we couldn't wait and hope the cavalry came riding in. Looking over at Camilla, I sensed she was having similar thoughts and would agree that we couldn't leave this area by force.

We walked a few steps with the man still holding my left arm. I pretended to trip and as I bent over, the man's grip loosened slightly. I bolted upright, twisted around, and swung my right elbow until it crashed into the side of his head. He stumbled, and his hand let loose of my arm. I twisted back the other direction and the knuckles of my left hand slammed into his nose, sending him to the ground on one knee.

Other than a couple of schoolyard fights in elementary school, this was the first time I had ever hit someone in anger or fright. I'm not sure where it came from but didn't want to wait around to evaluate or debate the merits of my hand-to-hand combat skills. All I knew was Camilla and I had a limited time to escape.

Most of the people in the immediate area stopped to watch the disturbance and—with Camilla at my side—likely assumed it was a disagreement over a woman. The Uber driver sped off, leaving our legs as our only means of escape.

I grabbed Camilla's hand, and we began to run. I managed a brief look back at the man as he tried to shake off the blows. He was already on his feet with his hand under his long shirt, searching for his gun.

Would he pull out a gun in this crowded area?

Before that question could be answered a woman came flying in from the direction of the cathedral, gun drawn. Though she had on a dark-colored wig, I assumed the woman was one of the agents who Hartley told us would be watching. She yelled at the man to get down on the ground. He hesitated briefly, but after realizing his gun lay on the sidewalk a few feet away, he got down on his knees and put his hands behind his head. He was familiar with the drill.

Despite being under the control of a petite woman about half his size, the man stared at Camilla and me with a slight smirk on his face. It was like he knew something we didn't; knew that he lost this battle, but the war was still far from over.

We slowed our run but kept moving. I didn't want to be caught up in any legal entanglements that would arise from an agent taking a man into custody in the middle of Geneva.

"Should we go back?" Camilla asked

"No. Let's keep moving. I don't think we want to be answering any questions for the local police. Plus, Hartley should be able to track us with the GPS in your spy phone."

Camilla accepted my answer and took my hand as we walked rapidly away from the scene. The walk took us across Rue de l'Eveche and up some steps that led up to a terrace named after the French poet, writer, and historian Theodore Agrippa d'Aubigny. We went down the other side of the terrace, turned left, and found ourselves at Madeleine Square, which offered outdoor seating for restaurants on each corner.

Camilla suggested we blend in and find a seat. Neither one of us felt like eating but picked a table in the shade that made it difficult for anyone to notice us. We both ordered Filets de Perche, small boneless fish filets advertised to be fresh from Lake Geneva. We nibbled on the food and kept a lookout, checking out each person who walked through the square.

After we finished and hadn't noticed anyone paying us any undue attention, we once again called for an Uber.

Back at the house, we were enveloped by a heavy cloud of emotional exhaustion. I wanted to go to sleep and wake up in a couple of days back in my own home in the States but knew that wasn't going to happen. The fact that an attempt had been made to abduct us for the third time in the past four days was enough proof that whoever we were dealing with would not let us walk away.

Even though Hartley listened to most of our conversation through Camilla's phone, we needed to talk to discuss our next move with him. I dialed the number he gave us, and he picked up after the first ring.

"I was wondering when you guys would call," he said without any preamble. "Are you okay? From what I was able to hear, you had some extra excitement."

"Yes. We're fine," I said. "Just tired of being chased, bullied, and having guns pointed at us."

I put the phone on speaker and Hartley proceeded to tell us that the Geneva police had the man who tried to abduct us in custody. His name was Amet Damir, a Turkish citizen who had lived in Germany for the last several years. His family had a legitimate and very profitable import-export business. However, the Damirs were deeply involved in several criminal activities, even though the German authorities have not been able to pin any convictions on any members of the clan.

Since we did not stick around to press charges, the only offense the local authorities could hold Amet on was carrying a concealed weapon, a severe crime in most of Europe. However, Hartley told us Damir was well-connected, and he expected a high-priced lawyer would get him released in a short time. There was a good chance Damir would disappear before any trial ever convened. Hartley would pressure the police to hold him as long as possible but didn't expect the Turk would be in custody for more than a couple of days. Hartley would have some local agents question the man, but again, didn't expect to get much cooperation.

Hartley believed the man who took the Alcuin information from us was Amet's older cousin Yusef. A car had been waiting behind Saint Peter's Cathedral and Yusef was gone before Hartley's agent could intervene or attempt to follow.

"What about our families?" Camilla asked.

"They're still safe," Hartley assured both of us. "There's been no one suspicious in the area of their homes. We'll keep twenty-four-hour surveillance going for the time being, so you don't need to worry about them."

Camilla and I both thanked Hartley profusely for helping protect our families. Then the discussion turned to deciding our next move.

"In my opinion, you should both go home and lay low," said Hartley. "Whoever is behind all this has what they wanted with the information and research you handed over today. We will keep working at our end to track this person down, but I don't see any more that you can do."

"What about the fact they tried to grab us again today? Shouldn't we be worried that they will try again?" I asked.

"That is a concern. But barring the two of you going into hiding for the long term, there aren't many options. We are confident the Damir clan will not bother you. Since one of them has been exposed, they are too smart and have too much to lose to make another attempt."

There was silence for a few moments, from Hartley on his end and from Camilla and me as we stared at the phone.

"What I can do, though," Hartley said, breaking the silent gap, "is arrange for transportation for the two of you to get home. Then I'll put some surveillance on you, at least for a few days. Matt, we already have agents watching your parents and daughter in Indiana, so they will stay in place. Camilla, I'll have other agents meet you when you land in London. Within a few days, we hope to get a break in the case and know for certain you are out of any danger."

We talked for a few more minutes, working out plans for transportation to our respective homes. We would catch an Interpol jet in the morning at the Geneva International Airport and fly to London, where I would transfer to a commercial flight to the States. In the meantime, Hartley said he would send the same agents that were at the cathedral earlier today to keep watch over us until we left Geneva.

"One more question before I let you go," said Hartley. "Do you truly believe the information you handed over could lead someone to the cup of Christ?"

Camilla and I looked at each other, both of us expecting

the other to answer.

Before we said anything, a blast ripped through the front door.

CHAPTER 17

We froze in our seats for a split second. But, with all that had gone on in the past few days, our nerve endings didn't take long to fire. Our reactions happened almost before our brains had the chance to record the fact that there was a gaping hole in the front door.

Camilla jumped up and started for the back door. I instinctively picked up the computer bag that sat on the table and followed. We were set to bolt off the deck, across the small backyard, and vault the short retaining wall, only to see a man we didn't recognize come into the yard. He was definitely not a friendly visitor, the gun he carried confirming he wasn't coming to borrow a cup of sugar.

I grabbed Camilla's hand and pulled her back into the house just before bullets pinged off the door frame. We heard someone breaking through the front door as two more shots shattered the glass in the back door.

We were trapped with no viable options.

The gun. Amid my panic, I had forgotten about the gun we acquired in Frankfort, which was now in a kitchen drawer. I started for the gun, but two more shots ripped through the kitchen windows, forcing me to turn back.

"This way," Camilla shouted and pulled me down the short hallway.

"I need to get the gun," I shouted, my words lost amid the chaos.

Camilla kept pulling me down the hall until we came to

what I assumed was a closet door. Once she opened it, I saw stairs leading down. “Wine cellar,” she said as we started down the stairs.

Our pursuers wouldn’t take long to figure out where we were hiding, so we needed to find something to fight back. There were several racks filled with wine bottles. Maybe we could launch the bottles at the men once they broke through the door. Not exactly great weapons against guns, but we were running short of viable options.

In addition to being scared, I was mad at myself for not getting to the gun in the kitchen drawer. At least Camilla had some experience shooting guns, thanks to her old boyfriend. Even bad aim would be better protection than a bunch of dusty wine bottles.

Camilla’s spy phone remained on the table upstairs, so I pulled out my phone to try and connect with Hartley. I quickly realized there was no cell signal in the basement.

The door to the wine cellar opened. Our time was up.

Two random shots rang out, scaring us, but not coming close to hitting us.

“Enjoy your final moments together,” came a mocking voice from the top of the stairs.

We heard the door shut. Then nothing. Only my pounding heartbeat and Camilla’s heavy breathing broke the total silence. We kept watch on the door for several minutes without speaking.

“You think they left?” she asked with a hopeful tone.

“If they’re willing to shoot their way into the house in broad daylight, they surely wouldn’t give up easily.”

That wasn’t the assuring answer Camilla wanted to hear. I put my arm around her and pulled her close. She was shivering, the adrenaline still pumping through her system. I was feeling the same rush but somehow kept my body from shaking.

Several more minutes passed with no movement or noise detected from above us. I did notice some type of change, though. I couldn't tell at first what it might be, but my senses were picking up something.

Camilla was the first to pinpoint the slight change. "What's that smell?"

I took in a few deep breaths through my nose and then it hit me. It wasn't a pleasant realization.

"Something's burning," I said, hesitantly. I didn't want to freak her out, but my imagination was already running wild with visions of the entire house burning down on top of us and trapping us in a fiery inferno.

I saw Camilla sniff the air and watched as a horrified look came over her face. She bolted up the stairs and reached for the door handle.

"What are you doing?" I shouted. "They could be waiting right outside the door."

"I don't care," she screamed down at me. "I'm not going to burn down here."

I raced up the stairs to stop her, but the door wasn't moving. Camilla was pushing, shoving, and even reared back to kick at the strong door. It remained solid.

"They must have found a way to lock the door. Let me try." I yelled.

My efforts at opening the door proved no more effective than Camilla's. We both pounded and kicked until we were exhausted. The strong door that hid us a few minutes earlier was now the obstacle preventing our escape.

Camilla stumbled to the bottom of the steps and dropped to her knees sobbing. "I hate fire. I hate fire," she repeated in between her sobs. I went down and tried to comfort her but didn't have any positive words to counteract her fears. The reality was the house was burning above us and we were trapped down here.

I desperately looked around the small basement for something to help break down the door; anything heavy enough to use as a battering ram. There was nothing.

Thoughts of our imminent death flashed through my

head as I sat down alongside Camilla. I was heartbroken by the realization Maddie would grow up without any parents. Then I thought of Camilla's parents and what they would feel like with the death of both of their children within a few weeks.

In the middle of the fear and sorrow, though, I felt a small sliver of peace. As that feeling grew, I wanted to somehow share it with Camilla. It was awkward and totally unlike anything I had ever experienced. I asked if I could pray for us. She nodded yes and then wrapped her arms around me as we sat on the floor and rested her head against my shoulder.

So I prayed—probably longer than any prayer in my entire life and certainly more heartfelt and sincere. I prayed for our deliverance. I prayed for our families. I thanked the Lord for the many good things in our lives and asked Him to bless Maddie in a special way as she grew up. I finally stopped, not knowing what else to say.

"Thank you, Lord, for Matt," I heard Camilla say in a small, tentative voice, her face still planted against my shoulder. "Thank you for sending him to be with me. Thank you for my parents and please watch over them."

I waited for more, but nothing more came out. Something told me her few words were just as meaningful as my extended dialog.

We sat there in our embrace, realizing that smoke was now finding its way into the cellar. It wasn't heavy, but becoming noticeable in the upper reaches of the underground space. It was only a matter of time until the floor above us would give way.

Camilla still wept softly as her grip tightened around my body. "I'm scared," she admitted in a shaky voice.

I didn't say anything because no words would help at this point. I pulled her as close to me as possible.

I heard a crashing noise overhead and assumed some part of the house had fallen. We were bracing for the collapse of the floor above us when suddenly the door at the top of the stairs opened. A man with a blanket over his head appeared. In the haze of the smoke, he almost looked like an angel.

"Let's go. Let's go," he yelled.

Two hours later we were safely tucked away in a non-descript hotel in the small town of Versoix, about ten kilometers north of Geneva. Camilla and I had adjoining rooms and were currently sitting in mine, along with the two agents sent by Brooks Hartley. Martin Kessler was the one who rescued us from the burning home. He was of German descent but spoke English with almost no accent. His partner, Nina Andersson, drove us to the hotel and found us some new clothes and personal items. All of ours were lost in the fire. Her looks and accent made it obvious she was from a Scandinavian country.

The two had driven to the home we were using in Geneva to watch over us until we were scheduled to leave in the morning. As they arrived, they saw the flames inside the home, and Kessler rushed in. Fortunate to find us in the cellar, he rescued us minutes before the entire house collapsed. Once in their car, we zoomed out of the neighborhood at the same time a fire truck and other emergency vehicles arrived.

"I feel horrible about the house. It belonged to an acquaintance of mine and he agreed to let us stay there for a couple of days," Camilla told the agents. "I'm not sure how to tell him."

"Don't worry about it," said Andersson. "We will talk to your friend and also work with local authorities to make sure his insurance company doesn't give him problems about paying to rebuild. Can you give me his name and contact information?"

Camilla passed on the information she had about Karl Verclammen, along with his cell number.

"Now, tell us what you can about what happened at the house," instructed Kessler.

I spoke up and told them about the initial shot through the front door, the shots fired from the man in the backyard, and our attempt to protect ourselves by going to the wine cellar—a move that nearly led to our deaths. We had only glimpsed one of the men while he was shooting at us, so were too distracted to get a good look. The only description either of us could give was of a dark-haired man who wore a dark-colored shirt; not enough detail for any type of recognition.

"How do you think they found you?" the agent asked. "Do you think they followed you home from your encounter at the cathedral earlier today?"

Camilla and I looked at each other and shrugged our shoulders. "I have no idea," was my honest reply. "We took extra precautions and didn't see anyone following us when we returned to the house."

Hartley called in the middle of our discussion. He started by apologizing for not providing us protection at the house and expressing his relief that we were both unharmed. He heard some of the gunfire through Camilla's phone before it was destroyed by the fire. He caught bits of the conversation between our two assailants but didn't pick up anything that could help lead us to whoever was responsible.

Hartley had us take a few minutes to describe our movements once again from the time we left the area of the cathedral through the attack and, ultimately, our rescue.

"Matt, check the pockets in your pants," Hartley directed once we finished going over the timeline.

"What are you talking about?"

"Humor me. Just check your pockets and see if you find anything unusual."

I followed his direction and emptied the contents of my pockets onto the table. I had my passport and billfold, along with a few Swiss francs and a couple of euro coins. Upon closer inspection, though, one of the objects wasn't a coin. Kessler picked up the small object to inspect it.

"Good call boss," he said so Hartley heard. "Looks like a small tracking device was slipped into his pocket at some point."

Thinking back, I remembered when Amit Damir grabbed me not far from the cathedral. During the commotion, he could have slipped the device into my pocket without me noticing. I also remembered the look he gave us once we got away, and Agent Andersson had him under control. It was a look of total confidence; like his plan was a success, even though he was being arrested.

"It looks like the tracking device is damaged," Kessler said as he was inspecting it closely. "I don't think it's giving off any type of signal now."

"That's good," replied Hartley. "At least we know what led them to the house. Since the device isn't working, they may believe you died in the fire."

Hartley went on to explain that he would convince the local authorities to release a statement saying two unidentified bodies were found in the burned-out home. He wasn't sure the deception would work for long, but it would at least buy us a little time. Whoever was out there looking for us was not going to give up.

We now needed to lay low for a few days, so we wouldn't be flying home in the morning. That part was disappointing. Camilla and I wanted to stay safe, despite the strong desire to see our families.

Before he hung up, Hartley informed us that he had received a call in the last hour from one of his agents in Paris. The agent visited the store where the phone used by our mystery man had been purchased and managed to get a picture from the store's security camera. The grainy screenshot was taken off a video, but still provided some details. Hartley said the man looked to be in his twenties or early thirties. He would run the photo through all the available databases but didn't think the quality was high enough to get a positive match. Hartley would send a copy of the photo, so we could take a look and see if there was any chance we recognized the face.

After completing the call, Kessler soon received an e-mail and pulled up the picture sent by Hartley on his phone. The photo was not great, just as Hartley said. The man had short dark hair and wore dark dress pants and a light-colored button-down shirt. Nothing in the man's features looked familiar to me or Camilla, although we couldn't be sure because of the poor resolution of the photo.

Once done examining the picture we realized we were starving. Andersson went out to a local Chinese restaurant and brought dinner for the four of us. We didn't hesitate to dig into the boxes of orange chicken, beef and broccoli, cashew chicken, and shrimp with lobster sauce. There were egg rolls for all of us, along with both wonton and egg drop soup. We ate our fill and then the two agents excused themselves, promising to watch over us throughout the night.

Once alone, Camilla and I made a quick inventory of our belongings. Besides the outfits we were wearing, we each had one complete change of clothes—thanks to Agent Andersson's shopping trip—plus some basic toiletry items. We were fortunate to still have our passports and a little cash. We also had my laptop computer, which somehow remained unharmed in our escape from the fire.

If we ever managed some extended time in which we weren't being chased or harassed, maybe we could solve the mystery of the Alcuin letter and find the item that had been hidden so many years ago.

"I trust you have good news for me," said Niklaus Griego as soon as he answered the phone.

"Yes, I believe I do," replied the caller.

"Go on."

"The materials you were hoping to acquire are on their way to our agreed-upon location and should be there within the next hour."

"And the other matter you were to take care of?" inquired Griego.

"That task has also been completed. An unfortunate fire took care of your two problems."

"You're sure?"

"Yes, I'm sure," the man snapped back. "There was a tracking device with your subjects that quit working at the same time the fire ended their existence."

"Very good," commented Griego. "Your fee will be forwarded by the end of the day."

Griego leaned back in his chair and smiled the most relaxed and confident smile that had crossed his face in many weeks. The quest that had only recently been thrust upon him was nearing its end; the quest that he had decided was his destiny. Only one step remained to claim what he now felt was his personal holy grail.

CHAPTER 18

The run started like normal. I ran through the streets of Bannister just like most other days over the past couple of months. I passed my father-in-law's newspaper office and ran the loop around Bannister College. I cruised down Main Street, by Joe’s Café, a drug store, and the local grocery store before heading out to the countryside, running along endless fields of corn.

Then things started to turn a little strange. I crossed an unfamiliar old bridge and ran into a dense fog that made visibility difficult. Apprehension came over me, mirroring the settling of the unusually thick fog. Soon, I couldn’t see my feet as they hit the pavement, causing me to slow down and then come to a stop. The disorientation played with my senses, making me feel like I was in a vacuum, devoid of sound, smell, or any visible stimulation,

Just as my panic levels began to rise, I heard a soft voice in the distance. I couldn’t quite make out what the voice was saying, though something about it was familiar. Fear kept my feet planted, despite the impulse to move toward the voice. I opened my mouth to reply, only to have the sound absorbed by the fog before it projected outward. The next time I heard the voice it was closer and stronger and the realization hit me like a tidal wave. It was Rachel. My wife. She was telling me to keep going.

“Don’t stop, Matt. Keep going. Finish what you started.” Rachel repeated those words over and over.

I strained to catch a glimpse of her and thought a shadow appeared in the boundary of my visual capabilities. The shadow failed to take shape or come into clear focus.

"Don't stop, Matt. Keep going. Finish what you started," Rachel's voice said again, louder this time.

I felt tears running down my cheeks as I strained without success to see my wife.

Suddenly, the fog broke, and Rachel stood only an arm's length away. "Don't stop, Matt. Keep going. Finish what you started," she said softly.

I wiped the tears from my face, suddenly invigorated. I saw her perfect smile and knew my facial expression was one of pure joy. Her blue eyes sparkled, and her dark hair smelled like lilac, her favorite scent. I didn't know how this was happening, but I didn't want it to end.

After several minutes of standing in silence and enjoying each other's presence, she once again said, "Finish what you started." Then the fog began to come back, and Rachel floated out of my sight. I attempted to reach for her, but she was gone before I could move.

"Rachel," I tried to shout, her name coming out in barely a whisper. "Rachel. Rachel."

I jolted awake, trying to get my bearings, not recognizing my surroundings. I soon realized perspiration covered my body and my heart pounded like I just finished a long run. As I sat up in bed, the vision of Rachel came roaring back, bringing both joy and sadness. Her words joined the memory, as vivid as if written down in front of me. "Don't stop, Matt. Keep going. Finish what you started."

"Camilla, are you awake?" I said for the third time while I continued to knock on the door separating our rooms.

I heard the deadbolt turn and waited until the door opened a crack. One of her eyes peeked through the opening, several strands of hair hanging down in front.

"I'm awake now," she said with a scratchy voice. She turned and looked at something in her room. "It's not even seven o'clock yet. Is something wrong?"

"No, nothing's wrong," I said to assure her. "It's just that I've been working on the Alcuin letter again, and I think I have it figured out."

The one eye I could see opened a bit wider. "Give me a couple of minutes."

Camilla opened our adjoining door a short time later wearing a t-shirt and a pair of jeans. Her hair was pulled back into a ponytail and her face looked freshly washed.

I sat at the desk in the room, the computer opened in front of me, and several pieces of the hotel stationery scattered around. The stationery contained my scribbles and notes from the past couple of hours.

Camilla noticed the notes littering the desk. "How long have you been working?"

"I couldn't sleep so got up and went to work. I think it was a little after four a.m. when I turned on the computer." I didn't want to tell her about the dream that spurred the early-morning research.

"Can I get some coffee before you tell me what you have discovered?"

"There's some on the cart. I had it delivered about an hour ago."

Camilla poured herself a cup from the carafe and came back to look over my shoulder.

"It took me a while to get a grip on the last section of the Alcuin letter, but everything finally fell into place.

"The first line translates into *Comes from a martyr of the church,* which doesn't lead us anywhere, as many churches are named after martyrs," I explained. "However, once I worked out the second line and started to cross-reference the two statements, a location became clear."

Camilla read the Latin version of the second line, which

said *A constant Ecclesiae est laus.* "What does it mean?"

"The translation is *Constant praise comes from a church.* I know that seems generic, but when I considered the first two lines as a complete description, I came up with only one place that makes sense."

"And that place is…?" she asked after I didn't continue.

"The Abbey of Saint Maurice, which happens to be in Switzerland and is only a couple of hours from here."

She took in the revelation for a few minutes. I assumed she was as amazed as me when I made the connection. After what we had been through in the last few days, somehow, we found our way to Switzerland, not knowing the culmination of a search that started with Camilla's brother could be a short car ride away.

"Okay. Before I get too excited, tell me how you came to that conclusion."

I took a few minutes to explain that the Abbey of Saint Maurice was named after the commander of the Theban Legion. According to legend, the entire Legion converted to Christianity and would no longer worship the Roman emperor. The Legion was martyred together in 285 A.D. while stationed near where the Abbey is now located. Completed around 515 A.D., the Abbey and parts of the church had been added to or rebuilt numerous times in the past fifteen centuries.

The fact that confirmed I was on the right track, however, was the practice of *Laus Perinnis*, or continual prayer that took place at the Abbey for nearly 300 years. The monks at the Abbey shared the responsibility to lift up prayer and praise continually, twenty-four hours a day, every day of the year. The practice began after the completion of the church and continued until the early 800s.

"With the martyrdom of Saint Maurice and the continual praise of the monks, this is the only place I found that met both descriptions in the Alcuin letter. Once I found out Charlemagne is believed to have stopped at the Abbey during a trip to Rome and left a gift for the monk's hospitality, I knew I had the right place.

"Guess what kind of gift Charlemagne is credited with leaving?" I asked as Camilla tried to process all the information.

She thought for a few moments. "It must be some kind of golden vessel."

"Very good. It's called the Golden Jug of Charlemagne, and I found a picture." I opened a page on the computer showing a jug with a rounded body, narrow neck, and thin handle. Gold covered the jug, along with numerous gems added for decoration. The lower part of the body looked just big enough to contain a cup. A cup that could be much more valuable than the golden jug.

"The jug is thought to have been made by Byzantine craftsman sometime in the eighth century, which would fit the period for it to be a gift to Charlemagne from Harun al-Rashid. A gift Charlemagne passed on to the monks at Saint Maurice."

"That's incredible," was all Camilla said as she stared at the picture.

"I agree. Before waking you, I sat here considering the implications of the cup of Christ being hidden in that jug, and I was overwhelmed. I don't think we can imagine the crush of attention this type of discovery would draw; not only from the church, historians, and the media, but also from those who would do everything in their power to prove it was a fake. Many would set out to discredit anyone associated with the find."

"So, what do we do?" Camilla asked. "Whoever has all of our notes could also figure this out and be on the way to this Saint Maurice Abbey. Plus, we are supposed to be staying out of sight."

"I'm sure Hartley and his agents will want us to stay put for at least a couple of days. I don't know if Interpol would follow up on this or not. Other than our amateur translation of the Alcuin letter, we have no real proof anyone would be going after a golden jug. Specifically, a jug that's been at an obscure abbey for several hundred years. Maybe if we had the original letter instead of a copy, someone might listen to us.

"I guess we can call Hartley and see what he thinks," Camilla said.

Fifteen minutes later my thoughts on the probability of Hartley or Interpol pursuing our deductions about the Alcuin letter proved true. According to Hartley, there wasn't enough proof to justify sending agents to a small Swiss town to protect a golden jug that no one had touched in centuries. He was glad to help protect us but said it would be a misuse of his authority to aid in our treasure hunt.

Disappointed, but not surprised, Camilla returned to her room to shower, while I did the same. An hour later we were back in my room eating a room-service breakfast and watching the morning news on an English-speaking channel. We wanted to know if anything was being said about the house fire from the previous evening. There was no mention of the fire, and I was ready to turn the television off when a news piece caught our attention.

"The leader of a religious movement based in Switzerland had a major announcement today," said the female news anchor. "Father Niklaus Griego, the Superior General of the Society of Angels, summoned a large group of media to the Society's headquarters in Saillon early this morning for a surprising revelation."

The newscast cut to a scenic shot on the balcony of an impressive stone building overlooking a picture-book Swiss mountain scene. A distinguished-looking man with white hair and a white priest's robe stood at a lectern addressing the media. **Father Niklaus Griego, Society of Angels** scrolled along the bottom of the screen.

"I stand before you now as a humble man, one who has been privileged to lead this Society for many years," Griego began. "Just as you can see the sun rising behind me to indicate a new day, our Society is about to embark on a new dawn; a new era that has been ordained by God.

"I know many will scoff at those words but let me assure you that the Lord has indeed shown us His favor. As proof, I'm here to announce an amazing discovery we have made and will soon share with the world. This discovery—a historical artifact—has been talked about and searched for endlessly since the time of Christ. After all these centuries, the Society of Angels has been abundantly blessed and will be able to present this important artifact to the world in a few short days."

Griego looked directly at the camera for his final words. "I am confident in saying that this is one of the most meaningful and important historical finds in our lifetimes. I look forward to sharing it with you."

The coverage cut back to the studio, where the anchor closed the piece. "Father Griego did not take any questions after his announcement and refused to give any more details on the artifact he claims has been discovered. He did promise to reveal more within the next week."

To say we were speechless would have been an understatement. I don't think Camilla and I could breathe, let alone speak.

"That's him," I said after sucking in a huge breath. "That's the voice on the phone call. That's the person who is behind all of this!"

Camilla turned red and the anger built behind her eyes.

"That's the man who had my brother killed," she spit out through gritted teeth. "How dare he talk about being blessed by God. He's a murderer!"

I took Camilla's hand and held it between mine as the rage flowed through her.

"I'm calm now," she stated, though her red face refuted her words. "So, what can we do? That man can't get away with this."

"I don't know if we can do anything," I said, trying not to sound too disappointed. "He's already found the cup, and I don't think we have any evidence to accuse him of any crime. I doubt our claims that it was his voice on the phone call would hold up in court. Besides, he seems to be a well-respected priest with a wide following. Who would believe us?"

We both hung our heads, the resignation of defeat beginning to take hold.

"What if he doesn't have the cup yet?" Camilla said suddenly.

"He just announced to the world that he had it."

"No. He only said the discovery had been made. He didn't say they had the artifact in their possession. Only that they would share it with others sometime in the next week.

"Think about it," she continued. "We just passed on all of our notes and information yesterday. If he had everything figured out before then and already had the cup, why did he pursue us with so much effort?"

"I guess you have a point," I admitted, beginning to see her reasoning.

"Even if he only needed our notes for confirmation, there's no way he already went to Saint Maurice and found a way to get Charlemagne's jug and remove the cup. The people there wouldn't just give it to him anyway. Someone would most likely have to find a way to steal it, and that would take a little time to plan."

"So what exactly are you saying?"

"I'm saying, we need to get to the Saint Maurice Abbey as soon as possible."

"Are you sure you did the right thing this morning?" asked Helmuth Moltke, speaking on the phone with Griego from his home on the outskirts of Munich. "I have always found in business that it is dangerous to make promises before I am one hundred percent sure I can deliver."

"I wanted to build a little bit of anticipation with the help of the media," answered Griego. "I know this will not be big news right away outside of our church members, but my announcement might get a few people talking. That word of mouth will help attract more attention when I show the world the cup of Christ. My office has already received calls from representatives of several prominent museums, inquiring about the nature of our discovery. We also received a call from an underling at the Vatican hoping to get some information."

"What are you telling them?"

"Very little, except that the find will have major religious and historical significance," stated Griego.

"So, what's your plan to acquire the artifact?"

"Saint Maurice is only an hour from here, but I know I cannot go myself and be involved with the acquisition of the relic. I'm sending some representatives from the Damir family to check things out and report back by the end of today. They will recommend a plan to acquire the relic with the least possible resistance. As far as they know, they are to take possession of a golden jug and pass it on to my son, Dominic, who is traveling to the area as we speak."

"Your plans need to work, Griego," Moltke said with some doubt. "You have put the Society in a position to reap an immense benefit once the cup is revealed. But your little press conference this morning also put everyone in a precarious situation if something goes wrong."

"Listen, my friend," countered Griego in an unfriendly tone. "After the elimination of our two biggest headaches last night in Geneva, anyone with specific knowledge of the Alcuin letter is no longer a threat to us. We are the only ones who know what has been waiting inside the golden jug in Saint Maurice for the past twelve hundred years.

"The next time you see me on television," continued

Griego, “the name recognition around the world for the Society of Angels will go to unprecedented levels. So, too, will our opportunities for immense profits. You need to be ready to capitalize.”

“I will be ready,” said Moltke. “You need to make sure I get that chance.”

Griego let out a long, slow breath after Moltke ended the call. *He needs to relax*, thought Griego to himself. *Everything is under control.*

CHAPTER 19

It was easy for Camilla and me to get out of the hotel without our Interpol minders noticing. The two agents were there to keep people away from us but weren't prepared to keep us away from the outside world. All it took was a simple request that one of the agents go out and get us some lunch. We made a quick trip down the back stairway of the hotel to avoid the other agent, and we were soon out of sight. They would know something was wrong when the food arrived, and we were not in the room. By then we planned to be in a car, bus, train, or whatever transportation would get us closer to the Abbey of Saint Maurice.

It turned out we caught a bus a few blocks from the hotel that dropped us off at the main train station in downtown Geneva. Twenty-five minutes later we were on a train with one-way tickets to Saint Maurice. The trip would take us along the north side of Lake Geneva, through Lausanne, and then turn southeast to our destination. There would be stops in Montreux, Roche, and Aigle before stopping in Saint Maurice two hours later.

We purchased lunch at a small café, taking the food onto the train along with our only possessions: my computer bag and our passports. If we needed additional clothes, we would have to find some in Saint Maurice.

As someone who lives in the flat Midwest region of the

United States, the scenery while traveling through Switzerland was like being on another planet. I didn't get a good look when we traveled into Geneva a couple of days ago, but now, as we headed to the western edge of the Bernese Alps, the views were breathtaking.

While only fourteen percent of the Alp's total area is within the Swiss borders, the small nation can boast over half of all the alpine ranges that tower above 4,000 feet. Four other surrounding countries—France, Italy, Austria, and Liechtenstein—share the totality of the majestic mountain range.

"Hartley is not going to be happy with us," Camilla said, breaking my focus on the scenery.

"No, he's not," I agreed. "I can't see him trying to come after us, even though he can probably surmise where we're headed."

"I do feel a bit bad since he put a lot of effort into helping us. I guess we'll have to apologize later."

We rode in silence for much of the next hour, me looking out the window and Camilla studying a guide on Saint Maurice she picked up at the train station before we boarded.

"Your prayer surprised me." The words escaped my mouth as I continued to gaze out at the passing mountain views. I wasn't sure if I was really planning to say them out loud or if I was just running them through my mind. But I saw Camilla's reflection in the window as she turned to face me.

"What did you say?"

Realizing I must have voiced the thought, I shifted to face her. "Your prayer. In the basement of the house. I didn't know if you believed. It surprised me."

"You know what they say: There's no atheist in a foxhole," Camilla stated flippantly, but without much conviction.

"I think there's more to it. You have avoided talking

about your thoughts on faith throughout this whole experience, but you've grilled me a couple of times. We're stuck on this train for another hour, so I think it's time for you to open up and tell me your true feelings. We've been through enough together, to be honest with each other. Haven't we?"

"You're right," she admitted. "There are just some things that are difficult for me to talk about: God, faith, salvation, Jesus….forgiveness. It's a long list."

Camilla looked away and I thought she might go silent and stonewall my efforts. Then she turned back toward me, took a deep breath, and began to talk.

"My parents were ardent church-goers while Ashton and I were growing up. My mother came from a Catholic background in Spain but converted to the Protestant faith after marrying my father. Despite the constant decline of practicing Christians in England, and especially in the London area, we were deeply involved in the Chelsea Community Church. Ashton and I worked hard to encourage enough teenagers to stay connected to the church, so we had a vital youth group during our time in school.

"After Ashton went away to the university and I was finishing up my secondary schooling, I began spending more time with a guy named Bryce who helped with our youth program. He was only a couple of years older, but in the eyes of a seventeen-year-old girl, he seemed so much more mature than the other guys my age. My parents were happy I was so involved, though they didn't realize that most of the evenings I claimed to be planning youth activities, I was spending time alone with Bryce."

Camilla looked away again but gathered herself and continued.

"A few months before I planned to enroll in university, I found out that I was pregnant." She didn't look me in the eyes and struggled to get this out. For my part, I tried not to show any surprise, hoping my facial expressions didn't betray my efforts.

"I didn't know what to do. I thought Bryce would help me, but he disappeared and left me to deal with the situation. I was in mental anguish for weeks. I considered abortion. I even considered telling my parents that I decided to attend a school in the States and move before I began to show. I think they realized something was wrong because I rarely left the house. When they asked, I either told them I wasn't feeling well—which was true most of the time—or I was busy studying for my final exams.

"I finally opened up to Ashton and told him the truth. Having someone to talk to about the situation took some of the weight off my shoulders, but I was still in a dilemma. I couldn't bear to tell my parents and see the disappointment in their eyes. Ashton convinced me that I had to speak to my parents and assured me they would be supportive once they got over the initial shock.

"It turned out that I didn't have to tell them."

Camilla paused. I think she was waiting for me to ask what happened. I gave her the most supportive look I could manage and waited for her to continue.

"On the day I planned to sit down and tell my parents the truth, I had a miscarriage. I was at the library studying when it happened but managed to make it to a nearby hospital. After calling Ashton, he broke the news to my parents. They were at my bedside within the hour."

The emotions were evident on Camilla's face as she continued to tell her story.

"Ashton had been right. My parents were unbelievably supportive and loving. They didn't judge me and let me explain everything in my own way and in my own time. They had to be somewhat disappointed, and I didn't blame them. As the days went by, they made sure I understood that while they didn't agree with some of my actions, they would always love me unconditionally.

"I didn't go off to university after that. It didn't feel

right anymore. My photography, which had been a simple hobby, began to be a form of therapy as I tried to tell a story with my pictures. I ended up getting accepted into a photography school and was fortunate to make some fantastic contacts who happened to like my work. Once I got the chance to do a few big projects, my hobby took off and developed into my career. There is no way I could have planned how things turned out."

We stopped at another station and the train schedule showed only two more stops before we arrived at Saint Maurice. After a few people disembarked and one new family sat down in our car, the train pulled out.

"I'm telling you about that part of my life because I realize it had an immense effect on my faith and beliefs. I was devastated when Bryce used me and then took off. I couldn't understand how someone who called himself a Christian could be so callous. On top of the hurt Bryce caused, there was the pain of losing the baby; a baby I was never sure I wanted until it was too late. It's impossible to put into words what it's like to lose something that was a part of you."

I think once the words were out of her mouth, Camilla remembered I had suffered a devastating loss. Not an unborn child, but a wife.

"You have gone through enough to have an idea of what that kind of loss feels like," she said in the form of an apology.

"It's alright. Go on," I encouraged.

"I continued to attend church for a year or two, but it was never the same. I didn't have the same longing in my heart. I went to make my parents happy. As I ventured out on my own, I stopped attending church almost completely, only joining my family on special occasions. My head told me that Bryce was the target of my anger, even though part of me held a grudge against the church, as well. That, combined with a low opinion of my part in the situation, caused my self-esteem and confidence to tumble. I didn't feel worthy to be loved by anyone, including God. Every time I entered a church, it felt like my guilt and anger were on display for everyone to see. It was almost unbearable.

"As crazy as the last few weeks have been, I've seriously thought about my faith for the first time in years. The heartbreak of Ashton's death and sitting through his funeral somehow prompted me to be more open to spiritual things. Your arrival, the Alcuin letter, and the situations we have faced in recent days; all of it has served to open my heart again and help me begin to forgive myself. I know that sounds crazy since most of what has happened should make me want to withdraw from any mention of faith in a higher power. I guess this all led me to realize how much I need the Lord and how much I miss being able to pray. The prayer you heard me say when I thought we were going to die in that basement was the first prayer to cross my lips since I lost my baby."

Sometime during her confession, our hands entwined, and we were sitting much closer together.

"I don't know what will happen once we are out of this mess," she continued, looking into my eyes. "But I know I need to build my relationship with the Lord again. I also know you have played a part in prompting a renewed motivation, and I thank you for that."

I wasn't sure what to say. I didn't feel qualified to prompt anybody in the area of faith. I struggled with my own most of the time and was only taking minor steps as my faith developed.

"I'm not sure what I've said or done that has helped you, because I'm often unsure myself," I admitted. "I am thankful, though, if I've been any kind of positive influence. It wasn't by my strength or knowledge."

"I guess we can accept each other as works in progress," Camilla said.

I nodded in agreement. Then she embraced me and held

tight.

Soon we overheard an announcement that the next stop was Saint Maurice.

CHAPTER 20

"What do you mean they took off?" Even over the phone line, Brooks Hartley made it clear that he was not a happy man.

"Martin came back from getting some food for their lunch, and when we looked in their rooms, both of them were gone." Agent Nina Andersson tried to explain to her boss how two people disappeared who were supposed to be under the protection of a pair of Interpol agents., "We were trying to keep people from going in. With the danger those two have faced recently, we didn't expect them to wander away from our protection."

"Did they leave anything behind?" asked Hartley, trying to stay calm.

"They didn't have much after the fire yesterday," answered Andersson. "Other than the new clothes I purchased, a computer was all they had. It wasn't in either room. Only their old clothes and toiletry items were left behind."

"There is no chance someone got by you and grabbed them?"

"No chance." Agent Kessler didn't want his partner to take the full brunt of Hartley's anger, so he took over speaking on Andersson's phone. "They must have gone out one of the back doors, which can only be accessed by a key card. Nina watched the only door someone not staying at the hotel could enter. There was no activity while I was away getting food. Plus, there was no sign of any forced entry to the rooms or any sign of a struggle. The two just left on their own."

"We will talk later about your performance in this situation. For now, I need the two of you to go after them. Lucky for you, I think I know where they're headed."

Hartley explained to his two agents about the phone call he received from Kincaid and Collins earlier that morning and about their search to find a hidden artifact. He told his agents to drive to Saint Maurice and then instructed them on how to proceed once they arrived.

Hartley thought there was at least a chance the two people he had been trying to protect could now serve to draw in the person or persons behind this whole mess. He didn't want to use Camilla and her friend as bait, but the pair willingly gave up protection and put themselves back into the game.

We disembarked from the train and found a small map of the area. Saint Maurice is located at a narrow point of the Rhone valley and serves as the entrance to an Alpine pass leading into northern Italy. Its location has made it an important stopping point for travelers for centuries. The narrow valley and canyon walls have also provided a strategic location for defense. Fortifications were built into the sides of the canyon in the 1800s and then upgraded to full-fledged forts during World War II.

The city of Saint Maurice is small, covering less than eight square kilometers and holding a population of under 5,000. Originally named Agaunum, the city's name changed to Saint Maurice in 1003 to honor its martyred namesake.

Our map indicated it was only a five-minute walk to the Abbey, so we started along Avenue de la Gare and turned left onto Avenue d'Agaune. The Abbey of Saint Maurice was in sight straight ahead, standing almost against a canyon wall. The Abbey was built over the sight of a first-century Roman shrine and had experienced many builds and rebuilds over the years, with the current version of the church erected in the seventeenth century. A Romanesque tower remained from the eleventh century.

We planned to stay as inconspicuous as possible, even though we hoped any others looking for the same relic would believe we died in the house fire. I wore a baseball-style hat purchased at the Geneva train station, complete with a Swiss flag on the crown. Camilla put her hair up, wrapped a scarf around her head, and added a pair of dark sunglasses. We attempted to blend in with other tourists as we approached the Abbey.

A sign near the Abbey advertised guided tours for fourteen euros, so Camilla paid the entrance fee, and we waited for the next English language tour to begin. There were two others on our specific tour, an older American couple from Arizona. We greeted each other and learned that Max and Earlene Sanders were from Prescott and were on a trip through Europe for their fiftieth anniversary. We introduced ourselves as simply Matt and Camilla and kept most personal information out of our conversations.

Large stone columns caught everyone's attention when first entering the basilica. The guide said many of them were made from stones used in previous versions of the church. The columns supported the Gothic arches, which provided perfect symmetry along the backbone of the basilica. Cathedral windows lined the upper reaches of the room, allowing rays of sunlight to pour in throughout the day.

I tried to concentrate on the information our guide, Oscar, provided in a continuous monologue but found my mind wandering away from the list of facts he spewed out. On most days the history teacher in me would be fascinated by the lineage of kings and other rulers who controlled Saint Maurice over the years. Names such as King Sigismund of

Burgundy, Conrad of Auxerre, Rudolph I, and Amadeus III were among the royalty who played a part in the Abbey's 1500-year history.

Our tour took us through the archeological dig just behind the main church. To an untrained eye, it looked like numerous holes in the ground, all covered by a massive, tented structure. A closer look revealed clues to the ancient construction of the original church. A group of ten workers were spread throughout the area, painstakingly removing soil one small trowel at a time. On another day, the story behind the dig would have been fascinating. Now, we just wanted to get on to the next stop on the tour.

We finally reached our desired destination: the room holding the Abbey treasures. Camilla entwined her fingers in mine and squeezed tight as we walked through the main entrance. I felt there was a deeper feeling of intimacy between us since she opened up during our train ride from Geneva.

"I never imagined there would be so many items," said Camilla as we tried to take in a vast number of displays. "I assumed it would be a small handful of relics relating to the history of this particular church."

I strained to find the specific relic we were looking for, but this wasn't the setting where we could be in a hurry. There were other tour groups in the room; what sounded like tours presented in German and French. Standing watch over the crowd were two competent-looking guards positioned at opposite ends of the room.

As we proceeded slowly, still walking next to Max and Earlene, our guide Oscar explained the history of the treasures.

"Most of the treasures you see in this room were given in honor of the martyr Saint Maurice by kings and officials, both from outside and within the church. The gifts started soon after the original monastery was built in the sixth century and continued throughout the Middle Ages. Vases, chests, reliquary, and other relics—most displaying the highest craftsmanship of their times—were protected by overseers of the Abbey through wars, pillaging, fires, and several rebuilds of the church itself.

"During the Middle Ages the importance of Christian relics grew to unprecedented levels," Oscar continued. "After the Second Council of Nicaea in 787, a relic was required for a church to be consecrated. Physical remains of a holy site or holy person were placed into a container or reliquary and then displayed in churches, often around the altar. The more important and numerous the relics, the more prestige awarded to the church.

"The reliquary themselves became a high form of art. Many held the bones of saints and were fashioned in the form of small caskets. Some took on the unique shape of the particular bones they held, including golden arms and one of our most renowned pieces, the head reliquary of Saint Candid, an original martyr from the Theban Legion."

We stopped in front of a glass display case holding what looked like a bust of a man on top of a box. The reliquary was made of silver, while the likeness wore a jeweled headband and a matching jeweled necklace. The silver box included a scene of what I assumed was Saint Candid being martyred.

We moved forward until we reached a row of the small caskets that Oscar described. Some were made entirely of silver or gold, while others were decorated with precious stones. One reportedly held the bones of the founder of the Abbey, King Sigismund, and his children. Saint Maurice's silver and gold reliquary held a place of honor in the center of the room.

The crowd followed a patterned route through the displays, each person or small group taking time to look at one display before moving on. We reached the end of the initial row of displays and turned to our left, following closely behind our new friends from Arizona. Max and

Earlene were pointing at the next display and appeared intrigued. I nestled in behind and gazed over their shoulders.

"This is one of our unique treasures," said Oscar, coming up beside us. "The small vial suspended from the gold and crystal reliquary is said to hold a thorn from the crown of thorns worn by Jesus Christ. The relic was given to the Saint Maurice Abbey by Louis XIV, also called St. Louis, in 1262."

I whispered to Camilla. "As unlikely as it sounds, with all we've been through, who are we to say that isn't a thorn from the original crown of thorns?"

Camilla rolled her eyes and shrugged her shoulders. I didn't know if she disagreed with me or wanted me to keep moving.

We passed two more displays filled with a variety of golden crucifixes, some inlaid with precious gems. Then Camilla, who had moved in front of me, stopped short and her hand went to her mouth, seemingly stifling a small scream. "There it is," she managed to say through her fingers.

The Golden Jug of Charlemagne was a bit of a letdown in real life. It was only twelve inches tall, which seemed much smaller than in the online picture we found. The elongated spout and narrow curving handle met at the body of the jug, which was made of two convex disks. The body then sat on a small golden base. The exterior was painted in an intricate pattern of greens and blues, while seven ice-blue gems ringed the perimeter.

We both stood and stared at the display. Knowing what could be hidden only inches from us was a bit mind-boggling, at least for me.

I started to realize it would be nearly impossible to get a chance to examine the jug. Who would believe an American professor who said the medieval jug held the cup of Christ? '*How do you know?*' someone would ask. '*Well, a 1200-year-old letter from a guy named Alcuin provided some clues, and this is where the clues led me.*' I would not only be denied any access to the jug but might be encouraged to seek psychiatric help.

An elbow in my side interrupted my thoughts. Camilla nodded toward the other end of the room. I followed her gaze and picked out where her eyes focused; or more accurately, on whom her eyes focused. A man just entering the room looked much like the man who tried to abduct us back in Geneva. Same dark complexion, dark hair and beard, and even the same demeanor. He had a different nose and more hair on his head but had to be another member of the Damir family.

The man looked intently around the room, taking in everything. I almost ducked as his eyes roamed in our direction but managed to stay upright and move my focus back to the display in front of us. After a few seconds, Camilla and I excused ourselves, telling Max and Earlene we had plans to see another local attraction. I slipped Oscar a small tip for his services, and we moved slowly toward the exit, not wanting to garner unwanted attention.

We emerged from the Abbey a minute later and headed straight down Avenue d'Agaune, back the way we walked from the train station. We didn't have a destination in mind but wanted to put some distance between us and the third member of the Damir clan we had encountered in the past few days.

Camilla looked behind us to see if anyone was following. No one appeared to be paying any attention to us, so we kept moving.

We reached the intersection that would take us back to the train station, but looked the other way and noticed a sign for a hotel. After a brief conversation, we headed toward the lodging and soon stood in front of the Hotel de la Mint du Midi. The structure was four stories high with pink stucco walls and numerous windows bracketed by white shutters. A few rooms had balconies with small wrought-iron tables and chairs. The year 1890 was chiseled into one of the cornerstones, testifying to the building's age. A *Restaurant* sign in the window made me realize we had not eaten since getting on the train.

I led the way through the front doors and into a large foyer, which featured a wood-paneled reception desk that looked as old as the building itself. The entrance to the restaurant was to our left and my nose smelled whatever was cooking. The enticing aroma was all I needed to turn in that direction, pulling Camilla with me.

"They went right where you said they would." Nina Andersson was standing down the street from the Hotel de la Mint du Midi, talking on the phone with Brooks Hartley. "Kessler and I waited outside the Abbey once we arrived in town and sure enough, the two of them came out thirty minutes ago. They walked for about five minutes and then went into a hotel."

"Was anyone following them when they came out of the Abbey?" asked Hartley.

"We don't think they picked up a tail," said Andersson. "We stayed back and watched for any followers, but there was no one."

"I hope it stays that way," said Hartley. "Do not let them know you are there but stay close enough to be ready if there's any trouble. Also, one of you tour the Abbey and check out the item I told you about. I don't think Collins and Kincaid would be crazy enough to try and steal it, but you should at least know what you are dealing with."

"I will send Kessler back to the Abbey before it closes for the day, and I'll stay in place in case they go out again."

"And one more thing," Hartley added.

"Yes?"

"Don't lose them again."

CHAPTER 21

Dominic didn't like the men who stood in his room. He was in the living area of a small, rented chalet just outside of Saint Maurice. There were two bedrooms, a small kitchen, and a patio with a magnificent view of the mountains. His own home in Saillon was less than an hour away and also boasted great views. Dominic wished he were home now.

Radic Damir, one of many cousins involved with the Damir clan, had just explained some things to Dominic and was waiting for the young priest to make a phone call. A large man named Axel looked on. He was not in the Damir family but appeared even more menacing—if that was possible.

Dominic tapped the phone number into his cell phone and waited. An answer came on the third ring.

"I have been anxious to hear from you, my son," said Father Niklaus Griego. "What have you been able to find out?"

"The two men you sent with me say they have found the golden jug. It is located in a display in the Abbey of Saint Maurice, just as you predicted." Dominic paused and looked at Radic before continuing. "They are confident in their ability to acquire the item within two days. There's one more thing though."

"What?" asked Griego.

"They want more money. They said the security in the

Abbey is more advanced than they expected, and it will take extra work to get the jug and get away safely."

Radic smiled as Dominic talked to his father.

Griego didn't reply for a few moments. "How much?" he said.

Radic held up five fingers on one hand and then closed his fist, indicating a zero.

"Fifty thousand Euros more," said Dominic.

"Very well. But tell them the item needs to be undamaged and in my possession within forty-eight hours. Any more than that and the pay will be cut in half."

Dominic relayed the message to Radic and received an affirmative nod in reply.

When Dominic completed the call, Radic and his massive sidekick departed the chalet. He was sure they were off to plan how they would steal the golden jug.

The whole situation made Dominic uneasy. The fact that a priceless relic would be stolen and most likely destroyed unnerved him; not to mention the high probability that someone would be hurt. Even if Christ's cup was inside the jug, was all this worth it? Would his father use the cup for the greater good or only for profit and power? Dominic believed he knew the answer.

Sunlight poured in the windows, waking me from a fitful sleep. Another new bed in another location somehow made sleep more elusive than all the thoughts and issues flowing through my mind could do on their own.

Standing and stretching my tired muscles and joints, I once again realized how much I missed the chance to go for a daily run; if not for the health benefits, then as a way to get my blood flowing and oxygen moving.

With no running gear, today I had to be satisfied with the incredible view greeting me when I stood at the window in my room. I pulled back the thin curtain and viewed mountain ranges in every direction. The Rhone River flowed just east of the hotel, and I glimpsed an ancient stone bridge constructed centuries before any motorized vehicles would cross the Alps.

The third-floor room was small by American standards. The head of a double bed rested against the wall opposite the window. A three-drawer dresser and a tiny chair looked like they had been used for decades by weary travelers. A wardrobe with a long vertical mirror on the front stood against another wall. A narrow door led to a bathroom featuring only slightly more space and maneuverability than the lavatories on a commercial airplane.

I showered and met Camilla in the hotel restaurant for breakfast. She walked in with damp hair, wearing the same clothes as yesterday. We hadn't taken the time to replenish our limited wardrobe before the local stores closed.

"Our first order of business is to find some new clothes," said Camilla. "I think I saw a shop as we walked from the Abbey yesterday."

"No complaints from me. I know I'm just a guy, but I've never been a fan of wearing the same clothes for multiple days. Even in college, I did laundry twice as much as my roommates. I hate to think how many days in a row some of them wore the same jeans and sweatshirts."

The thought made Camilla scrunch up her nose and shudder.

"Are we still moving forward as we discussed last night," she asked.

"After sleeping on the idea—or at least trying to sleep—I still think the direct approach is best. I hope the Abbot is available today and will agree to meet with us."

We decided to try to meet with the Abbot of Saint Maurice and be truthful with him, at least a certain level of truthfulness. We knew we couldn't steal the Golden Jug, so our only hope to see it up close was with the permission of the man in charge of the Abbey. We weren't sure if the Abbot would have the ultimate authority when it came to the museum, but he would be our best option.

I planned to present myself as a historian and tell the Abbot about a recent discovery of a letter written by Alcuin which alluded to something hidden within a gift from Charlemagne. Both of those statements were true. We would also tell him that our research led us to believe the gift was the Golden Jug, but that's where our true confession would end. We didn't feel that we could reveal the item hidden in the jug was the cup of Christ. Whether or not we would tell the Abbot about another party looking into the same discovery was still up in the air. We would wait and see how he reacted to our initial request.

The fact that the other party could use illegal and forceful means might spur the Abbot to let us see the jug. Or it might cause him to throw us out and put the museum on lockdown.

First, though, we had to find out if the Abbot was available to meet with us on short notice. Also, we had to stay as inconspicuous as possible as we moved around the small town of Saint Maurice. If the Damirs and Father Griego still believed we died in the house fire, we wanted to stay off their radar as long as possible. With any luck, by the time they found out we remained among the living, the cup of Christ would be safely secured, and the authorities could move in and shut down whatever Griego had going.

After breakfast and a trip to a clothing store near the hotel, Camilla and I emerged from our rooms in new attire. She wore a sensible pair of khaki pants, a blouse with muted hues of green and blue, and some new sandals. I went with a simple pair of jeans and a polo shirt. She donned a scarf and sunglasses as we left the hotel, while I added the same hat as yesterday. It wasn't a fashionable look, but it should keep any casual observer from recognizing us.

We made the brief walk back to the Abbey and asked

an attendant where the Abbot's office was located. The short, round woman with limited English skills gave us cryptic directions, but we managed to find the right office after a couple of wrong turns. I removed my hat and Camilla took off her scarf before we entered, giving each other reassuring nods while opening the outer door.

A lovely, middle-aged woman greeted us with a language-neutral "hello" as we entered. She gave the impression of someone who was accommodating, but also very much in charge, like a kind, but unwavering gatekeeper.

"We're here to see the Abbot," I said in English.

"May I ask your purpose," the woman replied.

"I am a college professor and historian visiting from the United States, and I've recently come across some information about one of the pieces in your museum." Pointing to Camilla, I continued. "My assistant and I are only in the area for a short time, and we would like to talk to the Abbot about our research and possibly get the chance to examine the piece ourselves."

I laid out our entire story in two sentences. The woman stared at us like she was giving us a silent lie-detector test, sizing us up on her believability scale.

"Do you have any identification?" she finally asked.

I pulled one of my business cards from my wallet, handed it to her, and showed her my faculty I.D.

"The Abbot is returning from a trip late this afternoon. I will check with him and then inform you if he can meet. How may I get in touch with you?"

I gave the woman my cell phone number and told her where we were staying.

"We would like to meet today, if possible, and are willing to stop by after normal hours if that would help."

"I will call you or leave a message at the front desk of your hotel sometime this afternoon if the Abbot returns on time and is willing to meet. If you do not receive a message, he will not be available."

Her tone made it clear there would be no begging or cajoling for a meeting. It would either happen or it wouldn't.

We expressed our appreciation before exiting the office.

The sun shined brightly from a cloudless sky as we left the Abbey. Tourist season was in full swing, which meant another active day in Saint Maurice.

"What should we do to pass the time until we hear from the Abbot's office?"

Camilla thought for a moment before replying. "This is a tourist area and the pamphlet I picked up yesterday describes several options. In the remote chance anyone is looking for us, they won't expect us anywhere but the Abbey. So, let's check out some other historical sites in town. We should be able to get back to the hotel by the middle of the afternoon and pick up any messages."

"Sounds like a plan. Let's start with the Castle of Saint Maurice and then we can check out those limestone caves. What were they called?"

"I think it translates to, the Grotto of the Fairies," Camilla said.

"So, it's off to the castle we go." I grabbed her hand and tried to act more lively and relaxed than I felt.

As much as we would like to play the part of tourists, we were risking a lot by being here and trying to complete this quest; a quest we inherited from Ashton and one we chose to do alone the minute we left the protection of Brooks Hartley's people in Geneva.

"They seem to be playing tourist."

"What do you mean, playing tourist?"

"They went back to the Abbey today for about twenty minutes. They didn't go into the main building but headed down a hallway leading to offices. There was no way to follow without being noticed. When they came out they followed a crowd of tourists toward a castle. Now they are buying tickets to tour the castle and some limestone caves."

Hartley was uncertain about how to instruct his agents to proceed. What were Kincaid and Collins up to? They went to Saint Maurice to see the golden jug, but what else were they planning? After all they had been through in the past week, he didn't feel they were the type to give up easily.

"Could you tell what office they went to in the Abbey?" asked Hartley.

"Not the exact office, but the area they were walking toward had offices for the Abbot and some other top administrators for the Abbey." Andersson was the agent talking to Hartley.

"What about anyone following them?"

"No. They were still clean."

"Okay. Here is what I want you to do," said Hartley. "Andersson, stay close to our wayward couple and make sure they do not try something stupid. Kessler, you stick around the Abbey and watch for anyone who looks out of place. Maybe take a stroll through the museum and see if anyone is paying too much attention to a particular relic. From all we have witnessed from the group so far, I expect them to show up there at some point.

"We need to stop the bad guys and keep the good guys safe," concluded Hartley.

CHAPTER 22

Abbot Joseph Haller looked forward to retirement. He was ordained as a priest at Saint Maurice in 1974 and then selected as the Abbot in 2008. After fifty years—including sixteen as the head of the Abbey—Haller's retirement had recently been accepted by Pope Francis and would soon be given emeritus status. Haller planned to keep a small home in Saint Maurice but also intended to travel for several weeks each year. There was no shortage of priests who had spent time at Saint Maurice and would welcome a visit from Haller at their various postings throughout Europe and the world. He would also visit his younger sister in Sorrento, Italy. Her home—overlooking the Bay of Naples—had long been one of his favorite places.

Returning from a short conference in Rome, Haller was weary from three days of meetings and a day of travel. His secretary, Mrs. Bieler, left a message indicating a history professor from the United States wanted to meet about one of the historical treasures in the Abbey's collection. Haller was not in charge of the treasures, but after being at Saint Maurice for five decades, he considered himself an expert on each piece in the Abbey's museum. He agreed to a short meeting as soon as he returned, scheduled to be at six p.m.

His trip went a bit quicker than expected, and his watch told him it was half past five as he opened the door to the Abbey's office area. Haller didn't expect anyone to still be working, so was surprised to see a light coming from the reception area of his office. Maybe Mrs. Bieler was staying around until the college professor arrived.

Haller froze upon opening the door to the office as his senses tried to assimilate the view in front of him: Mrs. Bieler was tied to her chair, her mouth gagged and her face showing the results of a severe beating. Both of her eyes were swollen shut and a trail of blood appeared below her nose. She had swollen lips and a blood-stained gag in her mouth.

Before he moved forward to help her or form words in his mouth, Haller was slammed from behind and crashed awkwardly and painfully into Mrs. Bieler's desk. He attempted to turn his seventy-five-year-old body to see who attacked him, but a huge hand clamped down on his neck and forced his face onto the top of the desk, drawing blood from his nose.

Haller did not consider himself to be a brave person. But, after surviving his early childhood and adolescence in Communist-controlled East Germany, he had been through more stressful situations than most. An uncle who held a high-ranking government position was the only reason Haller and his family had been able to get out of East Germany in the late 1950s.

The last sixty-five years had not included many instances of physical danger as most of his stressful situations included dealing with individuals, families, and the responsibility of administering the Abbey's business. A person did not reach Haller's level of responsibility and spend fifty years in the church hierarchy, however, without being able to remain calm in demanding situations.

His current situation was something different.

The powerful hand pushed Haller's head down, his eyes seeing only the wood grain of the oak desk as he tried to fight through the fog of pain and take stock of his situation. Mrs. Bieler was not making any sound. She was either unconscious or…. worse. As he took deep breaths to try to calm himself, Haller sensed someone moving in the small reception area other than the person holding him down, confirming at least two assailants were involved.

"Willkommen zuruck Herr Haller," *Welcome back* said the man walking around the room. He spoke in Haller's native language but with an unusual accent. "Wir haben schon auf Sie warten." *The two of us have been waiting for your return.*

"Your secretary was difficult to work with," the man continued in German. "Was she always that stubborn for you? She met our request, but we were required to spend more time in negotiations than we had hoped. How about you, Herr Haller? Will you be more cooperative?"

Haller chose not to respond to what he assumed were rhetorical questions.

"Another one of your colleagues was much more cooperative, so our negotiations with him went quickly."

The hand on his neck pulled back, and Haller was allowed to stand upright. The same hand pushed him toward his office door. He wiped his nose on his sleeve as he stumbled forward. The man doing the talking walked in front letting Haller see him for the first time. He was short and stocky with coal-black hair, a nose that was a size too big for his face, and a dark complexion. Haller surmised a Middle Eastern heritage, confirming the origin of the unusual accent.

The man entered the office first and once he cleared the doorway, Haller became aware of the Director of Security for the Abbey and the museum sitting in the chair behind the desk. Manheim Piquard—known as Sergeant Piquard to most around the Abbey—looked almost like he was napping in the chair. Only the small black circle and red stain on his chest told a different story.

Haller caught his breath as he realized Piquard was dead. The two had been friends for more than twenty years. Haller baptized Piquard's two children many years ago and dedicated Piquard's first grandchild a month ago in the

Abbey's cathedral.

"I thought you said he was cooperative," said Haller with a sense of great sadness in his voice.

"He was. That is why we didn't make him suffer." The man spoke about the murder the way most would talk about swatting a fly.

"Please have a seat Herr Haller, so we can have a discussion." The man pointed to a small couch; the couch where many people sat over the years, telling Haller of their troubles, confessing their transgressions, or chatting about daily events.

Once seated, Haller glanced again at Piquard and said a quick, silent prayer for the man's family.

The person attached to the hand that had held Haller down remained standing in the doorway; or more accurately, filling the doorway. He was built like a block of stone and looked just as immovable. It would take a tank to get by him and then it might be an even fight. With a blonde goatee, fair skin, and a slick bald head, the large man was not related to the other. He looked more like a bodyguard for a regiment of Nazis from eighty years ago.

Haller tried his best not to show fear, closing his eyes and searching his memory for all the verses he used over the years to help comfort and strengthen others. Isaiah 41:10 came to mind: *"So do not fear, for I am with you; do not be dismayed for I am your God."* Would his lifetime of study, reflection, and devotion make a difference in a time like this? Haller believed it would. A divine sense of peace came upon him as if it had been poured over his body. He opened his eyes and looked at the man in charge with unwavering eyes.

"How can I help you?" asked Haller.

The change in demeanor and calmness in Haller's voice disrupted the sinister aura of the shorter, darker man. The man was used to instilling instant fear that bordered on paralysis in most of his victims. The confidence displayed by this man of God shook his self-assurance for a moment, but he responded in the way he normally did when challenged: he lashed out with a hard backhand slap to the Abbot's cheek. "I will ask the questions in this discussion."

A red welt soon developed on the Abbot's face and his nose began to flow with blood again. Still, he looked at his attacker with a calm, steady gaze, wiping his nose with his sleeve, which was already stained with blood.

"Now, Herr Haller, before your arrival we learned some things from your associates. For instance, we know Mr. Piquard carried a key that opened the main doors to the Abbey's museum. A key that is now in my possession. We have also learned the security and safety measures in place to protect the items in the museum. Again, your friend Piquard was very forthcoming with information.

"We understand the only way to turn off those security measures is with a combination of two keys and at least one recognized thumbprint. I applaud your advanced security protocols. It's more than we expected.

"I have only one question for you Herr Haller and I expect a quick response: Where is your key to the security system?"

Haller hesitated before pulling back his priest's collar and removing a thin silver chain from around his neck. At the end of the chain was a small cross, matching the silver of the chain, and a key. He handed the chain to the man in front of him, looking him in the eyes the entire time.

"That is wise of you. Now I must ask you to accompany me to the museum as we are in need of your thumbprint."

Once again, Haller hesitated for a few seconds. The man's response was immediate and without emotion. "I assure you, Herr Haller, I am willing to detach your thumb from your hand if needed."

"I will cooperate fully and without delay," said Haller. "But I ask one small favor."

The man, who was still a bit unnerved by Haller's calmness, waited for the Abbot to continue.

“There could be others in the Abbey or around the museum at this time, such as the men and women who clean the premises each evening. I ask that you let me interact with them and make sure they stay out of your way. There is no need for them to get involved and there is no need for any more bloodshed.”

"I will grant your request. But if you try to warn anyone or signal for help, my young friend here will have no choice but to put his specialized training to use.” The man motioned to his large companion standing in the doorway.

Haller nodded his consent.

The trio exited the office area, shutting off the lights and locking the doors behind them. They walked the long hallway until reaching the lobby area where daily visitors entered. Haller indicated they should go through a door that said *Authorized Personnel Only*. The door led to another hallway, much smaller and lacking any embellishments on the walls like the public areas of the Abbey. They passed two offices, a storage room, and a break room used by the housekeeping and maintenance staff as well as the employees who provided daily tours. All the rooms were empty and dark.

At the end of the narrow hallway was another door. Once opened, Haller and his escorts were less than ten steps away from the entrance to the Abbey’s museum. As they approached the doors of the museum, a woman pushing a small cart appeared. She was twenty-five meters away, just exiting a side door of the Abbey’s main chapel.

“Hello Victoria,” said Haller in French, the primary language in the Swiss canton of Valais, which included Saint Maurice. “How is the cleaning going tonight?”

“Very well, Abbot,” the woman answered. “Thank you for asking.” Victoria pushed her cart in the opposite direction of the museum and was soon out of sight.

Haller was relieved; first that the woman didn’t move in their direction and also that she was too far away to see his face or the blood on his sleeves. He tried to wipe off the blood from around his nose but imagined the handy work of his attacker was still obvious. Haller often gave private tours of the Abbey to special visitors, so the cleaning lady would not assume anything unusual was going on when the Abbot and his guests walked the halls after hours.

The trio approached the doors to the museum and the man in charge pulled out the key he acquired from Piquard. He placed the key into the upper notch of the double lock and then produced the chain with the second key. The man tried turning both keys clockwise, but they would not budge. He tried turning them in the other direction and, still, the keys wouldn't turn. Frustrated, he looked to Haller for assistance.

Haller stepped forward and first turned the top key clockwise until there was an audible click. Then he turned the bottom key in the same direction.

"You cannot turn them at the same time," was all he said.

The large door leading into the museum was clear and looked as easy to break through as normal glass. In reality, the door consisted of a special bulletproof material that would take an industrial strength battering ram to break. Haller slid the door to the right and the three men entered the museum.

"So, this is all about money? You think the treasures in here will make you rich?"

"This is all about doing a job," answered the man. "We were asked to acquire an item and will be paid for our services."

"Well, whoever hired you must understand that every item in this museum is so well known, that selling them will be near impossible. Anyone purchasing one of these items would be tracked relentlessly by the appropriate authorities as well as representatives of the Vatican."

"Selling the item is not my concern. My job is to make

a delivery. Others can concern themselves with the details.

"Now, please Herr Haller, quit talking and help me deactivate the security system."

The man knew just where the control panel was located for the modern security system; knowledge he acquired from Piquard. He walked to a small alcove to the right side of the door and motioned Haller to follow. "I need your thumb, my dear Abbot."

Haller hesitated but his reluctance would serve no purpose other than to anger his captors. One way or another, his thumb would be used to shut down the security system.

The elderly priest stepped forward and placed the thumb of his right hand firmly on the small glass panel, which linked to a digital reader. A yellow light blinked two seconds later. The man nudged Haller out of the way and used the numeric keypad to type in the six-digit code, another important bit of information he coerced from Sergeant Piquard. The blinking yellow light turned red, indicating the security system was no longer active.

Haller expected the two men to begin opening every glass case and taking all the relics they could carry. Even though he said it would be difficult to sell any of the items, he was wise enough to know there were always anonymous collectors who would pay exorbitant amounts for historically valuable artifacts. When the men grabbed him and walked toward a specific display case in the back of the room, Haller was both surprised and curious.

Once they stopped in front of their target, the large man took an instrument out of his pocket. It looked like some type of dental tool or maybe a battery-operated screwdriver. His meaty hands pushed a button on the end of the tool and a miniature circular blade began to whir. It dawned on Haller the tool was similar to a diamond cutter, which would be needed to cut through the special glass encasing each piece in the museum. Even with the alarms disabled, forcing open the case would take time and create an unwanted disturbance. The hulk of a man showed surprising dexterity as he carefully and swiftly cut a hole in the case. In less than a minute, a fist-sized opening appeared. The leader of the duo reached through the hole and released a latch on the steel bars holding the display's cover in place.

Of all the pieces in the museum, the Golden Jug of Charlemagne would not be at the top of Haller's list of items to steal. Yes, it was old and was of decent craftsmanship, and the fact that it was rumored to be a gift from the man some called the Father of Europe raised its historical value. But numerous pieces in the room would be considered much more valuable and desirable, no matter what factors were considered. Haller knew that the main body of the jug had been altered at some point in its history and had recently been worked on at the Louvre Museum in Paris.

The shorter, darker man gently lifted the jug and inspected each side of the relic. He gave a slight shrug of his shoulders as if he was also wondering why this was the piece being stolen from the museum. The man eyed some of the other treasures in the vicinity, perhaps contemplating taking something for himself. He refrained from the temptation, handed the jug to his partner, and pushed Haller back toward the main doors.

"I thank you for your cooperation, Herr Haller," the man said as they exited the museum, pulled the sliding door closed, and entered the hallway separating the museum from other parts of the Abbey.

At this point, Haller was wise enough to know his usefulness neared its end. The two men had already killed without remorse. Why would they leave him alive to identify them? The only viable answer was *they wouldn't*.

Just as Haller contemplated this and prepared himself for what was about to happen, Victoria and her cleaning cart came out of one of the rooms down the hall and headed their way.

With little thought, Haller, yelled, "Turn around and run

Victoria. Get out!" He feebly shoved the smaller of the two men and moved as fast as his old legs would take him toward her, hoping his actions would at least help the woman get away.

Despite momentarily being caught off guard by the unfolding events, the man in charge calmly pulled a silenced handgun from his waistband and fired. The brief scream of Victoria the cleaning lady covered the sound of the long-time Abbot of Saint Maurice falling on the well-polished floor.

CHAPTER 23

Camilla and I returned to our hotel from a day of sightseeing and found a message indicating the Abbot would see us at six p.m. If all went well, the Abbot would believe our story at least enough to let us inspect the golden jug. Then we could find out if the clues we followed had guided us in the right direction.

Our day as tourists in St. Maurice had passed quickly. It was a history teacher's dream to see, touch, and absorb so much historical information in a small radius. I made my career by teaching United States history, but appreciated the sheer magnitude of world history; a history encompassing far more depth and breadth than the few centuries of the U.S.

The two of us took a tour of the castle of Saint Maurice, sometimes called the Governor's Castle. Constructed in the late 1400s, General Guillaume Henri-Dufour realized the defensive value of the castle's location and added artillery positions between 1831 and 1853. The castle did not see any actual battles but remained a Swiss military installation well into the twentieth century until being restored in the 1960s.

After grabbing a light lunch at the snack bar, strategically placed at the exit of the castle to entice Swiss francs or Euros out of weary tourists' pockets, we walked a short distance to the Grotte aux Fees or Cave of Fairies. The limestone cave structure and its stunning underground waterfall were known to locals for hundreds of years but initially opened to the public in 1864. Professor Chanoine

Gard from the Abbey College of Saint Maurice conducted tours in the cave to raise money for an orphanage he founded. Over the years additional passageways were discovered, including a recent exploration connecting the cave to another grotto more than 3,000 meters away.

I felt the results of the day's activities in my legs when I walked down the stairs of the hotel to meet Camilla. We ate a quick meal in the hotel restaurant before starting the short walk back to the Abbey of Saint Maurice to meet with the Abbot.

An obscure door on the north side of the Abbey was partially hidden by creeping vines and brightly colored flowers. The Abbot's secretary told us to look for a small sign over the door that said *Employees Only*. Once inside, we realized the entrance was at the opposite end of the same hallway we used early in the day to arrive at the Abbot's office. No lights were on as we approached the office and when we tried the door, it was locked. Camilla and I instinctively looked at our watches thinking maybe we were early, but confirmed it was almost exactly six p.m. We leaned against the wall across from the door, taking this small setback in stride. After all we had been through in the last week, waiting a few extra minutes was no big deal. The Abbot was probably late arriving back from his trip.

A woman's scream somewhere in the Abbey interrupted our moment of relaxation. The muffled cry didn't cause immediate alarm—almost like a small scream someone might give when surprised by another person. Nonetheless, it grabbed our attention, and we gazed down the long hallway. Within seconds two indistinct shadows crossed our vision, one large and one smaller. The shadows headed toward the Abbey's main entrance and then a brief swing of light across the stone floors told us doors had been opened and shut. Another scream soon rang out, followed by what sounded like a call for help. The words were not shouted in English, but the message still got across.

The hallway felt as long as a football field as we sprinted toward the sound. We stopped at two corners to peer down other corridors before we came to the correct turn. A small woman knelt on the ground hovering over an older man, a cleaning cart stood nearby. My first thought was one of the cleaning men collapsed and was maybe having a heart attack. The frantic woman kneeling over him started yelling at us in what sounded like French. The only thing I got out of her hysterical words was the mention of the word abbot. Camilla spoke just enough French to communicate with the woman as I looked more closely at the man on the floor.

Two things immediately surprised me. First, the man on the ground was the Abbot of Saint Maurice, Joseph Haller. I recognized him from a picture in one of the brochures we had picked up. Second, this man was not having a heart attack. He had been shot. I could see an exit wound just below his ribs on his left side and a pool of blood slowly oozing out from under him. Camilla noticed the blood at the same time, and I could tell she was trying to hold her emotions in check as she attempted to calm down the older woman.

Camilla turned to me. “Give me your phone.”

I handed it to her as she communicated with the woman. Camilla dialed a number and waited. She asked whoever answered if they spoke English, and after what I assumed was an affirmative answer, described where we were and that a man had been shot.

“Help is on the way,” she said, tossing the phone to me. “We need to try and stop the bleeding.” Growing up as the daughter of a doctor must have given her some confidence.

“Is he still alive?” I asked, wanting to help, but not knowing where to start.

Camilla checked for a pulse and found one. She rolled the Abbot just enough so we could see where the bullet entered his lower back.

“I don't think the bullet hit any vital organs, but at his

age losing so much blood is not good. Grab a couple of towels off that cart."

I went to the cleaning cart and snatched a pair of towels. I didn't know if they were clean or not but doubted it was important at this point. Camilla put one towel over the exit wound, took the bigger towel, and put some pressure on the entry point. When she pressed down the Abbot groaned and his eyes flickered open. Despite noticeable pain in his face, his eyes focused on the three people around him; two he had never met before and one he had seen for many years in the Abbey. He tried to say something before Camilla told him to be quiet and help was coming.

The Abbot raised his head with some difficulty and spoke in a whisper. "The golden jug. Did they take the golden jug?"

The mention of the golden jug surprised me.

A million thoughts screamed in my mind trying to find the right way to connect. The synapses and neurotransmitters eventually all fired correctly, and the pieces fell into place. Someone must have stolen the Golden Jug of Charlemagne and then shot the Abbot as they were escaping. The dark shadows we saw down the long hallway when the screaming started and the opening and shutting of the main doors were the culprits leaving.

My concern for the Abbot was overwhelmed by my utter disappointment in the realization that we had missed our chance. The jug might contain the true cup of Christ and now the jug was gone; maybe never to be seen again. A vision of Niklaus Griego holding the cup and presenting it to the world flashed through my mind and made me angry; maybe as angry as I had ever been in my life.

"Was there anything inside the jug? Maybe some type of cup hidden in the main body of the jug?"

Camilla looked at me like I was crazy. "What are you doing?" she said through gritted teeth.

The Abbot's eyes locked onto mine and his face took on

a quizzical look.

"How did you know?" he managed to whisper. "No one was supposed to know."

Part of me trembled with excitement, as his words seemed to indicate a cup was hidden inside the golden jug. That would mean our conclusions about the Alcuin letter were correct. Another part of me was still furious, knowing the jug—and the cup—were now gone.

The Abbot spoke again, saying something I couldn't understand. I leaned in closer. What strength the elderly man had was beginning to seep away.

"Cup taken… Louvre… Aachen…" His voice trailed off as he fell unconscious again.

Four hours later we were able to return to our hotel. An ambulance arrived minutes after the Abbot passed out. The emergency medical crew worked on him for about ten minutes before wheeling him out and heading to the local hospital. Soon the two bodies in the Abbot's office were discovered and the activity level around the Abbey increased exponentially.

Once the ambulance departed, Camilla and I were taken to a conference room, and the authorities descended upon us. Someone had shot the Abbot of Saint Maurice, murdered two employees, and made off with one of the Abbey's treasures. We were strangers and were there when it happened, so we had to know something; at least in the eyes of the authorities. They questioned Camilla and me together for over an hour before we were separated and asked all the same questions again. We were yelled at, questioned, and threatened in French and German, as well as English. I had to assume the cleaning lady—who we learned was named Victoria—was also getting questioned, although they would take it easier on her because she was a local and had been a loyal worker at the Abbey for more than twenty years.

The most repeated question was, "What were we doing in the Abbey after hours?" It was also the most difficult to answer since we came to ask the Abbot if we could inspect the very piece that was stolen. In the initial confusion of the shooting and the wait for the authorities to arrive, Camilla and I had the chance to decide how much we could reveal. In the end, we stuck pretty much with the truth, only leaving out a few details.

I was an American history professor with an interest in the medieval times. Camilla had a brother with similar interests who had died recently while doing some research. That research led us to information on some pieces in the museum at the Abbey of Saint Maurice. We were supposed to meet with the Abbot to get a private look at the pieces.

The fact that our names were on the daily schedule book in the Abbot's office and listed as a six o'clock meeting was in our favor. The desk clerk in our hotel also confirmed he saw us leaving only minutes before the scheduled meeting. It would have been impossible for us to commit two murders, steal an artifact, and shoot the Abbot in just a few minutes. Despite Victoria telling the authorities that we didn't shoot the Abbott, they still tested both of us for gunpowder residue on our hands. They were anxious to make an arrest and appeared disappointed they couldn't pin anything on us.

We asked about the Abbot before leaving and were told the most recent update from the hospital had been positive. He was expected to pull through, which was welcomed news.

Darkness had fallen as we made the walk back to our hotel. People were still walking the streets; most being pulled like moths to a flame by all the commotion at the Abbey. Just as we made the final turn a voice spoke from a darkened, recessed doorway. "You two had an interesting evening."

Startled, I grabbed Camilla's hand we were about to bolt. Before my fight-or-flight reflexes took hold, however, I realized the voice was somewhat familiar. As I tried to place it, Agents Andersson and Kessler stepped out from the shadows.

"What are you two doing here?" I asked while trying to calm down from what was one of numerous adrenaline spikes in the last week.

Camilla still had a vice-like grip on my hand. The brief scare, along with the events of the past few hours and days, was pushing both of us close to the edge. We were in desperate need of normality and to feel safe and secure.

"Director Hartley asked us to keep an eye on you," said Kessler. "Your recent history has shown that the two of you have a way of finding trouble."

"I think trouble has been finding us," Camilla managed to say.

"That might be the case, but we need to talk." This time it was Andersson speaking. "Can we accompany you to your hotel?"

A few minutes later the four of us crowded into my hotel room. Camilla and I sat on the bed, Andersson sat on the one small chair and Kessler remained standing. If a fire alarm went off, we would knock each other out trying to exit the small room.

The two agents explained how they had been watching us the past few days, both for protection and with the hope we would be the honey that attracted the bees. In this case, the bee was another member of the Damir family, confirming our suspicions after seeing the man in the museum the previous day.

"When we were waiting for you to come out of the Abbey tonight, we saw the two men exit and recognized one of them as Radic Damir," said Andersson. "He usually remains on the legitimate side of things in the Damir family business and lets others handle the dirty work. That's one reason he has been so hard to pin down on any charges over the years. None of the underlings would ever rat out someone up the food chain if they are caught, so Radic has remained clean. At least until now."

"You didn't stop them?" I asked

"It was a split-second decision, but Kessler followed the two long enough to see them get into a black Mercedes driven by another young man."

Kessler broke in. "It was a quick look, but I am pretty sure I recognized the driver." He looked at us as if to say, 'Guess who?'

Camilla took the bait. "Who was it?"

"I believe it was the same young man on the surveillance picture we looked at from the telephone store in Paris. We asked Hartley to look for pictures of anyone associated with Griego: newspaper photos, news coverage, or publicity shots. He found a picture released on the Society's website last week that appears to be the same face on the surveillance tape. Believe it or not, the young man is Griego's adopted son. His name is Dominic and he recently became a priest himself."

After seeing Griego on television, we were certain he was the voice we heard on the phone. Finding proof there was a probable connection confirming our theory, though, was jolting. It's like hearing rumors your favorite sports star is on steroids. Even if many assume it to be true, it's still shocking when actual proof is presented.

"Kessler was on his own and out-gunned, so he decided to let them go." Andersson was talking again. "He wrote down the license plate number and made local and national law enforcement aware of the situation. With two murders, an attempted murder, and a priceless artifact stolen, no one wants any mistakes. Hartley is coordinating the hunt from our main office and brought in the director of Interpol's stolen art division. Taking the golden jug just adds to the strands in the noose tightening around Griego and the

Damirs."

We let the information sink in for a few minutes.

"So, you let us go through a few hours of interrogation even though you knew what was going on?" Camilla was tired, still a little scared, and upset.

Andersson and Kessler glanced at each other. The silent debate between them was settled when Kessler spoke up, trying to defuse our frustration. "I'm sorry about that. It took us a little while to coordinate with Hartley. By then the local authorities were already questioning you. We made contact with the commander of the municipal police, but he felt pressure to follow through with their questioning on such a high-profile case. We could have pulled rank and demanded your release, but it was not the time to damage a relationship we might need in the future."

Camilla took a deep breath and looked away.

"Can we get some sleep now?" I asked.

The two agents nodded and began to exit the room. "We will check with you first thing in the morning," Andersson said. "Maybe we'll have some more news by then."

"Please don't try to leave again," added Kessler.

CHAPTER 24

As I wiped the sleep from my eyes, the memories of the previous night's happenings descended upon me. Those memories overwhelmed me with a deep, aching sadness. It didn't help that I had a repeat of my dream about Rachel urging me to keep going. Once again it was so real, I awoke in the middle of the night saying her name out loud. I swore the scent of her perfume still lingered in the room. Whoever said '*time heals all wounds*' was greatly mistaken. Time may dull the ache or allow me to make new and positive memories, but the wound will always remain.

Thoughts of my daughter Maddie helped to clear the cloud of melancholy hanging over me. Despite being exhausted after Kessler and Andersson left last night and Camilla went to her room, I called and talked with my in-laws and Maddie before she went to bed. They were doing fine and had seen no evidence anyone was watching them. Donald went out to run a few errands yesterday and felt safe. It was the first time he had left the house in two days. My colleague Ethan stopped by to check on them and let them know many at his church were praying for me and my family. Donald and Karen were appreciative of Ethan's willingness to help.

Maddie was very talkative—at least as much as a three-year-old can be. Some of her words were still undecipherable, but it did my heart good to hear her ramble on about something she was excited about, whether that something was real or imaginary.

I informed Donald and Karen that I would be home in a couple of days and would call them soon with the specific flight plans. I assured them Camilla and I were safe, and our little adventure was pretty much over.

Camilla's heart ached. Sleep only came when exhaustion overtook her in the early-morning hours. The weight of all that had happened in recent weeks filled the void left when the adrenaline of the previous night faded. Ashton was dead. Dr. Monteith was dead. The antique dealer in Frankfort was dead. Two people were killed at the Abbey yesterday. The Abbot was shot and in serious condition. She and Matt had somehow managed to survive several close calls, but their families had been threatened. These events happened because of something that took place well over a thousand years ago and a cryptic letter that found its way into her brother's hands. A letter that could lead to a cup that may or may not have been in the hands of Jesus Christ.

The weight and responsibility accompanying that knowledge were immense. No matter how many times Matt assured her it wasn't her fault, she couldn't stop thinking of the people who might still be alive if she had carried on with her life after Ashton's death and not stubbornly pressed forward. She had only wanted to know the truth, but the search for that truth had caused irreparable pain. With the theft of the golden jug, what truth may be out there might never be fully known. Worse, there was no guarantee those who had caused much of the pain would be held accountable.

Sitting on the edge of her bed, elbows on her knees and head slumped into her hands, Camilla began weeping, weeping out of sadness, despair, and disappointment. Soon the tears fell faster than she could wipe them away, dripping down her face and onto the carpet below. She wept until her inner faucet went dry; until some of her inner turmoil was washed away.

Then she began to pray.

I met Camilla in the hallway as we prepared to go for a late breakfast in the hotel restaurant. Her hair was still wet from a shower, and she looked tired. But there was something a little different in her demeanor as she came out of her door. She moved forward to embrace me and held me without saying a word.

"What was that for?" I asked after she took a step back.

She sheepishly dropped her head, then looked up and met my gaze. "Despite all that has happened, I'm blessed you have been through all of this with me. If you were not with me, I'm not sure what I would have done.

"I know you said it before, but this morning I am confident that you and I going through this together is somehow part of God's plan. I don't understand it all right now and I don't know how everything will work out, but I want you to know how much I appreciate you."

Caught a bit off guard, I managed a quick "Thank you" before taking Camilla's hand and heading toward breakfast.

As soon as we entered the restaurant, Andersson and Kessler caught our attention and motioned for us to join them at a table.

"We have some news," said Kessler.

We looked at them expectantly as we took our seats.

"The two men we believe were involved in yesterday's incident at the Abbey were caught early this morning."

This was welcome news, but surprising just the same.

Kessler continued. "A resourceful captain in the municipal police of the Village of Verbier, a ski resort about forty kilometers from here, happened to see a black Mercedes entering the village limits about one a.m. this morning. He wouldn't normally take notice because of all the late-night parties that are a regular occurrence in Verbier for much of the year. But it was a slow, uneventful night, and the captain happened to read the emergency bulletin sent out by Interpol. The bulletin described the car, the license plate number, and the individuals believed to be involved in two murders and a major theft in Saint Maurice. The captain reported the car and the Swiss Federal Police sent a unit to Verbier."

"A couple of hours ago the Federal Police arrested the two men at a chalet on the edge of Verbier." This time it was Andersson talking. "There was a short gunfight and one of the suspects was seriously injured. The other soon surrendered and both are now in custody.

"The one we believe is Radic Damir is not able to talk. He's in surgery right now to remove a bullet lodged in one of his lungs. The other has been identified as Axel Maret, a long-time thug for hire. From all reports, Maret is not the smartest man in the world, but, so far, he's not talking."

"What about the golden jug? Was it found?" I asked.

"At this point, the investigators on the ground at Verbier have not found the jug and there has been no word on the third person we believe was in the car when it left Saint Maurice," said Andersson. "The one we suspect was Dominic Griego."

Kessler broke in. "People are watching Niklaus Griego in Saillon and have been given the authority to speak with Dominic if he shows up there. There's also an attempt to get a search warrant for Griego's home and the Society of Angels headquarters. Director Hartley is pushing hard to make it happen, but with little concrete evidence, it will be difficult. At the very least, it will take some time."

"What are we supposed to do now?" I asked.

"Hartley arranged flights for you later today. Similar to the plans from a few days ago, an Interpol jet will be waiting at the Geneva airport to take you to London." Andersson pointed to me. "Then a commercial flight will be available to take you to the U.S. Details will be worked out before we put you on the plane in Geneva."

There was some relief and excitement at the thought of flying home. I couldn't wait to see Maddie. There was also a small amount of trepidation, mostly because the last time we relaxed, believing this whole affair was over, we soon found ourselves trapped in a burning house.

Part of me wasn't pleased that my time with Camilla would be coming to a close. There had not been adequate time to navigate our feelings amidst the craziness of the last few days. I had to admit to myself, however, that there was a flicker of something between us that I would like to have the time to explore. As Camilla said, all of this was part of God's plan, so I would have to wait for His timing.

"One more thing," said Kessler. "We received word from the local authorities that Abbot Haller is alert and doing well. He requested to see the two of you before we drive to Geneva."

That was intriguing news. The Abbot's response last night to my question about a cup inside the golden jug was puzzling. Despite his weakened state he seemed to be aware of what I was asking and tried to respond. Camilla and I thought the Abbot said something about the Louvre and then a word sounding like *ache*. When we discussed it after the Abbot left in the ambulance, we decided the Abbot's words made no sense. He must have been delirious from the pain.

Regardless, it would be our pleasure to meet with the Abbot.

We ordered a light breakfast and then accepted a ride from the two Interpol agents to the local hospital. Kessler ushered us in through the security detail still watching over Abbot Haller. The elderly man was pale, hair unkempt, and had tubes running from each arm. His eyes though, were alert, and he instantly recognized us as we stepped tentatively into his room.

"Thank you, young man," the Abbot said to the security guard. "Please give us some privacy."

The security guard hesitated, not feeling confident in our purpose or identity. "It will be fine," the Abbot assured him. "These two helped save my life last night."

Sufficiently pacified, the guard stepped out and left us alone with the Abbot.

Not knowing exactly what to say, we both stood silently. The room was like most hospital rooms: white and sterile with one small window to allow some natural light, and a myriad of monitors to track any bodily function. A tray with a half-eaten breakfast sat near the Abbot's bed and a cup of water with a long straw on a bedside table.

"Come closer," he said.

As we approached the bed, he feebly extended his hands as far as the tubing would allow. He held them open until Camilla and I each took hold of one.

"I wanted to thank the both of you for coming to my assistance last evening. I was certain last night would be my final night on earth, but apparently, the Lord has other plans."

He lightly squeezed our hands as he took a few deep breaths, gathering more strength. We introduced ourselves and found that one of the Abbot's assistants had already provided him with some of our background; information that must have come from the local police.

"I also need to ask you how you knew about the cup hidden inside the Golden Jug of Charlemagne."

"You remember that?" I asked, surprised he recalled our brief conversation.

"I do," he said. "Only because the cup was just recently discovered and removed. Few people knew about it."

"Did you say it was removed?" Camilla grabbed my other hand, squeezing with the astonishment we both felt.

If the cup was no longer in the golden jug, Griego might have a priceless artifact, but wouldn't have the object he truly desired. The head of the Society of Angels would not be a happy man; a fact that brought a smile to my face.

"Yes. Many of the treasures of Saint Maurice were displayed in Paris at the Louvre earlier this year," continued the Abbot. "The display honored the 1500th anniversary of the Abbey and also allowed some time for our museum to be upgraded.

"While at the Louvre, one of the curators discovered something inside the Golden Jug of Charlemagne. An x-ray showed a small cup of some kind hidden within the main body of the jug. After further study, the curators determined the jug had been cut open along its seams at some point in its history and then put back together. They received permission to re-open the piece, hoping what was inside would be an important historical piece."

The Abbot stopped, took a small drink of water, and continued.

"Experts were called in to perform the task and the cup was removed. They restored the golden jug to its original form, and it went back on display. After the cup was found to be a common wooden cup used throughout many centuries, the decision was made not to publicize any of the findings. I believe the people in charge didn't want others to know they cut apart a precious artifact only to find a plain wooden cup worth very little.

"Tell me, how did you know about the cup?" The Abbot looked drained from talking so much.

We placed his hands at his side, and Camilla and I pulled chairs close to his bed. The Abbot managed to keep his eyes open, so Camilla started in with our story, and I interjected when necessary.

Despite a gunshot wound to his side and what had to be a thoroughly exhausting experience, Abbot Haller became more alert as we talked. He interrupted only a couple of times to get some clarification and never indicated he thought we were lying or had misinterpreted the facts. When we came to the end of the story, he raised his right hand and slowly made the Sign of the Cross, an act he had performed thousands of times. He closed his eyes, but his lips were moving in what I assumed was a silent prayer.

Camilla and I knew the question we wanted to ask the Abbot. He must have sensed it, as well.

"The cup removed from the golden jug is now in Aachen, Germany," he said. "I believe it's in an exhibit in the Aachen Cathedral."

"Charlemagne's home." My research over the past several days paid off.

"Correct," said the Abbot. "The golden jug is believed to be a gift to the Abbey of Saint Maurice from Charlemagne. Therefore, after finding the cup inside the jug, the decision was made to donate the cup to the Aachen Cathedral Treasury, which is filled with artifacts from the time of Charlemagne. To the best of my knowledge, that's where the cup now resides."

I looked at Camilla and realized we would have a decision to make.

"What will you do now?" asked the Abbot.

"We are scheduled to fly home later today, but that's a question we'll have to discuss." Camilla's eyes told me her adventurous spirit was back. "Do you have any advice?"

The Abbot remained silent for a while, eyes closed. I thought maybe he had fallen asleep.

Then he continued.

"If the cup in Aachen is the cup of Christ, you need to determine what benefit it could be if revealed to the world. The cup has been hidden for twelve hundred years and during that time the word of our Lord has reached the far corners of the Earth. The cup had nothing to do with that. Many wars have been fought in the name of religion and millions have died. Many great acts of selflessness have also been performed because of the faith of the followers of Christ. The cup had nothing to do with the good or the bad.

"The cup is an object; maybe something to be admired, but certainly nothing to be worshiped. If faith comes only by seeing, is it truly faith? The cup might inspire some to seek faith in Christ, but as you have seen in recent days, it can also inspire selfishness, greed, and faith in earthly treasures.

"The only advice this old priest can give is to pray, wait for the Lord's answer, and then follow His leading."

A nurse entered the room and urged us to leave so the Abbot could rest. Camilla and I spent a few moments saying goodbye to a man who had managed to become a friend during our short visit. I shook his hand and promised to keep in touch. Camilla promised the same and gave him a quick kiss on the cheek, which put a twinkle in his eye.

The anticipation flowing through Niklaus Griego was like nothing he had ever experienced; not his wedding day, his first million-dollar business deal, and not even the day he first opened the doors to start the Society of Angels. This was historic. Something that would be talked about around the world.

Dominic arrived back at their home outside Saillon before the sun made its first appearance of the morning. After leaving Saint Maurice with the golden jug, Radic Damir instructed Dominic to drive to the nearby town of Martigny. Using mainly small roads leading through the mountains, the short trip took more than an hour, as staying out of sight was more important than speed. Dominic paid Damir the agreed-upon fee, took the jug, and switched to a nondescript Skoda for the drive home.

It was now mid-morning and Griego prepared to examine the golden jug. As tempted as he had been to destroy the jug to reveal what was inside the moment Dominic delivered it, Griego found the patience to make all the necessary preparations. He made the short trip to the chapel at the Society's headquarters and prepared a table in front of the altar. Placing the jug on the table, Griego looked up at the stained-glass window depicting the Last Supper and felt his anticipation rise to another level.

Around him were several tools to help cut open the jug. He hoped to save it, as it was a beautiful piece that served a noble purpose for the last twelve hundred years. However, his desire to keep the artifact from major damage was far outweighed by his lust for what he expected to be hidden inside.

After a brief examination, he pushed a small wedge into a seam on the bottom of the jug. The gold overlay was soft, and the wedge created a small opening. Griego took another wedge and made similar progress on the side of the jug. The wedges pushed easily into the gold, almost like a similar operation had been performed on the jug in the past. One more wedge and the seams started to pull apart. There was not quite enough space to see inside yet, but the seventy-year-old priest trembled with excitement as he placed a final wedge in the side of the jug and tapped it.

The Golden Jug of Charlemagne came apart in two halves for the third time since being created in the eighth century. The first time was to hide something of extreme value; the second was to remove what was believed to be something of little value. Now, the third opening of the jug served to crush a man's selfish dreams.

Griego was speechless. There was nothing inside. He examined both pieces in case there was a message or clue. When finding none, he violently threw the pieces toward the stained-glass window that now served to mock him.

"Noooo!" he screamed, his face red with fury and his entire body trembling with rage.

Griego began pacing around the altar, muttering to himself. "This cannot be. What clue did I miss? What mistake could I have made?"

He was thinking of ways to spin this with Moltke and

the few others who knew about his search for the cup when the doors to the chapel burst open. Spinning around, ready to berate whoever dared disturb him, Griego was stunned to see two men enter with Dominic between them, the young priest's hands in cuffs.

"What is the meaning of this? What are you doing with my son?"

One of the two men at Dominic's side raised his arm to show Griego a badge.

"We are with FIS and we have a warrant to search this property," the man said with authority. "Your son, Dominic Griego, is under arrest for suspicion of being an accessory to murder and robbery."

As more men from the Federal Intelligence Service came into the chapel, Griego rushed forward to embrace his son, only to be pushed away. As he turned to protest to the man in charge, Griego froze when an agent picked up a piece of the golden jug from behind the altar.

"I think we found something interesting," the agent said, holding up the relic for all to see.

Staring at the sight in front of him—a federal agent holding a piece of medieval history with the scene of the Last Supper as a backdrop—Griego wondered how things had gone wrong so quickly.

CHAPTER 25

Less than three hours after our conversation with Abbot Haller in the Saint Maurice hospital, Camilla and I were stepping onto an Interpol jet at Geneva International Airport. Agents Andersson and Kessler continued to serve as our babysitters, driving us to Geneva, and ushering us through security and onto the plane. The seventy-five-minute drive was filled with me talking to Brooks Hartley on the phone and trying to convince him to let us go to Aachen, Germany, instead of flying us to London. The back-and-forth conversation was about at a standstill when Camilla grabbed the phone from me.

"Brooks Hartley. I know my father did a lot for you and you and Ashton were friends. Matt and I need to complete what Ashton started and to do that we need to go to Aachen. I am asking you as a friend to help make it happen." She handed the phone back to me. In a few short sentences, she had expertly made Hartley feel obligated to send us to Aachen and guilty if he didn't.

The pilots soon filed a new flight plan that would deliver us to the Maastricht Airport in the Netherlands, located only forty-two kilometers, or twenty-five miles, from Aachen. The compromise we made with Hartley was that we were totally on our own once we got off the plane. We had to find our way to Aachen and then back home. Camilla and I gladly accepted those terms. It would be easy to call an Uber or catch a shuttle to Aachen. When we finished with our *little adventure*—as Hartley described it—we would take a Eurostar train to London. The train left Aachen each day, making a stop in Brussels before going through the Channel Tunnel to cross over to England.

Though not extravagant, the Interpol jet was comfortable and functional. The short flight proved uneventful, and we were soon shaking hands with Andersson and Kessler as we exited the plane. Within minutes we were on a shuttle taking us to downtown Aachen.

Niklaus Griego had never been in handcuffs. That changed when the FIS agents cuffed him and led him out of the Society of Angels headquarters earlier in the day.

He was no longer cuffed, but clothed in prison-issued garments, sitting in a small room across a table from his lawyer. The message his lawyer had delivered was surprising and infuriating. Griego didn't have time to figure out how the situation came about, but he still had resources to reach out to someone who could exact a little revenge on his behalf.

Griego finished writing on a piece of paper and slid it across the table to his lawyer. "Take this note and call the number at the top. The person who will answer is a friend. Read the message exactly as written and then hang up. Do you understand?"

The lawyer looked at the message as he nodded affirmatively. He didn't like being the gopher for Griego. In fact, he didn't like Griego. But the money his firm received as counsel for the Society of Angels was significant. He would deliver the message as instructed and hope what he was doing would not get him into trouble.

We were dropped off in Aachen's city center in the late afternoon. The westernmost city in Germany, Aachen sits close to the borders of the Netherlands and Belgium and has both historic significance and high-tech innovation. The local university boasts some of the best programs in the entire country of Germany for computer science and technology. The university's reputation and the growth of the tech industry fed off each other for several years, helping the population to grow to over 250,000.

Immediately after stepping off the shuttle, we found ourselves standing in front of Aachen City Hall. Built in the 1300's, the structure is not only the seat of the local government but also houses an impressive collection of artifacts, many from the time of the city's most renowned inhabitant: Charlemagne. The *International Charlemagne Prize of Aachen* is given out annually at City Hall, honoring those who have made significant contributions to the unification and integration of Western Europe. Past recipients included Winston Churchill, Bill Clinton, and Pope John Paul II.

Camilla tapped my shoulder and told me to look in the other direction. Directly south of City Hall, across a long, narrow courtyard, sat Aachen Cathedral. The cathedral—featuring a soaring steeple, a unique octagonal rotunda, and breathtaking seventy-five-foot-high stained-glass windows—made for an inspiring view. No wonder the structure was one of the original sites granted UNESCO World Heritage status in 1978.

We strolled, trying to take in the grandeur of the cathedral as we progressed toward the front of the huge structure. There was a specific entrance for the treasury in the Cloister, as well as a courtyard leading to the entryway for the main chapel, rotunda, and choir area. We contemplated an official tour, but since our time was short, we decided to do a quick self-guided tour through the cathedral.

Using a small booklet we picked up to guide us, we first entered the large bronze doors that had hung on the original structure when it was commissioned by Charlemagne. We moved into the Rotunda, which was more impressive from the inside than it appeared from the exterior. Its unusual octagonal shape rose to over ninety feet high, much of it decorated with marble and mosaics. Hanging down from on high was a gold-plated chandelier presented to the church by the emperor Friedrich I around 1180.

Looking past the Rotunda, the main altar became visible. Although assembled in the 1950s, the marble in the altar came from medieval times and stood exactly where the Carolingian Altar of St. Peter stood until around 1400. The front was decorated with seventeen gold reliefs from the early eleventh century depicting Christ in stages from his entry into Jerusalem up to his resurrection.

A few more steps and we were looking at the stunning windows of the choir area. Their incredible height made them some of the largest Gothic windows in existence. Sitting in the center of the choir was the Shrine of Charlemagne: a wooden box, gilded with silver, enamel, and precious stones. Inside were the remains of its namesake, transferred into the shrine from Charlemagne's original burial spot in the Persephone Sarcophagus, a piece we would see in the Cathedral Treasury.

Despite being impressed with what we were seeing, we realized our main purpose for this trip was still ahead of us. We retraced our steps out of the cathedral and headed toward the treasury. We paid the five Euro admission fee and proceeded into the Aachen Cloister. Compared to the actual cathedral, the cloister was a fairly simple building but remained an example of Gothic architecture from different ages.

Outside the Vatican, the Aachen Cathedral Treasury housed one of the world's most important collections of church treasures.

With heightened anticipation, Camilla and I didn't talk much as we walked through the displays. Where would they display the cup? Would we know immediately when we saw it? Would we feel something special because of what we knew about the cup? And the big question: What would we do with that knowledge?

We observed many things in the treasury: an intricately carved ivory book cover from the ninth century, the gold and precious stone-covered Cross of Lothair created in 980, and a bust of Charlemagne dating from around 1350. But no cup of any kind. A bit surprised, we made another tour around the exhibits assuming we had missed it in all the other treasures. Still no cup.

Camilla suggested we ask for the director or curator of the museum, so I approached a docent who was in the middle of a tour. The young woman was giving the tour in French but responded to my query in nearly perfect English. She pointed down a small hallway and told us the treasury's director was in his office today.

The sign on the door said Dr. Georg van den Brink. We knocked before opening the door and found ourselves in a small reception area. No one was at the desk, but a light was on in what we assumed was the director's office.

"Dr. Van den Brink?" Camilla said firmly.

"Ya. Ya," came a voice from the office. A string of German words followed, not registering with either Camilla or me. A distinguished-looking man appeared in the doorway, looking at us like he was expecting a reply.

"Do you speak English?" I asked.

"Yes. Very well. How may I assist you?" The man was short and still trim despite appearing to be in his sixties. He had a full head of white hair, nicely styled, and wore an expensive suit, along with a blue and gold silk tie.

I introduced Camilla and myself, using the history-teacher-doing-research spiel again. Before I explained what we were looking for, Van den Brink interrupted.

"Ah, yes. I was told you might be contacting me."

That was certainly a revelation to us.

"Who told you?"

"Your good friend from Saint Maurice, Abbot Haller, called me earlier this afternoon. He told me a young man and woman may arrive in Aachen who had an interest in the cup that was found inside an artifact from the Abbot's museum."

"We didn't realize he would call," Camilla said. "The

last time we were with the Abbot, we weren't sure whether we would be coming to Aachen or not."

"He must have known your intentions before you did," responded Van den Brink.

"I guess he did," I said. Camilla and I smiled at each other, realizing the old and weakened Abbot was as wise as his title suggested.

"Would you like me to take you to see the cup that interests you?"

"Yes, we would," answered Camilla. "We have already been through all the displays in the treasury and did not find any type of cup."

"The reason you failed to find it is because it's not on display yet. It's currently in one of our preparation rooms along with some other items being readied for a new exhibit," responded the director. "Follow me."

We trailed behind Van den Brink further down the hallway and then down one flight of steps until we came to a large steel door. He typed in a code, and we heard a click, allowing us to enter. The room was not large—maybe thirty feet square—and felt somewhat like a vault. There were heavy-duty cabinets of various sizes along one wall, while lock boxes and a workbench covered another wall. In the middle of the room stood a circular platform topped with an amazing rectangular piece of marble. Sitting on the marble was an ornate wooden podium table with carvings of angels around its center pillar. The craftsmanship was astounding. The one thing out of place was a common folding chair placed next to the table.

"This is the exhibit we are preparing that will include the cup you are interested in," said Van den Brink. "It's obvious we have some more work to do."

"What is the focus of the display?" I asked.

"It will focus on the fact that more than thirty emperors or kings were consecrated and crowned in the Aachen Cathedral, starting with Charlemagne's son Louis the Pious in 813 and continuing through Ferdinand I in 1531. In addition to the location, another common thread of each coronation was that every would-be ruler partook of the Holy Sacraments before being crowned."

"You are saying each king participated in a communion service as part of their ceremony?" Camilla looked at me as she asked the question of Van den Brink. I could see her mind working because mine was working in the same direction.

"Exactly, young lady. We have various items representing many of the men who were crowned throughout the ages. The exhibit will be a representation of the communion service that was common to each ceremony. We believed the cup we received from the Louvre would be a good example of the type of cup used in the ceremonies. It's plain, but Charlemagne began the tradition of using austere utensils in any ceremony he was involved in. That tradition remained for several hundred years.

"Somewhere around the year 799, our research shows Charlemagne did away with many of the gaudy and valuable objects in his everyday life. No one knows why, but some surmise that as his Christian faith developed, he wanted to have some small parts of his life reflect how Jesus may have experienced the same events, including communion. It is written by his biographer Einhard that Charlemagne was led through communion by his priest on the morning he died."

I was dumbfounded by what I heard. I wanted to shout: *I know why Charlemagne simplified parts of his life. It's because he had held the true cup of Christ in his own hands. He felt convicted about using gold and jewel-encrusted goblets for his communion services when the Lord he was trying to serve used only a simple cup.*

"May we see the cup?"

"Certainly. Let me get it for you." Dr. Van den Brink walked to the wall with the lock boxes and studied them momentarily. He pulled a set of keys from his pocket and stepped toward a box that had a square door a foot high and a foot wide. He inserted the key, swung open the door, and withdrew a wooden case a little smaller than the dimensions of the lockbox. He put the case on the nearby table and pulled on a pair of white cloth gloves.

Camilla and I inched closer to look over Van den Brink's shoulder as he opened the case. My heart was exploding out of my chest, and I assumed the same pounding heartbeat was going on within Camilla.

Using the care I'm sure he demonstrated throughout his career with thousands of historical objects, Van den Brink gently lifted the cup out of the box and set it on the cloth covering much of the table.

Speechless is the only word to describe how I felt. Maybe reverently speechless, if that's an accurate expression. The only thing that came to my mind that had been more awe-inspiring in my lifetime was when my daughter was born. Seeing an object that could have been held by Jesus Christ was beyond special. The saying *'that's something that doesn't come along every day'* would be an immense understatement. Maybe *'that's something that doesn't come along every millennium'* would be a little closer but would still fall short.

Somewhere in the past few seconds, Camilla intertwined her fingers in mine. Her emotions were evident as she squeezed my hand and leaned her body into me.

The cup itself was unimpressive at first glance. It stood about four inches high and roughly three inches across the mouth, with no handle. It showed some small imperfections, confirming it was hand-carved with primitive tools, at least compared to today's mass-produced items. The wood was caramel colored, with an intricate dark brown pattern highlighting a unique grain.

"One strange thing about the cup—other than the fact that it was most likely locked inside a golden jug for twelve hundred years—is that it is made of olive wood," said Van den Brink.

"Why is that unusual?"

"I have had several people look at the cup and they all say it is much older than Charlemagne; maybe as old as the first century A.D. The only areas producing olive wood at that time were Israel and Syria. There's no good explanation for why Charlemagne would have had an olive wood cup when practically every other wooden cup surviving from that period and in this area of the world has been made of birch or cedar wood. Perhaps it was a gift from someone, although a wooden cup seems like a strange gift to give a king."

"Perhaps not as strange as you think," Camilla said under her breath, just loud enough for me to hear.

"May I hold it?" I asked like a kid wanting to hold his first puppy.

"Certainly, but put on gloves first."

Camilla and I put on the gloves Van den Brink pulled from a drawer and then took turns holding the cup. I know the way we treated the cup and the expressions on our faces must have been confusing to Van den Brink.

"Why, exactly, are you so interested in this particular item?" he asked. "Abbot Haller mentioned you were doing research, and the cup might have some special meaning."

I looked at Camilla. She looked at me. Neither of us knew how much to say. She managed to reply.

"My brother was a medieval scholar at the University of Leeds in England and was researching some old letters from Alcuin of York. One of the letters gave a few clues about a cup holding special meaning to Charlemagne. Unfortunately, my brother passed away suddenly, so Matt and I took up the search and eventually ended up here in Aachen."

"I would love to see this letter and hear about your research," said Van den Brink.

"Uh, we're not sure when we will be able to release our findings," I added awkwardly, trying to come up with a legitimate excuse for not sharing more. "The Alcuin letter Camilla referred to is a recent discovery, so until some other experts finish their evaluation and make an official announcement, we're not allowed to give out too many details."

Most of my statements were not technically true, but we couldn't tell Dr. Van den Brink our real reason for wanting to find the cup.

"I understand," said Van den Brink. "But I trust I will be made aware when the final report is released." He went on without waiting for a reply. "I am sure you know Alcuin had a large impact on Charlemagne. One of Alcuin's major contributions will be in the same display as the cup."

Pleased with the change of direction of the conversation, I inquired about his reference to Alcuin.

"Alcuin was instrumental in the production of many manuscripts when he was in Charlemagne's service, including what we call illuminated manuscripts. Such manuscripts were often written in gold and silver ink and many times included elaborate and colorful illustrations. One of the most famous produced under Alcuin's direction is called the Coronation Gospel, which some refer to as the most important book of the Middle Ages. Charlemagne used the Coronation Gospels when he was crowned the Holy Roman Emperor by Pope Leo III in 800. The manuscript was also used at many other coronations over several hundred years."

"I believe we saw the manuscript upstairs in the treasury," said Camilla.

"No, you undoubtedly saw what is called the Aachen Gospels, which is another fine example of an illuminated manuscript from Charlemagne's time. The Coronation Gospels have been housed at the Imperial Treasury in the Hofburg Palace in Vienna. They will soon be loaning us the manuscript to display for three months."

We replaced the cup in its case with care, and Van den

Brink returned the case to its lockbox. It was excruciating to see it locked away after all we went through to find it. For now, though, I think Camilla and I agreed it was the best thing. We still had to sort out in our minds what we were going to do with the information we possessed.

As we were returning to the main level of the building and thanking Dr. Van den Brink profusely for allowing us access to see the cup, my phone began to ring.

"Where have you been?" I heard when I answered. "I've been trying to call for several minutes." The voice belonged to Brooks Hartley and he sounded agitated.

"We've been in an underground room at the Aachen Cathedral. There's probably no cell service." I tried to reply calmly, but Hartley's tone of his voice worried me.

"Get out of there now!" he screamed. "Move! Now!"

CHAPTER 26

I grabbed Camilla's hand and pulled her toward the closest exit while I stayed on the line with Hartley.

"What are you talking about? What's going on?" I asked the Interpol agent.

I barely heard Hartley's explanation and exhortation as I attempted to run and listen. Camilla had no idea why we were suddenly rushing from the building and kept asking "What are you doing? Why are we running?"

All I managed to decipher from Hartley's explanation was something about Griego knowing we were in Aachen, and we needed to get away from the cathedral. The words '*help is coming*', also rang in my mind, but my brain wasn't working fast enough to put all the pieces together. We bolted toward the main exit doors, barely avoiding an elderly couple as we turned the final corner. With one hand holding the phone and the other pulling Camilla, I hit the crash bar with my hip at full speed. The heavy exit door flung open so hard it ricocheted off its stopper and almost took out Camilla as she came through the opening.

The bright sun of the late afternoon briefly stunned me, causing Camilla to bump into me as I slowed, shielding my eyes. We had three choices: go straight, left, or right. Neither of us was familiar with the area, so I headed left, hugging the stone wall lining the street. Two steps later, something suddenly punctured my cheek with enough force that the instinctive action to raise my hand to my face caused me to drop the phone. When I bent down to retrieve it, bits of the stone behind me exploded and sent shards into the side of my face again. Camilla screamed at the same time my brain kicked up the flow of adrenaline another notch, realizing someone was shooting at us.

Of all the things a person might visualize happening in life, getting shot at usually isn't one of them. It's impossible to simulate what your reactions might be when a projectile is coming toward you at over a thousand feet per second. A projectile that has the potential to instantly end your earthly life. Some might freeze; others might have the ability to shoot back. My reaction reverted to one of my basic instincts: run.

My fingers scraped the ground as I picked up the phone and stuffed it in my pocket in one quick motion. At the same time, my legs began churning, my eyes searching for a place to take cover. Camilla had a near-vice grip on my hand as I dragged her behind me. I attempted to determine where the shots were coming from—again not something I ever thought I would have to worry about in real life. My eyes roamed as my brain calculated. A gleam to my right caught my attention.

Camilla noticed the gunman at the same time I did and screamed, "Matt, watch out!" just as we found cover behind a statue of Charlemagne standing outside the cathedral's gate. Another bullet bounced off the bronze figure as we huddled together behind its concrete base.

By this point, others in the area were yelling, screaming, and searching for places of cover. I peeked around the statue and could see the gunman walking directly toward us, gun hand extended straight out, simply waiting for his opportunity. He was wearing black jeans and a dark button-down shirt, with wrap-around sunglasses hiding his eyes. He had jet black hair, cut very short. I could see a large tattoo extending above his collar and up his neck.

He fired again, the bullet chipping the concrete only

inches from my head. Another shot hit the sidewalk just to our left and then another on the right. I think he was enjoying this, effectively preventing us from fleeing until he managed to finish the job. My overloaded mind failed to come up with a plan of action that had any chance of success. This was the end. I pulled Camilla into me and held her tight, bringing a quick reflection of our similar experience in the burning house. We were miraculously saved once, but….

Camilla suddenly pushed herself away from me and bolted to our right. Startled, I looked that way and noticed a small girl curled up, crying loudly only fifteen feet away. Camilla's instinct was to protect the child. She would need only four or five steps to reach the girl, but it took the gunman just two of those steps to zero in and squeeze the trigger. After one shot missed behind her, the next hit Camilla in the side, jolting her into the wall a few feet short of her goal. She fell to the ground awkwardly, managing to reach out her hand as she came to rest with an audible groan. The young girl stretched to put her small fingers into the offered hand just as Camilla's eyes flickered shut.

Overflowing with emotion and rage, I yelled something unintelligible as I stood and tried to move toward Camilla. The man advanced with a silenced gun pointed at my head, blocking my path. A curl of a smile appeared on his thin lips as he looked me over, appraising his conquered prey. It was a smile projecting confidence, success, and superiority.

I hoped he sensed something other than fear in my eyes as I glared back at him. The Bible says I am supposed to love my enemy. Reality, though, is a challenging teacher and, in this instance, I am probably flunking the test.

"Father Griego sends his greetings," the man said in a thick, Eastern European accent.

Without even a small twitch of hesitancy, the man pulled the trigger.

A searing pain surged through me, followed by a blinding flash. Then all went dark.

The bright lights and pain hit me again, this time in reverse order. With a healthy dose of disorientation mixed in, I had no idea where I was or who I was for a few moments. The surges of pain inside my skull helped to clear my head, and I began to open my eyes. I tried to raise my hands to block the light, but something prevented them from moving. I heard a painful groan when I attempted to sit up, soon realizing the sound came from my own throat.

"I think you better lay still, Mr. Kincaid." The voice was familiar, despite the haze in my mind. A hand laid on my shoulder making sure I didn't move.

Several more blinks of my eyes and my brain started to engage. It was like everything had been shut down and was now trying to reboot. Whatever kind of inner processor I had was beginning to send out signals and the pathways began carrying those signals at full speed again.

A slight turn of my head brought another surge of pain but allowed me to see the person connected to the voice. Brooks Hartley. He was smiling.

"Welcome back. You have been out for a while. Nearly two full days to be exact."

A wave of memories flooded over me. The Aachen Cathedral. Holding the cup. The call from Hartley. Running into the street. Gunshots. Camilla being hit.

"Camilla?" My scratchy and feeble voice cracked as I inquired, expecting to hear devastating news.

Before Hartley had a chance to respond, two nurses and a doctor entered the room and began checking me out, pleased I was awake. Some brief tests satisfied them, and the doctor completed the visit with a few scribbles on my chart. They were smiling much like Hartley when they left, warning the Interpol agent to be brief.

Once they left, I looked at Hartley waiting for him to

speak. He stood directly over me with a serious look on his face. His moments of hesitation seemed like days as I tried to brace myself. Finally, the smile returned. “She’s going to be fine.”

The next few days were a whirlwind of medical tests, explanations and updates from Hartley, and some sweet reunions.

Hartley described the man who came after Camilla and me outside the Aachen Cathedral. His name was Vlad Glazkov, and he was a hired gun from the former Soviet Union. We were still alive because a local Aachen police officer got to the scene just as Glazkov was pointing a gun at my face. The officer fired a fraction of a second before Glazkov, hitting the Russian and throwing off the trajectory of his kill shot by millimeters. The bullet grazed the side of my head, causing a slight fracture in my skull and a severe concussion. Glazkov did not survive.

Camilla’s injuries were more severe. Her gunshot wound included a lacerated liver and punctured lung, while the bullet itself ended up lodged very close to her heart. She was quickly transported to a hospital and rolled into surgery within thirty minutes of being shot. Despite an extended recovery time, doctors assured her there should be no long-term effects from the wounds, aside from a couple of small, unattractive scars.

The hows and whys of our attack were tougher to explain. First, we assumed Griego and anyone associated with him believed Camilla and I died in the house fire in Geneva. Second, if someone in Griego’s circle found out we were alive, how did they know we were in Aachen? Only a select number of people had that information, most of them Interpol agents.

A day after I regained consciousness and felt a bit more

coherent, Hartley described what his people discovered. Once Radic Damir was wounded and his associate captured early the morning after the murders and robbery at Saint Maurice, Constantine Damir—the patriarch of the Damir clan—became involved in the situation. He sent an underling back to Saint Maurice to kill Abbot Haller in an act of revenge, believing the Abbot was the one who identified his son and facilitated Radic's capture. When the hitman observed Camilla and me during our visit to see the Abbot in the hospital, Constantine directed him to leave the Abbot alive for the time being. We were tailed during the drive to Geneva airport. Then, a low-level associate in air traffic control was either bribed or threatened to reveal the updated flight plan taking us to Aachen.

Constantine knew Griego would want to be informed about the new development and got word to him in jail through his lawyer. The lawyer left the meeting with Griego and called a wealthy businessman named Helmuth Moltke in Munich. Interpol had been monitoring Moltke for several weeks because the millionaire was suspected of acquiring stolen works of art for his massive collection. A recently approved wiretap picked up the conversation, and Moltke immediately made another call from the same phone. The agents monitoring Moltke passed the content of the messages up the line, eventually reaching Hartley, who knew we were in trouble. Hartley assumed Griego had studied enough about Alcuin and Charlemagne to understand we were most likely going to the Aachen Cathedral and treasury. There was no way for him to know our ultimate goal at the treasury, but under his current circumstances, Griego probably didn't care. He simply wanted us out of the picture.

Several people were arrested in the days after the shooting; days I was unconscious. An Interpol alert even led to the capture of Klein and Schmidt, the two who killed Ashton and Dennis Simons and tried to do the same to us a couple of times. They were picked up trying to cross the border between Germany and the Czech Republic.

It turned out Dominic Griego was a somewhat reluctant pawn in his father's schemes. The young priest willingly revealed all he knew about the activities surrounding the Alcuin letter and some other questionable practices of the Society of Angels. The story was big news in many parts of Europe where the Society was deeply ingrained. Many *true believers* loudly vocalized their firm beliefs that Griego was innocent, but their numbers began to decrease as more information became widely available. The fact that Moltke, one of the Society's most influential supporters, also faced charges of numerous crimes made saving the thirty-year-old religious movement unlikely. Despite those challenges, there were already rumors about who would take over the reins from Niklaus Griego.

Another piece of good news arrived when I heard that the Golden Jug of Charlemagne had been recovered. Even though Griego took it apart hoping to find the cup, experts had already looked at the jug and were confident it could be repaired. It would be back at Saint Maurice in less than a month.

The original copy of the Alcuin letter was still missing. Authorities continued to search through the Society's headquarters and other properties, as well as Griego's home, but so far nothing resembling a twelve-hundred-year-old letter had been found.

Hartley did his best to keep my name and Camilla's out of the news. As far as the majority of the public knew, we were simply tourists in the wrong place at the wrong time when a crazed gunman appeared near the Aachen Cathedral. No connection between the attack in Aachen and the events in Saint Maurice was ever mentioned publicly.

Late on the fourth day after being shot, a nurse entered to tell me I had some visitors and wondered if I was up to it. Despite being tired and still battling severe headaches, I gave the nurse a thumbs up, curious about the visitors. Seconds later, a little bundle of energy came through the door with big round eyes and a smile I had sorely missed.

"Daddy." Maddie skipped into the room with the innocence and joy only a three-year-old could portray. She stopped when she saw me in the bed with an IV in my arm and my head wrapped in a bandage but attempted to crawl into the bed to join me. Donald and Karen came in right behind Maddie and picked her up to allow her to give me a huge hug. Somehow the pain in my head disappeared as tears welled up in my eyes and rolled down my cheeks. No hug had ever meant more to me.

It had been less than two weeks since I left Maddie and my in-laws, but it felt like months. There were tears all around while I briefly tried to explain some of what happened. I let them talk about their decision to make the transatlantic trip and the adventure of traveling with a toddler. Mostly, though, I enjoyed their presence, relishing the humble act of holding my daughter's hand.

Karen gave me a massive envelope stuffed with get-well cards from friends and colleagues. She said Ethan Montgomery helped them arrange the trip to Germany and delivered a donation from his church to assist with the costs. Ethan told the Hendersons to let me know that he was looking forward to our weekly chats starting up again. Even Ethan might be surprised by what I would tell him.

The next day I was allowed to see Camilla. She had been weak after her surgery, and they were monitoring her very closely to avoid any infection that might set back her recovery. Donald assisted me into a wheelchair and then pushed me to Camilla's room. Her parents were there, having flown in from Spain almost immediately upon hearing about the shooting. It was bittersweet meeting them after all that had gone on with Ashton's murder and now Camilla being shot. They were gracious under the circumstances, allowing me a few minutes alone with Camilla. I wanted Maddie to meet her, but the time was not yet right.

The reunion was awkward at first. The days since we had last spoken nearly equaled the number of days we had been together traipsing through Europe, trying not to get killed. We both cried. They were tears of happiness and relief, I believe. Going through such a dramatic experience has a bonding effect, but it would take some time to see if that bond had any longevity.

We mostly talked about the joy of seeing our families. I also filled her in on the news about the man who shot us and about Griego and all the arrests. Not wanting to tire her too much, we agreed to talk again the next day, and I left her to rest.

CHAPTER 27

The doctors agreed to release me from the hospital a full week after being shot. My headaches had subsided, the slight skull fracture was healing well, and I showed no side effects from the concussion. The first flights available back to the States were for the next afternoon. The Hendersons, Maddie, and I all stayed in a suite at the Mercure Hotel, not far from the hospital.

Camilla would require another couple of days before being cleared to travel, so I took a taxi to the hospital on the morning of my departure. Maddie wanted to come with me to see her new friend—a connection developed during brief visits over the past couple of days—but this needed to be a discussion between just Camilla and me without any distractions. Two important topics needed to be discussed: what to do about the cup and what to do about our relationship. I had a definite answer in mind for one of those questions but remained unsure about the other.

Camilla was up and sitting in a chair when I entered her room.

"You must be feeling better," I said, handing her a bouquet of bright yellow daffodils I purchased from a street vendor outside the hospital.

"I am now," she said. "These are beautiful. Thank you, Matt."

We continued with some small talk for a few minutes, both of us trying to steer the conversation where it needed to go, but both hesitant to go there.

Taking the lead, I said, "So, how do you feel about knowing where the cup of Christ is right now?"

"I am not sure I can fully comprehend all that's happened," Camilla began. "I've had many hours to think in the past week and still find it difficult to know my true feelings. There's certainly excitement and wonder, but also some apprehension about what would happen if that knowledge is made known on a wider basis."

"I've been feeling the same way. I keep thinking about what Abbot Haller said. '*The cup is just an object. Maybe it's something to be admired, but nothing to be worshiped.*' Will the benefits of revealing what we know outweigh the potential uproar and arguments over authenticity and rightful ownership? We've seen first-hand how the desire to possess the cup can lead to tragic results."

"But how can we not make the world aware of this discovery? It would be one of the most important historical pieces ever found." I wasn't sure if Camilla was serious or just playing devil's advocate.

"Do you believe the cup being revealed would have a profound and positive effect on the Christian faith?"

Camilla thought momentarily before answering. "When we first started our search, I would have said *yes*. Seeing such a holy relic, with all its meaning would have to deepen a believer's faith and draw in some unbelievers."

"And now?"

"As I have been trying to process all we have been through, the one thing I know for certain is my faith has grown and become deeper. But that growth didn't happen because of the cup. It happened because I began to let go of some roadblocks and insecurities that kept me from a closer relationship with God. Those were barriers in my heart and my soul. Seeing something tangible, even as awe-inspiring as the cup Christ used at the Last Supper, didn't get me through those barriers. It was something much more personal and much deeper.

"If I use my experience as a guide, I would have to say my answer now is *no*, I don't believe the cup would have a lasting effect. Of course, there would be some hysteria when the news is first published, but a year or two from now it would probably just be a draw for tourists and a few historians. There would also probably be the occasional radical claiming the cup had some special powers."

"So you're saying we should keep the secret to ourselves and let an artifact of literally Biblical proportions remain a secret?" I put pressure on Camilla, but we needed to make sure we both considered the argument from all sides.

She laid her head back against the chair and closed her eyes. Despite her previous statement, it was obvious Camilla was still going through some inner turmoil. A couple of minutes passed with neither of us speaking. When her eyes opened, I could tell a decision had been made. She sat up straight and looked directly at me.

"Yes, Matt, I am sure. I believe we need to walk away and not reveal the things we have discovered."

A big smile filled my face, as much from relief as anything else. I knew when I walked into the room that I wanted to keep our knowledge about the cup a secret, but I worried Camilla wouldn't agree. Having her arrive at the same decision was a huge load off my mind. When I told her my thoughts, she seemed relieved, as well.

"My biggest regret will be not getting the royalties from all the pictures I could take of the cup," she said in jest.

Matching her wit, I said, "And I will miss having my picture in Time Magazine and earning Historian of the Year honors."

A carefree laugh proved to be great medicine.

We spent some time discussing her recovery and plans for traveling back to England. I passed on a sweet message from Maddie and the Hendersons and then began to say my goodbyes.

Many things remained unsaid between us.

Camilla stood on unsteady legs and opened her arms. I embraced her delicately, not wanting to aggravate her injuries. The emotion level in the room rose, though no words were spoken.

Once I found my voice, I said, “Camilla, it’s hard to describe what has blossomed between us in the past couple of weeks. I’m not sure of what's going on in my mind, let alone being able to decipher what you’re feeling. But, I know I don’t want this to be goodbye, at least not permanently.”

She turned her head and gave me a brief kiss. I took it as a sign to continue.

“In the middle of all the crazy things we've been through, the Lord has somehow prompted each of us to grow in many ways. I have no idea what that means for the long term. I only know that you are a special woman, and I would love to spend some time with you when we’re not being chased or shot at.”

Camilla kissed me again and then stepped back.

“Well, it is about time you said something nice to me,” she said with a mischievous grin. Turning more serious, she added, “I feel the same way, Mr. Matt Kincaid. I can promise you that we will find time together very soon.”

EPILOGUE

My breath came in a controlled rhythm, the beat of my heart almost matching the sound of my feet striking the pavement. The crowd around me moved at the same pace, making me like a minnow in a massive school of fish.

I stayed true to my word and joined two of my students—along with 35,000 others—in running a half marathon race. The first few miles went at a comfortable pace as the huge throng of people began to spread out. By the midway point, I started to experience a bit of fatigue, but by the looks on my students' faces, I felt better than them. Three more miles and the two students who had been so cocky when challenging me to run this race dropped off my pace. Once the end came into sight, I felt like a runner again, passing several people as I sprinted across the finish line.

I placed in the top twenty percent overall, my final spot being recorded as 6,122nd place. Not bad for being part of the largest half-marathon race in the country just two months after being shot.

Training for this race was part of the healing process after the ordeal with Camilla. I filled most of my days since returning to Bannister with extended play times with Maddie, long talks with my in-laws and Ethan Montgomery, and a nice long run each morning. Preparation for the current semester also took up some time, as I agreed to teach a new class on Medieval History, focusing on the influence of

Charlemagne in the formation of Europe. Ashton Collins would have been thrilled.

I grabbed some refreshments to help rehydrate after the race and began to search the swarm of people for my family. After several minutes I had about given up when I heard a familiar but unexpected voice calling my name over the din of countless others. I turned to my right until I zeroed in on the source: Camilla.

I jogged over to where she waited. Beside her were Karen and Donald, with Maddie sitting atop Donald's shoulders.

"Surprise," Camilla said as I approached. The Henderson's had approving smiles on their faces.

I grabbed Maddie and hugged her before turning back to Camilla.

"And a very nice surprise it is." With Maddie still in one arm, I reached out my free arm and embraced Camilla.

She wrapped her arms around both of us and whispered in my ear, "I'm ready for us to spend some time together."

Three Months Later

Abbot Haller reclined in his favorite chair, a small fire going in the fireplace to ward off a constant chill. His sister returned from a trip into town and handed him a package forwarded from his home in Saint Maurice. Haller smiled when he saw the return address.

It had been half a year since he was shot, but his retirement provided plenty of time to recuperate. Spending the last month in Sorrento with his sister was proving to be a splendid idea.

He opened the package and pulled out a letter along with a large, sealed envelope. The envelope was made of a type of clear material and Haller could see an aged document inside. He read the letter first.

Dear Abbot Haller,

We have been pleased to hear your recovery has gone well and you are in good health. We are preparing for the upcoming Christmas season and have much to be thankful for. Camilla and I have continued to work through all that happened on our adventure earlier this year and that process has helped us grow closer together. She still travels a great deal for her photography career but has secured numerous assignments in the U.S. so visits our small town of Bannister, Indiana, whenever possible. She and I are still discussing and praying about a more long-term arrangement.

You will find the Alcuin letter enclosed in this package. Yes, it is the original letter that prompted most of the tragic events last June. We believed the letter was lost until recently when Camilla received it by courier at her London flat. It appears Dominic Griego finally deduced where his father had hidden the letter and, while awaiting trial, arranged to have it rescued and sent to Camilla. He included a message expressing his deepest sorrow for her brother's death and the other happenings that affected so many.

The appearance of the original Alcuin letter only added to the pressure Camilla and I have felt. We discussed at length what we should do with the letter and the knowledge we possess. Rarely does a day go by that we don't wonder if we have made the right decision to keep the letter and that knowledge a secret. Maybe Christ's cup needs to be revealed to the world, but as you once said, it is only an object and not something to be worshiped.

Trusting in your wisdom, we are now giving you this letter to do with as you see fit. It can be a roadmap to be followed toward the true cup of Christ like it was for Camilla and me. Or it can be a forgotten letter that never reaches its destination. We pray the Lord will grant you discernment.

We hope to see you again,

Matt Kincaid and Camilla Collins

Haller was intrigued by the Alcuin letter. Matt and Camilla told him about its contents when they visited him in the Saint Maurice hospital several months ago, but it was a special privilege to read it in its original Latin form. Handling the protected pages with great care, he slowly made his way through the letter. His Latin was rusty, but he managed to read the text without too much difficulty.

"Extraordinary," he said to himself when finished.

Haller sat in contemplation and silent prayer, staring out the window near his chair for more than an hour. The view of the Bay of Naples, despite its beauty, faded as his thoughts deepened. With the sun disappearing on the horizon and the heat from the fire beginning to falter, he rose and approached the fireplace. Hesitating only briefly, he stooped and added some fuel to the fire.

The pages of the Alcuin letter soon turned to ash.

Separating Truth From Fiction

The vast majority of historical characters in the book are real and several of the events described took place.

Pope Leo III suffered an attack by his enemies in 799 and took refuge with Winigis, the Duke of Spoleto. The Pope traveled to meet with Charlemagne in Paderborn later that year. On Christmas, 800, Pope Leo anointed Charlemagne as the first Holy Roman Emperor. Leo's position as the Pope had been reestablished in large part due to Charlemagne's support.

There is no record of a late-night meeting in the forest outside of Paderborn or the exchange of a special gift.

Charlemagne himself was a fascinating character who helped unite most of Western Europe and laid the foundation of what would become the countries of France and Germany. Often called the *Father of Europe*, Charlemagne also prompted the Carolingian Renaissance; a time of increased focus on learning and education, including reading, art, and architecture. In addition to these efforts, Charlemagne made policies that led to reforms in the church. The standards for clergy rose dramatically, and many liturgical practices were standardized.

With the need for educated people to help administer his kingdom, Charlemagne convinced Alcuin of York, among several others, to join his court. Alcuin revamped the palace school and helped establish schools in the cathedrals around the kingdom, bringing in the liberal arts and improving the overall quality of education. His liberal arts curriculum would be the foundation for education for several centuries and even has an impact on today's methods. Alcuin was part of Charlemagne's court from 783-790 and again from 792-796.

Alcuin was not with Charlemagne when Pope Leo III visited Paderborn in 799.

For the last eight years of his life, Alcuin served as the Abbot of the monastery at Saint Martin of Tours. He continued to teach extensively and considered Rhabanus Maurus one of his most accomplished students. Rhabanus eventually became the Abbot at Fulda in 822 and was named the Archbishop of Mainz in 847. He retired to Winkel and, at least according to some legend, died at the Graues Hause in 856.

Rhabanus did not keep a secret letter from Alcuin.

Charlemagne received many gifts from various places during his reign, none more unique than an elephant from Harun Al-Rashid. Even though the two rulers never met, Charlemagne and Al-Rashid had a unique relationship as rulers representing the East and the West, Christian and Muslim. Much like Charlemagne, Al-Rashid had a great love of learning. He established the House of Wisdom, which grew into one of the world's largest libraries and most important educational centers.

Of the many gifts the two rulers exchanged, the Golden Jug of Charlemagne was, most likely, not one of them.

The Golden Jug of Charlemagne does exist and is displayed at the Abbey of Saint Maurice. The story of Saint Maurice and his martyrdom with his Theban Legion is true, along with the practice of Laus Perinnis, or continual prayer, which took place at the Abbey of Saint Maurice for almost 300 years. The other treasures of Saint Maurice described in the book are also real, as is the fact that some of the treasures were on loan in 2014 to the Louvre in honor of the 1500th anniversary of the Abbey of Saint Maurice.

Other locations mentioned in the book around Geneva,

Saint Maurice, and Aachen are described accurately including Saint Peter's Cathedral (Geneva); Castle of Saint Maurice and Grotte aus Fees (Saint Maurice); and Aachen City Hall and Aachen Cathedral (Aachen). (The interior layouts of some locations were changed to fit the story.)

There is no Bannister, Indiana, or Bannister College, although there are several small college towns around the Hoosier state that would be similar to Bannister. The Indianapolis Mini Marathon is the largest half-marathon in the United States and includes a 2.5-mile loop around the Indianapolis Motor Speedway. However, the actual event is held in May each year, not in the fall as described in the book.

There are several theories out there concerning the cup of Christ, but as described in the book, there are huge historical or practical holes in virtually all of the legends. In Europe alone, more than 200 vessels claim to be the Holy Grail.

The heritage described of the Saint's Chalice that remains in the Cathedral of Valencia in Spain is accurate, at least according to one written theory. Pope John Paul II did use the chalice for Mass in 1982 as did Pope Benedict XVI in 2006.

Two of the best-known relics associated with the Holy Chalice or the cup of Christ are the Nanteos Cup and the Goblet of San Isidro. The Nanteos Cup resides at the Nanteos Mansion in Wales. Legend claims that the wooden cup was brought to Wales by Joseph of Arimathea. The relic was stolen in 2014 but recovered in 2015. The Goblet of San Isidro burst into the news in 2014 when two historians wrote a book claiming that the stone cup was indeed the Holy Grail. The goblet can be seen at the Basilica of San Isidro in Leon, Spain.

Does the true cup of Christ exist? If so, what would be the impact of revealing it to the world? Would it be admired or worshiped? Praised or reviled? Fought for? Studied?

What objects do you worship? What objects keep you from an authentic relationship with Christ?

To learn more about the author, visit
jeffraymondfiction.com

Made in the USA
Middletown, DE
02 August 2025